Brutal Scars

JANE BLYTHE

Acknowledgments

I'd like to thank everyone who played a part in bringing this story to life. Particularly my mom who is always there to share her thoughts and opinions with me. My wonderful cover designer Letitia who did an amazing job with this stunning cover. My fabulous editor Lisa for all the hard work she puts into polishing my work. My awesome team, Sophie, Robyn, and Clayr, without your help I'd never be able to run my street team. And my fantastic street team members who help share my books with every share, comment, and like!

And of course a big thank you to all of you, my readers! Without you I wouldn't be living my dreams of sharing the stories in my head with the world!

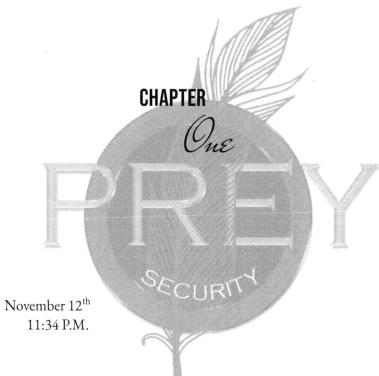

CHAPTER *One*

November 12th
11:34 P.M.

The water was cold.

It was November, so that was to be expected, of course, but there was nothing that Mason "Scorpion" Markson hated more than the feel of cold water on his skin.

That was why when he decided to build a career in the military, he had opted for the Army with the ultimate goal of joining the elite Delta Force, rather than the Navy to become a SEAL.

There was just something about the way water clung to you, permeating into your being with its icy coldness even as it sat against your skin, that he hated. It wasn't the same in the shower, the water was warm and soothing. Swimming pools were fine, too, and lakes, actually he didn't even mind the ocean on a summer's afternoon when everything was hot and bright.

But like this?

In the middle of the night, halfway through fall, when the daytime temperatures were dropping and the nighttime ones even more so, there was nothing pleasant about the ocean. The wind was howling, whipping the water up into huge waves, making swimming difficult, and if the case wasn't so personal to Scorpion and his team, he would almost wish he was back home in the peace and quiet of his cabin.

Okay, so he wouldn't really. He took every case seriously, but this one was a whole lot more personal than most.

This op was about family.

His own family was pretty typical. Older sister and a younger sister, parents divorced when he was ten, reasonably amicable and he and his sisters had bounced between their mom's home and their dad's for the rest of their childhood. He played football and baseball, got what he asked for on Christmas morning, made good grades, got a job when he was old enough, played video games, all the usual stuff.

Then there was his second family. The men who had served with him in Delta and now at Prey Security as part of Bravo Team might not be biologically related to him, but it didn't make them any less his brothers. Brothers born out of blood, sweat, and tears. They watched each other's backs, fought side by side, and were there for each other no matter what.

With targets painted on their backs by a notorious human trafficker they had come so close to catching, that bond had grown even stronger. They now lived off-the-grid on a remote compound deep in the forest, they spent most of their time together, and when one of them needed something they were there.

Like now.

As they closed in on Russian oligarch and human trafficker Leonid Baranov's second in command each one of them was determined to get answers.

They needed them because part of their family was slowly falling apart.

Axel "Axe" Lindon's voice echoed through the comms. "We might have a problem."

The very fact that Axe had come on this mission with them said they had more than one problem. Almost five years ago, their Delta Team had raided a property belonging to Leonid Baranov, hoping to finally locate and detain the well-know trafficker. Instead, Baranov had evaded them and they had managed to rescue several of his sex slaves.

Among them was Beth. Having lived most of her life being abused by her mother, and a litany of boyfriends her mother paraded in and out of her life, before finally being sold and eventually winding up as one of Baranov's prisoners, she didn't know her last name or anything about the real world that existed outside of the abuse she had been subjected to. It had been a long path to healing, but he and his team had been there for her all the way, especially Axe.

When Beth was ready, he had proposed and the two had been married for three years now. Everything had been going well for them until Beth disappeared almost sixteen months ago.

Poof.

Gone like a wisp of smoke.

No matter how hard they tried—and Prey had a lot of resources to pull on—they hadn't been able to locate her.

Not a single trace.

Until she turned up on the compound one night seven months ago with no memory of who she was or what had happened to her in the eight months she had been missing.

Seven months of living with a wife with amnesia, who didn't know who he was, who wouldn't let him get too close to her, who was slowly floating further and further away from him had taken a toll on Axe. Nothing he did seemed to help, and while he had initially taken time away from the team to spend with Beth, this was the first time since she went missing that he had gone on a mission with them.

"What's the problem?" Gabriel "Tank" Dawson asked. Tank had been the stand-in leader for Bravo team while Axe was away, but with his return, Tank had happily stepped back down, pleased it would give him a little extra time with his girlfriend.

"That is," Sebastian "Rock" Rockman announced.

Looking around to see what had captured the two men's attention, Scorpion saw a small but ever-growing light in the night sky.

Helicopter.

Patrick "Trick" Kramer must have noticed it at the same time Scorpion did because he said, "Helo."

"What are the chances it isn't heading to the same yacht we are?" Rafe "Panther" Neal asked facetiously.

They all knew the answer to that question.

Zero.

The chances the helicopter wasn't heading to the yacht where they'd gotten word Baranov's right hand man Tomas Butcher was rumored to be staying were non-existent.

"We have to get there before it does," he said. They were close. Only a hundred yards separated Bravo Team from the yacht. If they didn't get there first there was every chance Butcher would board the helo and be gone before they could detain him.

Without Butcher they might never find Baranov, never get the answers Beth needed to move forward, never get her the closure of knowing she was no longer in danger from a man who didn't like others playing with his toys and who saw her as his possession. Baranov was like a ghost. Every time you thought you got a lead on him it evaporated. Despite being on pretty much every country's top ten most wanted lists, he somehow managed to remain off-the-grid, using his vast wealth as a shield, a cloak of invisibility.

Bravo Team had closed most of the distance when the whir of the rotors filled the air. Anger and disappointment warred inside him as he and his team began to scale the side of the yacht, knowing the helo was going to whisk away the man they were searching for before they had a chance to do anything about it.

They were so close.

And they all needed this so badly.

Honestly, Scorpion wasn't sure how much longer Axe could go on with his wife so close and yet so very far away. It was killing both Axe and Beth slowly, bit by bit, until sooner or later there would be nothing left.

It sucked watching people you loved, who you thought of as a brother and a baby sister, waste away like that.

Family was everything. Whether the one you were born into or the one you created, it was what mattered. There was nothing he wouldn't do for either of his families, and nothing turned him off more than someone who treated their family like they were nothing, like they didn't matter.

They reached the top of the yacht just as two figures, a man and a woman, hurried toward the now-waiting helo.

"Stop!" Axe yelled, aiming his weapon at Tomas Butcher.

The man turned, surprise covering his features before they broke out into a smug grin. "Sixty seconds till boom," Tomas called out above the thumping of the helo's blades.

Damn.

The yacht was wired to explode.

Nothing seemed to go right with this mission. There had been no clues when Beth was taken and none when she returned. One of only three remaining survivors of Baranov's sick, twisted games had been killed just hours before they were set to meet with him to learn what he knew, and now Baranov's right-hand man was going to get away, taking whatever secrets he knew with him.

Tomas Butcher and the woman were already on the helicopter. Going after them was only going to get them killed. There was nothing to do but jump off the yacht and pray they could make it far enough away before it blew up.

Helplessness clawed at him. He wanted to fix this for Axe and Beth, take away the threats hovering above them so maybe they could finally heal, find their way back to one another, and live out the happy ending they both deserved.

Instead, there was nothing he could do.

No way to fix it.

As he landed in the freezing water again, Scorpion felt it cling to him like quicksand, slowly pulling him under, leaving him feeling completely out of control of his life and the people in it. Without control there was nothing to stop the worst from happening.

Problem was, he didn't know how much worse things could get.

∼

November 12th
   11:43 P.M.

. . .

It was peaceful out here.

A gentle breeze, cold but the nice kind that just gave your skin a tingly chill, clear sky, and stars twinkling like fairy lights. Tall trees dressed in the pretty colors of fall, the occasional soft hoot of an owl, and a few bats flying overhead. There was something almost magical about the countryside, especially this time of year.

Even the fact that it was dangerous to be out this late, leaving the tent after the nightly worshiping of the stars was strictly forbidden, and definitely punishable if caught, couldn't take away from the beauty and serenity of nature.

Funny thing was, that even though she was deep undercover in a dangerous cult, Jessica Bowen had never felt this kind of tranquility before.

Maybe a long time ago, when she was a very little girl before one accident had changed the entire trajectory of her life.

Had it really been eighteen years already?

It didn't seem possible.

Seemed like a lifetime ago.

In a way it *had* been a lifetime. At least what should have been an entire childhood and adolescence lifetime.

For her, childhood had ended at the age of ten. One day she had been a happy, exuberant, playful little girl, who hadn't had a clue what the real world was like. Her world had existed of school, friends, gymnastics, sleepovers, and playing with friends. She'd had extravagant birthday parties her event planner mother used as ways to promote her small business. Christmases had been huge affairs filled with presents, games, and more food than any family could eat. School had been a fun place. She'd been popular, gotten good grades, and other than her tendency to talk too much in class, she rarely got in trouble. Gymnastics had not only been a fun after-school activity, but she'd shown real promise, and almost been good enough to try out for the Olympic team.

Then it was all gone.

No more fun, no more play, no more dreams of springing across the balance beam on her way to a gold medal.

All of it had come crashing down around her.

Still, Jessica knew she shouldn't complain. Plenty of people had things way worse than she had. No longer was she that young girl carrying the weight of the world on her shoulders. She had been rescued and gotten out of a life that could have wound up consuming her.

Not just her, her two little sisters were safe, too. They would never have to do what she had just to survive. Thankfully, they had been too young, just nine and seven by the time they were all put in foster care, to realize what she had been forced to do to support them and make sure they had a roof over their heads and food on the table.

Their lives had been relatively normal. Somehow, they had all lucked out when they entered the system and had been taken in by a cop and her husband. Raised together, they had been well cared for, known safety and support from their foster parents, and were both now happy, well-adjusted college students.

Jessica might have had to give up on her dream to become a lawyer, but she loved what she did, and couldn't say that she regretted her choice to follow her foster mother into the police force.

Although when she had joined up, she had never thought she would be here.

Out on a remote compound, infiltrating a cult that was dangerous enough that there were legitimate threats that the Seeds of Life could wind up killing thousands, maybe even millions, of innocent people.

Not if I have anything to say about it.

Hurting innocents was at the absolute top of her hate list.

Top top.

Nothing was worse as far as she was concerned.

Okay, so maybe she was a little jaded when it came to that particular topic, but who wouldn't be after being forced to do what she had?

Luckily her past had helped her learn how to control her fear instead of letting it control her, and it turned out she was a bit of an adrenalin junkie, because it wasn't the fear of what would happen to her if she was found out that kept her up at night, but the fear of failing.

If she failed to get close enough to the cult leader who went by the name of Genesis, then she couldn't gather the intel they needed on the cult's plans to eliminate the unbelievers, so only the righteous would survive. Of course, Genesis himself got to decide who the unbelievers were and who would be saved.

For six months now, she had been embedded in the cult, doing everything she could to attract the attention of Genesis' second in command, a man who quite predictably went by the name Exodus. While Genesis was all about creation and rebirth, Exodus was all about the rules. All of the rules were made up, and quite frankly, pretty ridiculous, not that she would ever let on she thought that way.

Thankfully, her acting skills were pretty top-notch, and so far, nobody seemed to suspect a thing.

During the day she worked in the fields, tending the crops, everyone worked there now that it was harvest season. There was also cooking, cleaning, minding the children, and tending to the men because, of course, that was a woman's job.

Seemed men in cults were no different than those in the real world, they all believed that women existed for the sole purpose of catering to their every whim. They didn't care if they hurt you so long as they got what they wanted in the process.

Okay, again she was a little jaded on that subject thanks to her past.

Tempting fate as she did every few days, Jessica slipped between the trees on her way back to her tent.

It was a risk to sneak out of the tent to send coded messages to her handler, but it had to be done. The only way to save the lives of thousands of innocents was for her to relay all intel she could as often as she could. Often, she didn't have much to pass along, she hadn't yet made it into the cult's inner circle, but she kept her handler apprised on the number of cult members—which continued to grow almost daily—and any rumors circulating amongst them.

It was wearing having to constantly be playing a role. The people here were nice, gullible, but searching for something better. They thought they had found it here amongst a group of people who believed that the stars were where the future lay. According to Genesis, once you found the star that matched you, you'd be transported to another dimension, one without pain and suffering.

Of course, that sounded intriguing to these poor souls.

All they wanted was to find a peaceful way to live. But this wasn't it. The stars didn't talk to you, there was no such thing as a star twin, and they weren't going to be magically transported to some perfect place free from pain.

Most of them had no idea that the cult didn't just care about the stars and happiness and everyone living happily ever after. They didn't realize that Genesis had much bigger plans, and that they included killing thousands of people just because he wanted to restart the world the way it appealed to him and didn't mind hurting others to do it.

"Jessica, you shouldn't be out there," a voice hissed as she slipped back inside her tent. It wasn't really hers, it was shared with a dozen of the other single women. Married couples were housed in tents on one side of the community space, families on the other, single men and single women in the middle, although separated of course. It was forbidden to take a husband or wife unless you received Genesis' blessing.

"Couldn't help it," she whispered back to Sarah, the woman whose bunk was right beside Jessica's. Pasting a dreamy look on her face, she gave a content sigh. "I can't stay away from them."

"The stars?" Sarah asked.

"Mmhmm, aren't they beautiful? Do you hear them singing?"

"Singing?" Sarah squealed. "You can hear them singing? Jessica, do you know what it means? It means that your star twin must be some-where close by!"

"Mmhmm," she said again, keeping the dreamy look on her face as she swished past, and dropped down onto her bed which was really more a cot with a scratchy brown blanket and a lumpy pillow.

"You're so lucky," Sarah said, and the envy in her tone was clear as she also crawled into her bed.

Lucky?

That was about the last thing Jessica would ever call herself. It hadn't been lucky that her dad had been paralyzed in an accident. It hadn't been lucky that her mom had been unable to cope and became depressed, eventually getting hooked on pills. It wasn't lucky that taking care of the house, her sisters, and her parents had all fallen on her. And it hadn't been lucky that her older brother had compounded it all by inflicting unimaginable pain on her.

Closing her eyes, she rolled over to face the tent wall so Sarah wouldn't see the tears winding silvery trails down her cheeks. Strong girls didn't cry, they knew that it didn't change anything, but every so often, Jessica allowed herself a moment to be weak, to remember what had happened and how she had overcome it.

This was one of those moments.

Tomorrow she'd be strong again.

CHAPTER *Two*

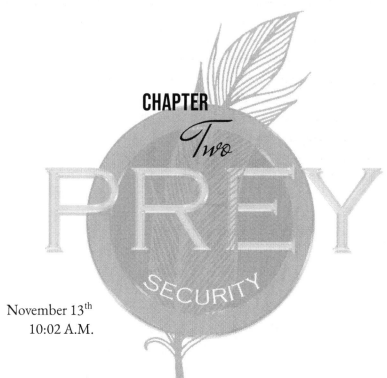

November 13th
10:02 A.M.

Finally, vacationing with the family.

Scorpion needed the break, especially after last night's close call.

Thankfully, they'd made it into the water and far enough away from the yacht that the blast hadn't injured them. Although it had still tossed them about, and it was safe to say, he now disliked the cold ocean even more. They'd regrouped once they were on their boat, but Tomas Butcher had made it away in his helicopter and they hadn't managed to track where he'd gone.

It felt like it was getting less and less likely that they were going to get the answers Axe and Beth needed, and he hated knowing that Leonid Baranov might remain a free man until he died of old age.

Wasn't fair.

Men like him didn't deserve to walk the earth with sweet, innocent women like Beth.

Feeling drained, he dodged around a group of excited children as he headed for the airport doors. It had been a long year, and he was looking forward to doing nothing but relaxing. Nothing to worry about, no *one* to worry about.

Everything that had gone down with Axe and Beth, then with Tank and his girl Tillie, then right on the heels of that there was the mess with Rock and his girl Ariel who had finally gotten the happy ending they should have had as teens, had taken a toll. As much as he loved his family, so much had gone on that all of them were running on empty.

They all needed a break. Scorpion knew he certainly did.

Two weeks chilling on a beach with his parents, sisters, his older sister's family, and younger sister's husband, sounded like heaven. His little sister and her husband of almost a year were expecting their first baby in just over two months and had wanted one last vacation where she didn't have a little one to tend to. At first when they'd arranged the family trip, he hadn't been sure he'd be able to make it. His work was unpredictable at the best of times, then adding in the Beth situation made it even more so.

But their boss had insisted. Billionaire former SEAL Eagle Oswald had founded Prey Security after being forced to medically retire from the Navy following a career ending injury. Not willing to give up what he loved completely, he had started Prey, quickly growing it into the largest and best private security company in the world. Now married with two small children, three-year-old Luna and nine-month-old Apollo, he had even more appreciation for family than he had before.

Knowing how many blows Bravo Team had received this last year and a bit, he had insisted that all of them take a break. Two weeks off. No exceptions.

Vacationing felt weird, almost wrong, his job had been his life for so long that walking away from it and his team felt like there was a piece of himself missing, but he had to agree with Eagle that this was something they all needed. Tank and Tillie needed time to continue growing their relationship. They all knew Tank wouldn't be able to last much longer before he asked her to marry him. And Ariel had been through so much and was still healing from her fourth—and hopefully last—surgery on the hand that had been broken when she and Rock had been abducted, the two of them needed time to spend together, no distractions.

Just as Scorpion set foot in the airport, allowed himself to relax, accept this vacation was happening and take a break—even *enjoy* the break—from work mode, his phone rang.

"Ignore it," he muttered to himself, rolling his suitcase along behind him as he headed for the check-in counter.

Whatever it was could wait until he was back.

This vacation had been mandated by his boss, there was nothing so important that he should answer a call before the vacation even started.

It had been almost a year since he'd seen his parents and sisters, and that had only been for a few hours last Christmas Day. Talking with them on the phone—something he did as often as he could—wasn't the same. His two little nephews were growing like weeds, and he wanted to be part of their childhoods, not just some uncle who dropped off presents on Christmas.

His cell started ringing again.

"The team is fine, everyone is safe," he reminded himself, even as his steps slowed.

Was it too much to ask to have two weeks to himself to spend with his family?

And yet ...

What if there had been a development on Beth's case? What if Panther had been able to track where the helo had gone after it took off with Tomas Butcher inside? Sure, Panther was supposed to be taking a break, too, going camping with his eight-year-old son, but he knew the man wouldn't be able to resist at least attempting to get a lead for them to follow when they got back.

When the phone started ringing a third time, he finally yanked it from his pocket and answered. "What?"

"Sorry, Scorpion, I know you're on vacation, and normally I would never interrupt that, especially since I'm the one who ordered Bravo Team to take a break, but this can't wait and I knew you'd want to be told," Eagle said without preamble.

Scorpion had gotten to know Eagle fairly well during his time with Prey's Bravo Team and knew his boss would never call unless it was a matter of life and death. Maneuvering out of the throng of holidaymakers, he moved to a quiet corner of the airport, or at least as quiet a corner as you could find in a busy airport. "What's going on."

"Got a call from an old friend of yours. David Bowen."

David Bowen? There was a blast from the past. The two of them had met in boot camp and instantly became friends. They'd both had plans to try to make it onto a Delta Force, but David had wound up leaving the Army after his first four-year deployment was up. Since their paths had taken them in such different directions, they'd wound up losing touch. "What did Dave want?"

"His sister Jessica has disappeared. He believes she's joined a cult."

"Okay," he drew the word out.

David's sister Jessica had been a beautiful girl, but most definitely a spoiled brat who instead of helping her family during a really rough patch had been selfish and made things worse. Five years younger than David, she'd been just a kid when he'd known her, but what he did know about her he couldn't imagine that she'd managed to make much out of her life. Didn't have the discipline to attend college or hold down a job, she was too entitled, too childish. Probably paid her bills by charming a boyfriend into taking care of her.

Yeah, he could totally imagine her batting her long lashes, aiming her big baby blues at some hapless dude, and getting herself whatever she wanted.

"What does that have to do with me?" It wasn't as though he wanted the girl in trouble. She might be selfish and spoiled, but she was still a human being, and the little sister of a man who had once been a good friend. Prey often did rescues, so an extraction wasn't out of the question. But why was it life or death, interrupt his vacation worthy?

"We know the cult," Eagle informed him. "It's Seeds of Life, they have links to a terrorist group that believes all life but for a few enlightened individuals should be poisoned."

They were hardcore, the cult and the terrorist group, although it was hard to make a distinction between the two. Not only did they believe that other than the enlightened few who joined the cult everyone else should be wiped off the face of the earth, they were going to follow through on that and make it happen. They'd been on a watch list for years, as a man who called himself Genesis slowly charmed those who were desperate to find a place to belong and a purpose for their lives into joining his cause.

Why was he not surprised that Jess had gotten herself mixed up in something like that? How could she keep being so stupid and irresponsible? It was time the girl grew up, she had to be in her late twenties by now, old enough to know better than to fall for something as stupid as joining a cult. Her brother must be going crazy with worry. Despite being in boot camp and then away on deployments, David had always done what he could to take care of his family, Jessica included, not that the spoiled princess would ever say thank you for that.

Vacation time was officially over before it even began.

"I'm on my way."

~

November 13th
   11:52 A.M.

Man, this was hard work.

Jessica was no stranger to working hard. When her life fell apart, she'd taken over pretty much all of the housework. Cooking, dusting, vacuuming, mopping, laundry, and caring for a toddler and a preschooler while trying to get to school at least a couple of days a week. It had been exhausting, and she'd wished her lazy, good for nothing older brother would have helped out.

But he believed that housework was women's work.

Only she hadn't been a woman, she'd been a little girl, barely ten years old, while he was fifteen. If they'd worked together, it would have been so much easier, but it hadn't been until tragedy tore her family apart that she realized he wasn't just lazy and spoiled but evil as well.

As exhausted as she had been as a kid trying to juggle running a household, it was nothing compared to the backbreaking work of tending a farm.

The jobs here on the Seeds of Life commune were never ending. At least it felt that way. The weather might be getting colder as the days of November ticked on by, but today there was clear blue sky and sunshine, and sweat pooled in her lower back, and dripped down into her eyes as she toiled in the garden.

How many more minutes until midday?

Life here was regimented to the extreme. They rose at five to bathe and dress, ready for breakfast at exactly six in the morning. After that it was chores, chores, and more chores. There were the chickens to feed and eggs to collect, the cows also had to be fed and then milked. There were also sheep, pigs, and horses that needed to be attended to and then there were the huge fields full of food. Weeding, watering, pruning, and harvesting. It didn't seem to matter the time of year there was always so much to get done.

Midday was lunchtime, before afternoon chores started all over again until six in the evening when they would finally stop for dinner. Food here was nothing extravagant, bread made from the wheat they grew themselves, fruit from the orchard, vegetables from the garden, and sometimes meat from their animals. While in theory it all sounded like a nice way to live, living off the land, growing it all yourself, it was some people's dream, but not like this.

Not when your whole day consisted of tending those gardens and the animals to provide for the two hundred or so people that lived there. Then it was just plain hard work that never ended because the garden was always growing, and the animals needed to be cared for rain or shine.

"Ugh, it has to be almost lunchtime," Martha whispered, straightening from leaning over the tomato vine she had been harvesting.

Talking while working was strictly forbidden. If one of Genesis' men who patrolled the gardens while they worked caught them, they would both be punished. Punishments included everything from being locked in the "reflection shed"—a tin shed set in the middle of the commune that had no windows and only the one door. In the summer it was like an oven, and in the winter a freezer—to public floggings, to being expelled from the community.

While Jessica did everything she could to be as perfect as possible, she never passed up an opportunity to gather any intel she could. Anything, no matter how small, could be the key to unravelling the entire cult.

Angling her body, she did a quick scan of the area, and noted that the only guard nearby who was there to "protect" them should anyone not of the enlightened chosen few who had joined the cult infiltrate, had his back to them. Bending down so she was mostly hidden by the tall tomato plants should the guard wander this way, she cast Martha a quick glance.

"Must be almost midday," she whispered.

Martha rolled her eyes. The woman was not like most of the other cult members. They all walked around as though they'd had a spell cast on them and were unable to think for themselves, they obeyed with an almost otherworldly devotion. It was the kind of devotion that was going to lead to them doing bad things they never would have done had they not fallen under Genesis' spell.

But not Martha. Jessica suspected that it had been the nature side that had attracted her to the cult. The getting back to basics, growing your own food, living off the land, and going off grid away from all the hustle and bustle of the rest of the world. While that was an attractor to all who had joined the cult, most had quickly succumb to Genesis' charms.

So far Martha was yet to fall for those charms, and sooner or later it was going to get her kicked out of the commune. Or worse.

Jessica had an awful feeling that those who were told to leave left permanently.

As in were killed.

This was more than just a cult, it was a terrorist group, and they couldn't risk letting someone leave who might possibly have information that could be given to the authorities and used against Seeds of Life.

Already Martha had endured several punishments in the months Jessica had been there, and if the woman didn't start being more careful she could wind up dead.

"You take the rules so seriously, Jess," Martha said, lifting her arms up above her head to stretch them, drawing more attention to herself. "I don't see why we can't talk while we work. It doesn't make us slower, if anything it passes the time more quickly and we could get even more done."

"Genesis knows best," she murmured. In a place like this, you never knew who might be listening. Any one of the women working around them could be one of Genesis' inner circle and they would never know it until they reported back to the revered leader, and they were punished for stepping out of line.

Another eye roll. "You girls are always so paranoid. If Genesis is who he says he is, a messenger of the Goddess Moon, who wants to help us find peace and happiness in a new world, then he should already know everything that's going to happen. We shouldn't have to hurry the harvest in case the time comes, he should know when it's coming."

Hands on her hips, she looked the picture of indignant. Martha's patience with Genesis and his beliefs had run its course, and Jessica prayed that the woman left and was able to get out without winding up dead.

"Genesis is the prophet," an angry voice growled, and they both looked over to find the guard who'd had his back to them before now standing just a few feet away.

Immediately, Jessica dropped her gaze. They weren't allowed to interact with the guards in any way, including making eye contact. Since speaking with them was absolutely out of the question, she just stayed on her knees, hands curled in her lap, gaze locked on the ground, the picture of submission even as she gave the same eye roll as Martha, only internally.

"Then how come he tells us we have to work without talking because we must hurry, that the end is coming soon? When is soon? Why doesn't he tell us the date if he knows it already?" Martha shot the questions at the guard whose face grew redder.

"How dare you disrespect our leader," the guard snarled. "Come with me."

Martha harrumphed like the whole thing irritated her. "You know what? I'm done with this place. I'm packing my things and leaving."

"Only the prophet can give permission to leave," the guard told her snidely.

"You can't keep me here," Martha exclaimed. "I'm not a prisoner. I came here voluntarily because I thought this was the place for me, but now I know that it's not. I'm leaving and there is nothing you can do to stop me."

Although her gaze never lifted, if she wanted an in with Exodus, she had to be the epitome of obedience, she saw Martha's feet stomping past. She felt the guard's eyes on her, wondered if she was going to be summoned to face Genesis, but then he turned and walked off after Martha.

Jessica so badly wanted to follow Martha, talk the woman into not doing anything stupid, and find out if Genesis really was letting people leave if they wanted to or if he was doing as she suspected, but she couldn't.

Even if it meant sacrificing Martha.

It hurt.

A lot.

She was a fixer, she didn't like to see people hurt, but this mission was too important to mess up in any way. All she could do was pray that Martha would get safely out of the commune and keep her focus on getting into the inner circle and getting the intel needed to stop the terrorist threat.

Jessica prayed that when this case was over, she was still able to look in the mirror and respect the person she saw looking back at her.

CHAPTER
Three

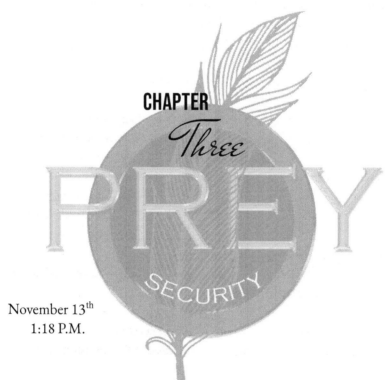

November 13th
1:18 P.M.

This was absolutely not how he had envisioned his day turning out.

Absolutely not how he *wanted* it to turn out either.

But Scorpion owed it to his old friend to at least come in and hear the information they had gathered on the Seeds of Life cult. Then he could offer some insight into Jessica so whoever was going in to get her out had the best chance of convincing her to leave the cult.

After that, he could walk away with a clean conscience and go join his family on their vacation.

"Uncle Scorpion!" a little tornado with blonde pigtails and sparkling blue eyes ambushed him the second he walked into the conference room at Prey's main building in the city. It was closer to the airport and he didn't intend to make this a long stay.

"Hey, squirt," he said as he bent down to pick up Eagle's three-year-old daughter Luna. The little girl giggled as he lifted her above her head and flew her around the room like an airplane.

"More! More!" she squealed delightedly.

There was no way not to smile at the child's enthusiasm, and Scorpion did a few more circles of the room.

"Me!" Apollo shouted from his mother's lap, his blue eyes holding the exact same confident gleam that his father's did. Like the two of them never even considered the possibility that they wouldn't get what they wanted.

"Apollo wants a turn, too, Uncle Scorpion," Luna immediately said. She was a fabulous big sister and it was the cutest thing ever to see her take care of her baby brother. In both looks and personality she was the spitting image of her mother.

Setting the little girl on her feet, he reached out to take Apollo.

"Careful, this little guy weighs a ton," Olivia said as she handed over her son.

"He's gonna be a big boy like his daddy," Scorpion said as he lifted the baby up high and zoomed him around the room, making airplane sounds as he did so.

"I'm going to be a dolphin like Daddy," Luna piped up.

"SEAL," Eagle corrected, his amusement evident.

"Oh." Luna's brows furrowed. "I forgotted. I like dolphins betterer than seals."

"Then you should totally be a dolphin," he told the little girl as he handed Apollo back over to Olivia. As much as he loved hanging out with any of the Prey kids, he hadn't come here today for playtime. He'd come to give as much intel as he could on Jessica so he could get his old friend's sister safely extracted.

Although knowing the stubborn, spoiled girl it would probably be easier for the poor soul who went in after her to just tranquilize her and carry her out.

"Okay, Loo-loo, Uncle Scorpion and I have some things to discuss," Eagle told his daughter.

"Why don't you go play with your dolls," Olivia suggested, pointing to a pile of Barbies down one end of the table, while simultaneously setting Apollo on the floor beside her chair with a pile of brightly colored wooden blocks.

"Mama, can you make me braids?" Luna asked as she eyed the dolls and then her mother.

"I have to help Daddy with his meeting," Olivia told her daughter.

Eagle's eyes were soft as he looked at the two most important women in his life. "If I help Mama, I bet she can do your braids and help with the meeting all at the same time. Mama is supermom after all."

Luna giggled and clapped her hands as she went to stand beside her mother, and as he watched Olivia begin to braid Luna's long, blonde locks, a long forgotten memory surfaced. One day he'd gone by the Bowen house to pick up David. It had been just after Thanksgiving, and they were returning to base after the holiday. He'd arrived a little early, and Jessica—then just fourteen—had opened the door and told him he could wait in the kitchen. While he'd waited, he'd been able to see her in the living room, she was braiding one of her sister's hairs while singing nursery rhymes to the crying toddler.

At the time he'd thought it was odd because she seemed surprisingly good with the two small children considering her brother's claims she never helped at all, and that he had to pay for a maid and a nanny out of his meagre income to keep the family afloat.

Shrugging off the memory, Scorpion looked at Eagle and nodded. Just because he knew a bit about the cult, it didn't mean he wasn't interested in learning everything there was to know so he could report to David what he knew before he got on that plane.

He was a little surprised that David wasn't here himself. Scorpion was sure that Eagle wouldn't have objected to Jessica's brother joining them.

"As you know, Seeds of Life is a cult created by John Jenkins, better known to his followers as Genesis," Eagle began. "The cult was founded about three years ago, and has grown to include nearly three hundred men, women, and children. On the surface, they believe in living without the influence of modern technology. They live off the land, grow all their own food, and are almost completely self-sufficient. Upon joining the group, you must send a letter to your family members informing them that you have joined, and that you will no longer have contact with them."

That was exactly how cults operated, cutting off their members so there was no one to provide rational thought and disagree with the leader's claims and beliefs. "David got a letter?" he asked.

"About a month ago. Seems Jessica left to join Seeds of Life six months ago, but he only just found the letter and called us looking for you."

A month?

David had known for a month his sister was in danger but had done nothing about it?

"When you look a little deeper into the cult, you learn that they believe they can commune with the stars, and if you find your "star twin," Eagle did air quotes, "you will be transported to a new plane of existence. Dig deeper again, and you find that they wish to rid the earth of all unbelievers—those who aren't enlightened—and after a couple of the early members of the cult managed to get out and talk to the cops, Seeds of Life was deemed a credible threat. It is believed that they intend to start poisoning water supplies, but only those in Genesis' inner circle are privy to all the details."

This was a dangerous group. It was about so much more than growing your own food and pretending you could talk to the stars. Why didn't Jessica see that? Why did she always have to be so selfish?

Didn't she think about the impact her joining a dangerous cult would have on her brother and sisters? Hadn't the family been through enough without her creating more drama?

Rubbing his hands down his face, Scorpion sighed. "I can see Jessica getting mixed up in something like that. She doesn't have the best track record when it comes to making smart choices. Her dad was a truck driver, he was in a horrible accident when she was ten and was left completely paralyzed. The mom didn't handle it well and fell into depression and addiction. David was fifteen at the time of the accident, and while he did his best to hold everything together, even after graduating and going off to boot camp, it was difficult. The three sisters ended up going into foster care when Jessica was fifteen."

One accident had changed everything for the family, and they all still bore the scars to this day.

"Jessica didn't help out at all, in fact she made things harder for all of them by being spoiled and insisting on things they couldn't afford. She never pulled her weight, it all fell on David's shoulders. I haven't talked to David in a while so I have no idea what Jessica has been up to, but I doubt it's much. Honestly, I thought she was more likely to take the sugar daddy route than the off-the-grid cult one, but who knows. Like I said before, she doesn't make the best decisions." He frowned when he noticed Olivia pause in the middle of a braid, both her and her husband shooting him somewhat odd frowns.

Assuming it was because of Jessica and her inability to help her family out in their time of need, he brushed it off.

Bottom line was, he was reading more into it than there was because he didn't like what he was about to do next.

But there was no other choice.

David had been a great friend and they'd been there for one another during the long, hard days at boot camp. He owed it to the other man to do whatever it took to get his sister out of the dangerous cult.

Looked like he wouldn't be going on vacation after all.

"I'd like to volunteer to be the one to go in and bring Jessica home."

～

November 18th
    7:32 P.M.

As far as ideas went, this was either going to be one of her best or one of her worst.

Jessica shook her head as she glanced around at the mass of people lying outside in the grassy field. Another night of lying around in the dark, staring up at the clear, inky black sky, where a million diamonds twinkled down at them. The air was cool with the gentlest of breezes, but after toiling all day under the sun, it felt refreshing instead of cold.

It was a beautiful night, like most of the nights since she'd arrived here six months ago. Too bad she couldn't enjoy it.

But that wasn't why she was here and given the gravity of the situation there was really nothing to enjoy.

As she looked around at the hundreds of people lying flat on their backs in the grass, she searched for the one face she'd been looking for for days now.

Martha's.

Pushing the boundaries as hard as she dared, Jessica had asked around about the woman, but no one had seen her or heard from her since that day in the fields. All of Martha's things had been gone by the time Jessica returned to their tent that evening, and she prayed Martha had just gone back to her old life and wasn't lying dead somewhere out here in the forest.

Nobody had told her about this side of going undercover.

Sure, she knew that she would be putting her life at risk, she even knew that she might have to say and do things that she didn't like. But not this. In her wildest dreams she wouldn't have expected to have to stand by and let someone possibly be murdered just to keep her cover.

Naïve of her perhaps, but she had never expected to be given such a big undercover case with such high stakes, and so maybe she had been thinking more about that and how amazing it would feel to be able to crack it wide open, to consider all the other details.

Now that she was face to face with those details, Jessica found she was walking around with a ball of nausea in her gut.

Different than the fear that had been there this whole time since she walked down the road to the commune and asked to join. That fear had been heavily laced with adrenalin. It was the kind of fear that would help her, keep her instincts honed and sharp, so she could complete this op successfully and help take down one of the most dangerous terrorist groups in the country.

This nausea now was just guilt that she might have played a part—however small—in an innocent woman's death.

She didn't like that.

Knew what it felt like to have other people stand by and do nothing while you got hurt, and had vowed to never be that person. It was part of her reason for becoming a cop. Her dream had always been to be a lawyer, but since she didn't have the money to go to law school, nor the time to work the multiple jobs it would take to get there, she'd settled on the police force, knowing she would at least make a difference.

And she could make a difference in this job, she just didn't want it to be at the expense of innocent people.

Movement around her brought her attention outside of her own head and back to her surroundings. It was dangerous to let her guard down even for a moment. Genesis' inner circle was constantly roaming around and more than once she had felt their eyes on her.

Since she had never been called in to be reprimanded by Genesis for breaking a rule, she had to assume—or hope—that they were watching her because she had caught Exodus' eye and he wanted to claim her and bring her into the fold.

Evening star gazing time over, everyone began to get up, and she did, too. Together they began to make the trek back to the sleeping area. The women's long, white, flowing dresses fluttered in the breeze, the men's white shirts did the same. Some talked softly amongst themselves, others hurried to get back to the tents to get some sleep before another long, hard day of grueling work.

While she walked along with them, Jessica kept her gaze roaming, wanting to get a glimpse of Exodus or even Genesis himself. The cult leader was rarely spotted, he left it up to his men to watch over the teams working the fields while he spent his time in his tent, or out alone in the forest, meditating.

At least that was the rumor.

Sometimes he came to join them for the evening star gazing, and once she'd even caught him watching her, although she had quickly averted her gaze as they were not permitted to stare at the prophet.

Instead of finding Exodus or Genesis, her gaze landed on a man she recognized.

A man who had no business being here.

A man she had crushed on as a child but knew would never see her as anything but David's bratty, spoiled, selfish younger sister, even if none of those things could be further from the truth.

A man she had at one time wanted to trust, had tried to trust, but who had thrown that trust right back in her face.

A man she hated.

Mason Markson. Although he went by Scorpion, a name she'd always thought suited him much better.

There was no reason in the world that her brother's best friend from basic training should be here. Not a single one. Although she had made no attempt to keep tabs on the man who had stood by and allowed her to suffer out of loyalty to her brother, she knew that he had made it onto the elite Delta Force. David had bragged about it to her once like the accomplishment of his friend should somehow rub off onto him and make him better than her.

A man like Mason wouldn't get suckered into Genesis' cult, he wouldn't believe that the stars really talked to anyone, and with even the hint of the terrorist activities surrounding the cult he would never allow himself to get entangled with it.

So what was he doing here?

Anger flooded her system as she figured out the most likely reason.

Let her make one guess. He was here to "rescue" her because she was so stupid and had gotten herself mixed up in a cult.

Jerk.

The nerve of him.

How dare he look down on her when *he* was the one who was a criminal. Just because he'd never gotten caught for what he'd done didn't make it any less illegal.

Instead of treating her like she was no better than mud on his shoe, maybe he should be thanking her for not tanking his career by going to his superiors and informing them just what kind of man he was.

Damn, he made her blood boil like nobody else could.

The only person she hated more than Mason was her despicable brother, and she'd always known he wasn't a nice guy. While it was just excessive teasing and tormenting before their father's accident, it had taken a sadistic and cruel turn after.

Now Mason was looking at her with that infuriating smug look that told her everything she needed to know. He thought she was pathetic, a loser, and from the expression on his face it was a fifty-fifty chance whether he kissed her or tanned her hide when he caught up with her.

Not that either was happening.

Childish crush aside, she had no desire to kiss Mason even if he did have the most kissable set of lips she'd ever seen. And she was definitely not into spanking, not that there was anything wrong with it if both people were into it, but it wasn't her thing. She liked her lovers on the rough side but not arrogant, and Mason was definitely way too arrogant for her tastes.

Too bad for him he wouldn't be catching up with her either. She was here to do a job and she wasn't leaving until it was done. No jerk from her past was going to change that no matter how sexy he looked.

The worst part about it was that he *did* look sexy.

Just because she wasn't interested in anything—not even steamy, hot sex—with him, it didn't mean she wasn't a woman and he wasn't one very attractive man.

But outside beauty was nothing if it wasn't backed up by inner beauty. One thing she knew for sure about Mason Markson was that he was as black as the night sky inside. Already he'd burned her once, and she had no intention of letting him mess up this case for her. It was a career builder, and after everything she'd been through she deserved to build a life for herself that didn't include pain and torment.

Mason was nothing but.

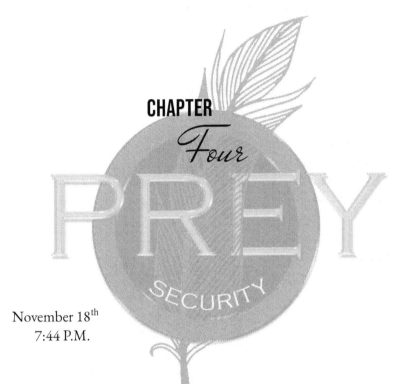

CHAPTER

Four

PREY

SECURITY

November 18th
7:44 P.M.

Scorpion scanned the crowd for his prey.

He didn't want to be there, but since he and David had been through a lot together, he felt he owed it to his old friend to come in and rescue his sister.

So he'd come.

Eagle had insisted it wasn't necessary, that he could send in someone else from Prey to find and extract Jessica, but Scorpion felt obligated to be the one to do it.

Four days ago, he'd arrived at the commune, his backstory complete and verifiable should they choose to look into him. From what they'd been able to put together from those who had left the cult in its early days when they realized it was more than just a group of people who wanted to reject the modern world and live off-the-grid, it would take him at least a month of initiation before he'd make it to those who were already part of the enlightened.

That hadn't happened.

After just a couple of days he'd passed all their tests, said all the right things, and now here he was, spending his first night star gazing with the others.

With going on three hundred people in the cult, he thought it might take some time before he was able to track Jessica down, but it seemed he was wrong.

There she was.

His gaze landed on none other than Jessica Bowen herself. Although she was a few years older than the last time he had seen her, she looked the same. Long golden blonde locks that hung all the way down her back in a mess of waves brushing her backside, eyes that could be blue one second, green the next, and gray the second after that. Long, slender legs, and a perky set of breasts just visible beneath the floaty white dress she wore, she was stunning, no doubt about it, but too bad the personality didn't match the package.

Right now, she was looking through the crowds of people heading back after the nightly stargazing time. Searching for whatever loser she followed here? That was David's story, that his sister had fallen for a loser who had wound up getting them both mixed up with the cult.

Typical Jessica drama.

Only this time she was in way over her head.

While he watched her, he noted the minutia of her expression. She didn't have a lovey-dovey expression on her face like she was looking for a man she loved enough to give up the creature comforts of home and follow to a place where she would be required to get her hands dirty every single day.

Neither did she have the same semi-vacant expression that the rest of the cult members had. Stargazing time was supposed to be the most sacred time of the day, kind of the equivalent of going to church. This time was vital to their eternity, if you didn't find your star twin you would be destined to remain here on earth and be poisoned along with the rest of the population. These people took it seriously, they focused on the stars, and walked away afterward doing their best to look pious like they were making strides in finding their connection.

The expression on her face conveyed neither.

It was serene in a different way, like she was carefully keeping it blank so no one knew what she was really thinking.

When her gaze finally met his, there was a moment of shock, like he was the last person she expected to find here, but it quickly passed, and her eyes narrowed in frustration.

Not what he was expecting.

If she'd recognized him at all—and he hadn't been sure that she would since it had been thirteen years since they had last seen each other, and back then she'd been just a fifteen-year-old kid—he would have thought she was either afraid, having realized this cult was hardcore, or she would have been grateful to see him assuming he was here to rescue her.

But that wasn't the case.

Even across the distance between them he could feel anger radiating off her in waves that seemed to be increasing in strength with each second that ticked by.

His own eyes narrowed.

Scorpion knew he'd been lied to.

Jessica was here for a reason and it wasn't what her brother had told him, or because she believed in Genesis and his mission. There was no man hanging around her, and she'd been walking with the other women, which meant she was staying in one of the women only tents. If she was here with a lover, where was he? And why wasn't she more afraid of these people? It was clear she hadn't just experienced a magical, religious stargazing experience.

What was going on?

Despite the fact that she turned her back on him in an obvious attempt to ignore him and shut him out, he followed after her. Working his way through the crowd wasn't easy, there were a lot of people, and they were whispering amongst themselves, all hyped and excited after their special time.

When he reached her, Scorpion snapped a hand around her bicep and tugged her away from the others, deeper into the woods. It was a risk to slip away from the others. If they were caught they would both be punished, but he had to know what was going on. He'd come here with the idea of finding her and saving her.

Maybe it hadn't been with the best of intentions. He was here because he felt like he owed David, but maybe he also wanted to lecture Jessica, tell her off for how she'd treated her family when they'd needed her to rally, and make her see that it was time to grow up.

But regardless of his reasons, he hadn't been here to take risks. Get in, get through the orientation, find Jessica, tell her he was getting her out of there, wait until dark, and then hike her out of there, deliver his lecture and then hand her off to her brother.

Now things had changed, and he needed to know exactly what he was dealing with so he could figure out his next step.

While Jessica didn't fight him as he guided her away from the throng of star lovers, the second he stopped she ripped her arm out of his grip and spun to face him. Pure fury shot out of those blue eyes of hers.

"What are you doing here?" she growled.

Annoyance spiked. He was doing her a favor, too, by coming here, not just her big brother. The least she could do was show him a little gratitude. Surely, she wasn't so stupid that she hadn't figured out there was more to this group than stars and living off the land. Months she'd been here, she had to have picked up the clues and heard about what Seeds of Life believed should be done to all those who didn't believe.

"Rescuing your ungrateful butt," he snapped. Was it really too much to ask that she say thank you and ask how quickly he was going to get her out of there?

"Of course," she sneered. "Perfect Mason Markson swooping in to save the day with his special forces powers." An eye roll of epic proportions followed. "You forget that I know for a fact that you are not as perfect as you pretend to be."

He didn't have a clue what she was talking about.

Nor did he care.

Better to just take this opportunity while everybody was distracted heading back to the tents to settle down for the night and get out of there. Whatever was going on with Jessica wasn't his business and he had no intention of making it his business. The quicker he handed her off for debriefing the quicker he could wipe his hands of her and head off on his family vacation.

"Let's get out of here." When he went to grab her arm again, throw her over his shoulder, and haul her out of there if she wasn't going to cooperate, she dodged out of his reach.

"Did it ever occur to you that maybe I don't need saving?"

Honestly?

No.

It hadn't.

"Let's go, while nobody is around," he said again. It had been hard sneaking it in, but he had a single vial of sedative sewn into the lining of his pants. Scorpion hadn't really thought he'd need it, because why wouldn't Jessica want to be rescued from the terrorist cult, but he'd thought it was better to be safe than sorry.

Now he was glad of that.

Knocking her out would give him a couple of hours to hike out of here and call in Prey to take custody of Jessica. They'd make sure she was debriefed and then returned to her brother who could deal with her however he wanted.

"You're going to ruin everything," Jessica hissed.

Shoving aside his preconceived notions of Jessica, the kind of person she was and the reasons he thought she'd be there, Scorpion took a moment to really look at her. Her posture was confident, her attitude as well, she knew what she was doing, and she was focused solely on that purpose.

Just like that he got it.

Jessica wasn't here for personal reasons, she was here for work.

A cop.

She was an undercover cop working a case.

November 18th
8:04 P.M.

"Leave," Jessica ordered, fuming. Honestly, it felt like a volcano had gone off inside her and she was seconds away from erupting. If she didn't know she was putting her life—and the life of this arrogant man although she cared less about that at the moment—in danger by being out here, and even more so by screaming at him and telling him exactly what she thought of him, she would have exploded already.

How dare the great and mighty Mason Markson come here thinking he knew what was best for her, potentially messing up all her hard work.

Nope.

No way.

This case was too big. Too important. She had been playing this role for six months now and she was making progress. No jerk from her past who thought he was better than her was going to ruin that.

The audacity of it had her literally fuming and she had to curl her hands into fists so she didn't lash out at him. Normally she wasn't a violent person, had never hit anyone in her life, but this man pushed her buttons like nobody else could.

Instead of leaving, he glared at her. "You're a cop."

Jessica was somewhat surprised he'd figured that out. She didn't believe he was the brightest bulb, and she knew he wasn't a good guy. Mason had known what had been happening to her when she was a teen and he had done nothing to stop it. She had no idea how he made it into the military, let alone into special forces, and then got a job with the world-renowned Prey Security.

"Duh." Okay so that was a slightly childish response, but this man absolutely brought out the worst in her. "Contrary to what you seem to think, I don't break the law. That would be you and David." She would never forgive her brother for what he'd done to her, and since Mason knew and hadn't stopped it, he was just as responsible as far as she was concerned.

From the look on his face, Mason was shocked by her admission. Well good for him. Did he think she wasn't aware that he knew what David was doing to her?

What an idiot.

Maybe he really had thought all these years that she hadn't realized he was in on what her brother was doing. For all she knew they split the profits, thought it was their dirty little secret, and since she hadn't reported them, they'd gotten away with it.

Not reporting them wasn't to help either of these men out, it was because she hadn't wanted to think about what had happened to her. After being put in foster care she'd wanted to forget all about it and focus on a new life. Part of her feared that made her a coward because she knew hiding from a problem didn't make it go away, but she'd finally been in a good place and she had feared focusing on the past would ruin what could be her future.

Standing here now though, as an adult who was finally happy with herself and in a good place, staring down the man who had participated in her suffering she wished she'd told the cops what David and Mason had done to her. It would feel so good to know they were paying for their crimes.

But this wasn't about her and her past, this was about stopping a terrorist attack from being perpetrated on US soil. She was not going to fail at this, and Mason could mess everything up if he didn't leave and pretend he'd never seen her there.

"Leave before you ruin everything," she ordered. Why did he have to choose now to pretend he was all noble and cared one iota about her and her safety? It would have been nice if he'd felt that same way when she was a thirteen-year-old kid being pimped out by her scumbag brother so he'd have money to spend on himself and not their struggling family.

"These people are dangerous."

"Duh." Wow, he really thought she was stupid, didn't he?

"Genesis isn't who he portrays himself to be."

"Duh," she said again. How was she supposed to reason with a man who thought she had the intellectual capacity of a toddler? "What part about this is my job did you miss? That's why I'm here, to stop Genesis before he can follow through on his plans. Now leave before you blow my cover."

Jessica turned her back on him, completely and utterly done with him and his absolute stupidity. Mason kept acting like she was the one who was stupid, but he was the one who couldn't seem to get that she was trained for this, it was her job, and she was good at it.

The longer they stayed out here, the more they risked getting caught. She had no intention of being found to be breaking any of the rules because if she wanted to get into the inner circle, she needed a perfect track record. It was time to get back to the tents. Already he'd cost her any chance to get eyes on Genesis tonight. At least she could go and get some sleep ready for another day of hard toiling tomorrow.

There was too much to do to spare another second of her time on this idiot of a man. Best to forget he was even here. If he wanted to waste his time playing hero to a woman who didn't need saving, then that was his own prerogative. Mason was nothing to her and how he chose to spend his time was none of her concern.

She was part way back to the path where the last stragglers were still making their way toward the tents when a hand snapped around her wrist, stopping her.

"Let go of me," she growled, trying to break his hold but he held firm. Big as he was—and he was mighty big and pure, solid muscle—she could probably take him down, but that was likely to draw attention to them, and that was the last thing she needed. Already, he'd put her entire mission at risk. She wasn't going to go and make things worse.

"If you're staying, I'm staying."

Arrogant much? "You somehow managed to figure it out yourself. I'm a cop. This is my job. If my superiors didn't feel it necessary to provide me with a babysitter, I don't see why you're volunteering for the job."

"Maybe they didn't realize how dangerous this was."

Damn. He just couldn't stop insulting her.

Knowing what kind of man Mason was, it shouldn't hurt that he thought so little of her. She had never done anything to him, yet he'd stood by and allowed her brother to force her to prostitute herself, and now, without having anything to do with her since she was a teenager, he was here telling her she was useless at her job and needed him.

She didn't need him.

She didn't need anyone.

The path she had forged for herself was all because of her own hard work, no one had been there for her except those last few years after she and her sisters went into foster care. There had been no one to have her back while she tried to hold her family together. Even now, she took care of herself, her sisters, and paid for their father's care.

That this infuriating man thought he was staying here to do her some kind of favor because he saw her as weak, pathetic, and incapable of taking care of herself was the biggest insult of all.

Speaking through gritted teeth, she somehow managed to keep the words quiet so as not to attract attention when really, she wanted to scream them at the top of her lungs. "I don't know why you hate me, and frankly I don't care because the feeling is absolutely mutual, but I am not the stupid, useless woman you seem to think I am. I have been doing this for six months and managed to keep myself alive and safe. I report to my superiors and I make the sacrifices I need to make to keep my cover. You being here is not going to be a help to me, it's going to be a hindrance, because I'm going to have to constantly worry that you're going to do something stupid and not only ruin my case but put me in danger by having to cover for you as well as myself."

Pausing to draw in a ragged breath, all those feelings of worthlessness she had battled so hard to overcome, rushed back after one conversation with this man.

It was the last thing she needed right now when she had to keep her head firmly in the game.

"I. Don't. Need. You."

"Too bad."

"Too bad?" she spluttered, but Mason had already released her wrist and walked past her, following the last few people as they headed for the tents.

Why did this have to happen to her?

Hadn't she been through enough?

Why did the universe now feel the need to trap her here with a dangerous cult and the world's most infuriating man?

How was she going to pull this off without losing her mind in the process?

CHAPTER *Five*

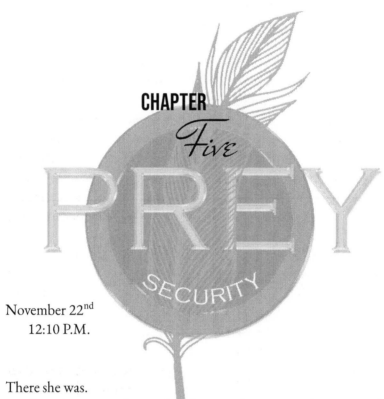

November 22nd
12:10 P.M.

There she was.

Scorpion stopped scanning the crowd as soon as his gaze settled on Jessica.

No matter what they were doing, over the last several days he was constantly looking out for her. Every time he saw her, something odd settled in his chest. He kept telling himself that it was just that she was his responsibility while he was there, but he knew it was a lie.

In truth, there was no reason he had to stay. He'd done his duty, come to rescue a friend's sister, only to find out that she didn't need saving after all. Leaving with a clear conscience was easy. There was nothing for him to do there, if Jessica's bosses had thought she needed backup they would have assigned another cop to infiltrate the cult.

So why couldn't he make himself leave?

It would be easy enough to slip away, but the thought of leaving Jessica there alone felt wrong for some reason.

Although, she would likely not believe him, it wasn't because he thought she was incompetent, or stupid, or incapable of doing her job. It was because ...

He wasn't even sure.

It just felt wrong to leave. So, he wasn't. Prey was expecting him to be in orientation for at least a month, so no one would know that he was already here, part of the cult, and not in contact with Jessica yet.

Maybe that was why he was having trouble walking away.

If Seeds of Life was willing to bypass the orientation process and let him just jump into things while he knew some of the older people and women who had been there before him were still there, then there was a reason. Scorpion suspected the reason was that they were getting ready to start enacting their plans. Leaving Jessica alone there just as things were about to start heating up seemed totally wrong.

So, he was staying.

Whether she liked it or not.

From the frown on her face when she spotted him, he knew she absolutely did not like it. In fact, she totally hated it.

Hated him.

That she had made more than clear.

As she helped a few other women lay out lunch for the men, their white dresses floating around them, giving them an almost ethereal look, she steadfastly refused to meet his gaze again. Men and women were forbidden from interacting unless they were already in a committed relationship when they came here, or they had been paired up by Genesis himself. But he wasn't asking for her to sit down and ream him out again—or even to have a reasonable, adult conversation—he just wanted her to acknowledge him.

Which was stupid given he hadn't thought of her in well over a decade.

It was what she'd said earlier.

He couldn't get it out of his head.

She had accused him and David of breaking the law, and from the look on her face, she believed that to be the truth even though he knew it wasn't. She was the one who had.

Crazy woman.

Only watching her these last few days she certainly didn't look crazy.

The opposite in fact. He watched her all the time, and she was playing her part to perfection. She seemed to know exactly what to say, and he could see her making inroads into getting herself into Genesis' inner circle. She was cautious and careful to follow all the rules, she worked hard, rose with the others, cooked breakfast, served the men before eating, and then worked in the fields. Lunchtime and dinner she had to help cook and serve before being allowed to eat.

There were no complaints from her about the hard work, no whining about broken nails or dirty hair, no whinging about the lack of clothing choices or the fact that she slept in a cot in a tent. It was like the woman he thought she was had never even existed because this woman was nothing like the Jessica he had been led to believe she was.

The more Scorpion watched her, the more he realized that he might have been wrong about her. He hadn't actually spent much time with her, his opinions were based mostly on what her brother had said. But the woman David described and the woman he saw throwing herself completely into her case were not the same woman at all.

David had lied to him.

That much was clear. Because there was no way the spoiled girl who had used all the money her brother had sent them for bills on clothes and makeup for herself, who had sold her body for more money, would grow up to become a cop who could so seamlessly play this role.

Good actress was one thing, but this level of commitment to a role was another.

Who was the real Jessica? And why had David lied about her?

It made no sense. Scorpion hadn't even known Jessica other than that she was his boot camp friend's little sister. There was no need to paint her as anything other than his kid sister. It seemed so pointless, but if there was one thing he had learned in his years in Delta Force and now with Prey, it was that nothing happened without a reason.

As Jessica set down a bowl of soup in front of him, he wondered what David's reason for lying about her had been.

She gave no indication that they had a shared past, that she knew who he was, or that they had ever met before as she moved on to fill the bowl of soup of the man sitting beside him.

Unable to take his eyes off her, he watched as she moved on down the line at the huge outdoor wooden table where they were seated. Not that she appreciated him watching her. Even though there was no outward sign of her irritation, he could feel it as though she were broadcasting it loud and clear.

Any time he got near her, she would hiss in his ear to just keep out of her way. Of course, he wasn't going to do that. For now, she was just going to have to make her peace with the fact that she had a partner in this case. He would not leave until he helped her bring down the terrorist cult leader, whether she wanted him to or not, and then he was going to figure out who Jessica Bowen really was.

"She's hot," the man beside him whispered, and Scorpion realized he'd been watching her too closely.

A stupid mistake, and one he knew better than to make. If he was here to watch Jessica's back, then he was going to have to do a better job of it. One slip up, and not only would he ruin her months of hard work, but he would be putting both of their lives at risk.

It was clear from what he'd seen that Jessica was good at her job, he'd never had trouble playing a role before, so he was going to have to match her skill. His acting skills weren't as good as hers, but he had a feeling he had a lot to make up for. Whatever she thought he might have done, he hadn't, but it didn't matter, it had obviously hurt her nonetheless, there was no other reason she'd hate someone she hardly knew.

"I'm not here to meet a woman," he said, somewhat haughtily. While it was permissible for the men to talk quietly amongst themselves during mealtime, he had no interest in talking to any of the men, even less if it was about Jessica. For some reason he felt a stab of something that was way too close to jealousy for his liking at the thought of another man being interested in Jessica.

"Seems like you are, the way you've been staring at her. Seen you do it before, too. You know her?" the man persisted, obviously not catching the leave me alone vibes Scorpion was sure he was shooting off.

"Never met her before," he muttered, embarrassed that as trained as he was, he'd made it so obvious that he was watching Jessica. No wonder she wanted him as far away from her and her case as she could get him.

He was going to have to do better.

The last thing he wanted to do was put Jessica in more danger than she already was. It was clear she was committed to her case, wasn't leaving until she achieved her goals, and he believed she could do it, too.

Maybe he should leave.

Was he staying to prove to himself that he had been right about her all along and she really was the immature, selfish, and spoiled woman he had always believed her to be? Or was he here because he really did want to watch her back and make sure the sister of an old friend stayed alive?

Scorpion knew he better figure out the answer to that question and quickly, otherwise he was a liability to both Jessica and himself.

$\sim$

November 24th
    11:02 P.M.

She knew he was following her.

Did he think he had some sort of magical powers of silence that allowed him to walk through the forest undetected?

Stupid man.

Of course, she could hear him. He was a mere mortal after all, even if he seemed to think otherwise.

Damn, he was so arrogant it was becoming a distraction.

That and the fact that she found herself watching him, seeking him out when she should be focused on more important things.

Like the reason she was there.

Jessica was getting more annoyed with Mason by the day. Strike that, by the hour. Could she strike that again and say by the minute? Because the man was super level annoying. Like master level. He followed her everywhere, made sure they were working the same fields or tending the animals at the same shifts, watched her near constantly, and couldn't seem to understand basic English.

How many times exactly had she told him to leave her alone? A hundred? A thousand? It felt like a million.

Yet he didn't get it, refused to back off, refused to leave her alone, and refused to give her space. Refused to trust that not only did she know what she was doing, but she was good at what she was doing. Acting was a skill she had been forced to develop so nobody learned how bad things had gotten at home. Now it was a skill she could put to good use to save lives.

It was the fact that his presence here reinforced her knowledge that he thought she was an incompetent, useless, good-for-nothing woman that bothered her the most.

Exactly the same way she'd felt when her brother pimped her out.

Time had healed those wounds, but they left behind horrible, lumpy, jagged scars that were still tender when rubbed the wrong way.

Mason was an expert at rubbing her the wrong way.

Despite the dozens of times she'd told him to leave, here he was, following her again. If he kept it up, he was going to blow her cover. Didn't he at least get that this case was important to her?

"I know you're there," she hissed. If she didn't get him to go back to his tent now it would be too late. Tonight was the night she was making her move and she wasn't letting any arrogant jerk from her past ruin that.

Mason stepped out from between the trees and shot her what she was sure he thought was a sexy smirk that would have women falling at his feet.

Her panties absolutely did not get wet at the sight of it.

Not. At. All.

And if that was a lie it was only a teensy weensy one.

"Not many people can hear me when I'm following them," he said.

Rolling her eyes was the only appropriate response to that ego dripping statement. "Well, yay for me then."

"Seriously. I spent years in the military learning not to let someone know I was following them. My life and the lives of my teammates depend on it. But you always seem to know when I'm around."

Jessica fixed him with a glare. Did he think saying stupid things like that was supposed to make her like him more? Because that wasn't happening. Okay, she could begrudgingly accept that she found him physically attractive. After all, she was a woman, and he was one hell of a good-looking man.

But that was it.

Attraction, nothing more, nothing less.

Right now, she didn't have time for something as meaningless as attraction.

"What part of this is my job did you not get?" This was getting beyond a joke. She was about a day away from reaching out to her handler and asking them to do something about Mason. There wasn't a whole lot they could do, not without breaking her cover or raiding the cult before she had all the information she needed, but maybe if they talked to Prey, they could somehow force Mason to leave. Surely he—like she did—had a way to connect with his team. They could tell him he had to leave. At least she hoped so.

Expression growing serious, smirk fading away, all pretenses that he was trying to get along with her gone, he said, "Tell me why you think I broke the law."

Not the direction she had expected this conversation to go.

Why was he asking her that?

Now was a terrible time to be discussing the past, and she failed to see how it had any relevance to their current situation.

"Stop being ridiculous, we both know you did. But don't worry, I'm not going to go running to your boss to blab. Unless threatening that would make you leave," she said hopefully. She wasn't above blackmail when it came to this, this case was too important to let a man like Mason ruin it.

Mason didn't comment. His gaze had gone far away like he was focused on something else, listening to something. Then he grabbed her and shoved her up against a tree, using his body to pin her in place.

She would have fought him, but she heard the same thing he had.

Voices.

One of them belonged to Genesis, another to Exodus, and at least two other men who she recognized as some of the guards who watched over them.

The next second a gunshot went off, and the unmistakable sound of a body hitting the ground.

"We have to go," she whispered. "If they see us here, they'll kill us." Tonight, she had been planning on making her first move to show she had found her star twin. It was why she was out there, wandering around, she'd wanted to get found, only not by Mason.

But being found like this?

It was a death sentence.

They were eliminating someone who wanted to leave the cult, she was sure of it. Any second how Genesis and Exodus were going to see them. All her hard work would be for nothing. Not only would she not get the intel they needed to bring Seeds of Life down, but she was also going to wind up dead, which meant her little sisters would have no family left.

"If we go, they'll see us," Mason whispered in her ear, his lips close enough she could feel the warm puffs of air as he breathed out. Slow and steady. Not concerned in the least. At least he had that going for him, he didn't panic in an emergency.

And this was an emergency.

They were seconds away from certain death.

Every instinct she had urged her to run, hide, but Mason was right, if they moved now they would be seen. If they stayed where they were there was a chance—a *slim* chance—that Genesis and Exodus wouldn't notice them in the dark as they headed back to the camp.

"Too late," she murmured. Behind him, she saw the two men step through the trees, their gazes falling on her and Mason.

It was over.

Her body tensed as she waited for the coming gunshot that would end her life.

Or maybe they would drag her and Mason off, interrogate them to see if they were spies.

If they found out that she was an undercover cop and Mason worked for one of the best private security firms in the world, then the two of them would be tortured before they were executed.

Knowing she was taking a huge risk accepting this assignment and actually getting caught were two different things. Terror pulsed inside her even as she stayed rooted in place.

Next thing she knew, Mason was trying to rip her clothes off her. What was he doing? He was going to get himself killed for touching her alone, let alone doing the forbidden by being out here at night.

Exodus was fixated on her. She'd been trying to attract his attention from the beginning, and it had worked. She knew he'd been talking her up to Genesis as a potential partner. Genesis was looking for a beautiful, angelic-looking woman he could impregnate and bring into his new world. With her long, wavy blonde locks, eyes that seemed to shift from blue to green to gray, and delicate features she fit the part.

Genesis wasn't going to like anyone else touching her. Neither was Exodus. In fact, fury marred both their faces as they looked at Mason.

When she turned her gaze to him, she saw determination and acceptance in his expression.

Her heart dropped.

Was he doing this to protect her?

Why would he do that?

The man she knew Mason to be wouldn't care if he got her hurt or even killed. Was this his way of trying to make up for the mistakes he'd made in the past? For not doing something to protect her when she was a helpless teenager whose brother was forcing her to sell her body?

Or was it possible she'd been wrong about him all along and the man she believed him to be wasn't the true Mason after all?

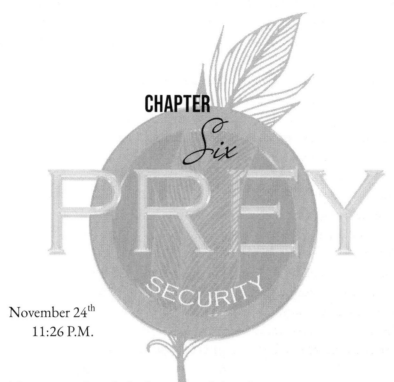

CHAPTER *Six*

November 24th
11:26 P.M.

This was not how he had envisioned this playing out.

Actually, nothing about this whole thing was how he thought it would work when he decided to be the one to come in and extract Jessica. She wasn't the woman he'd thought she was, she wasn't here for the reasons he thought she was, and this cult was a lot more dangerous than he had realized.

"Get away from her, she's mine," Genesis growled.

Scorpion froze, chancing one glance at Jessica and silently pleading with her not to do anything stupid. If she didn't go along with this then both of them were going to wind up dead.

As he saw it, there was at least a ninety percent chance that he wasn't making it out of here alive, but the same didn't have to be true for Jess. She was here on a mission that seemed to be working. She'd caught the attention of the cult leader, and she might actually stand a chance at achieving what she'd come here for and dismantling the cult before it could follow through with its plans.

If he had to die for that to happen it was a sacrifice he was prepared to make.

Either he was killed for being out here where he wasn't supposed to be at a time where he was supposed to be in his tent sleeping so he was well rested for the coming day of toiling the land, or because he was pawing at an unwilling woman. In the end, dead was dead, and if he could make it look like he'd been the one to prey on Jessica and she hadn't done anything wrong, he could hopefully spare her life.

It was the right thing to do and ...

He couldn't shake the feeling that he owed Jessica. Big time. For some reason her brother had been lying about her. There was no other explanation because the woman before him bore no resemblance to the woman he'd been led to believe she was.

Right now, it didn't matter why David had lied, all that mattered was keeping Jessica alive. Scorpion couldn't pinpoint exactly why her safety and her life felt so important to him personally, nor did he want to examine it too closely.

"It's not what you think," Jessica stammered, stepping around him.

Although he tried to make a grab for her and stop her from doing anything that was going to put her in even more danger, she moved quickly and gracefully. Making his attempt to keep his body between her and the threat the two armed men presented too obvious which would only up the danger even more, and it was already clocking in at extreme.

"He's my brother," Jessica said, gesturing at him even as she crept closer to Genesis. Somehow, she managed to sound both contrite and submissive, with a hint of confidence. "I felt something on me, thought it was a spider. I'm a little ... afraid of them. My brother was helping me try to find it and get it off me."

Exodus huffed, clearly not believing the lie, but Genesis gifted Jessica with a smile. "We all have fears, my child."

"What were you doing out here at night?" Exodus asked. "It is forbidden. Punishable by up to ten days in the reflection shed and a public flogging." The man's eyes sparked a little too much, his tone a little too excited at the idea of whipping another person. While Genesis was more self-deluded, self-aggrandizing, classic cult leader who wanted to be a God to as many people as possible, Exodus was more plain old psychopath. He garnered his pleasure through other people's pain.

Still, what he'd said was true. It was forbidden to be out at night after the stargazing. Everyone was supposed to stay in their assigned tents until five in the morning when they woke for morning chores and breakfast.

How was Jessica going to explain their presence here in any plausible way?

Obviously, he shouldn't have worried because the woman dropped to her knees, tears tumbling down her cheeks, the picture of submissive innocence. And he felt Genesis already begin to relax, falling for her sweet little innocent girl act.

"I was weak, my Lord. I am sorry," Jessica cried. "My brother is new here. He came after I shared with him our goals, he is a true believer as am I. But we have a sister, and I am so very worried about her. When I first came here, I told them both about Seeds of Life but neither were ready to hear the truth. Now that my brother has had his eyes opened, I wanted to know if he had any luck in convincing our sister that this is the only place she should be with the war coming. I'm so sorry, my Lord, I deserve to be punished for my disobedience. I was weak, but I will become stronger."

Jessica finished on a sob, and it took everything he had not to grin and clap her Oscar-worthy performance. Wow. She really was good at this. If she hadn't decided to become a cop, she could have had a successful career as an actress. Somehow, she managed to infuse genuine feeling and emotion into her words. They felt real and that made others believe them.

With talent like that, what had made her decide to become a police officer?

Did it have anything to do with her past and the things she'd done as a teenager?

Maybe she'd had a brush with the law and been caught prostituting herself. It was possible, given her young age, that instead of charging her, a cop with a big heart had decided to cut her a break, get her counselling and off the streets for good. That could have been her turning point, and she could have decided to use the second chance to help others like herself.

Genesis stooped and offered her his hand. "It is okay, my child, we all have moments of weakness. It is in acknowledging them that we learn to grow strong."

Giving an enthusiastic nod as though she truly believed that this man was as close to a god as one could get, she even managed to produce a genuine blush as she looked at his hand holding hers.

"Thank you so much for understanding, Prophet," she gushed, sounding more like a giddy schoolgirl than a woman who had successfully infiltrated the cult and worked hard for months to make inroads. There was no way Genesis or anyone else was going to suspect her of being a spy, not with this performance she was giving. "I ... I don't want to be weak. I want to grow strong, like ... you. I feel ..." she trailed off as though troubled and uncertain if she should proceed.

Having hooked him, Genesis leaned slightly toward her. "What, my child? You may speak freely. Perhaps it was not a random event that led us together tonight, perhaps it was fate."

Nodding eagerly, Jessica continued. "I felt ... drawn here. To this place. I came to meet my brother to ask about my sister, just like I told you, but ..."

"There was something more to it?" Genesis asked.

Another nod, this one earnest. Who knew you could communicate so much with just a nod of your head?

"Yes, exactly. I don't know what it was, it was like I was *supposed* to be here. Like something was calling me here to this spot right at this very moment. Does that sound ... stupid?" she asked tentatively.

"No, my child. Not at all." Genesis looked up at the sky, which was clear tonight, thousands of stars twinkling down on them. "They communicate with us in many ways."

Scorpion had no idea if this man actually believed all this nonsense about talking stars, or if it was just a way for him to lure in those who were desperate to believe in something, to find a place to belong. If Genesis truly believed, it made him that much more dangerous. True believers would do almost anything to protect the source of their belief.

"You and your brother will join me in my tent, beautiful angel,"

Genesis announced. Still holding her hand, he tugged on it slightly, drawing her closer, and Scorpion had to fight off a bolt of jealousy.

Not only was Jessica not his, but he knew she had nothing but loathing for the man she had come here with the express purpose of destroying.

"Really?" Jessica shot the man a winning smile. "You want me and my brother to come and spend time at your tent? I feel like I am unworthy to step foot in your sacred space, Prophet."

"You were led to me tonight, sweet angel. I do not ignore what the stars tell me, and right now they are telling me to keep you close."

She'd done it.

Jessica had gotten the cult leader to see her as the angel he was searching for, *and* she'd managed to save both of their lives.

The woman was flat out amazing, and Scorpion found himself wanting to know everything about her, including how he'd hurt her so badly and how he could make up for it.

~

November 24th
11:59 P.M.

Phew.

That was a close one.

Jessica hadn't been sure it would work, but Genesis was falling all over himself to ingratiate himself with her. He might be a dangerous terrorist, but he was also a true believer in his cause.

While that did make him that much more dangerous, because when you cared about something you tended to protect it with everything you had, it also made him easier to manipulate. All she'd had to do was imply that it was the stars calling out to her to be out there at the exact same time as he was, and he was ready to take that and run with it.

Thankfully.

Because otherwise she and Mason could both be dead right now.

Instead, tonight not only had she saved herself and Mason, but she had gotten exactly what she came here for. Now that she was that much closer to becoming a part of Genesis' inner circle, she would have access to everything. Her bosses were going to be thrilled. And shockingly enough it was partly because of the man walking quietly beside her.

She slid a quick glance Mason's way. Was it at all possible she had been wrong about him?

It seemed so unlikely given that she knew he had turned a blind eye to what her brother was doing to her, but that man and this one who had been willing to die just to give her a chance at living didn't seem to match up. Just because she didn't know how all the pieces fit together— yet—she was willing to admit that maybe things weren't as black and white as she had assumed. Maybe there was a reason for the way things had gone down all those years ago.

Please let there be a reason.

Stupid though it might be, the man was growing on her, and she found herself wanting to believe he was a good guy. Maybe it was because he had been so persistent in his refusal to leave her alone here. It was definitely infuriating—although given the sacrifice he had been willing to make for her less infuriating than it had been an hour ago— but in a weird kind of way it was also ... nice.

There had never been anyone who cared enough to completely ignore her wishes and do what they felt was best for her.

Sure, she was capable and competent, and she didn't need a partner for this case, but in its own annoying way, what Mason had done for her was nice.

While he didn't glance her way as they walked through the forest toward the part of the commune occupied by Genesis and his inner circle, Jessica could sense him watching over her. Just because he didn't have a weapon on him, it didn't mean he couldn't take these men down if he had to. His hands were his weapon, and along with that toned, muscles body of his, he could do a lot of damage. He was one well trained killing machine, only Genesis and his men had no idea of it.

A warm feeling of safety bubbled up inside her, and her smile turned genuine and not just a part of her ruse to keep her role in tact and get the intel she needed.

"Since he is your brother, you may both sleep in there," Genesis said when they reached his tent. It was a little way aways from the others, and much larger, but it was still a tent. As the three of them stepped inside, Jessica saw that there were two sleeping areas, divided from the main living space, which consisted of just a table and chairs, two rocking chairs, a small wood stove, and a roll top desk.

"Thank you, my prophet," she said, keeping her tone sweet and innocent.

Genesis cupped her cheek, and she felt Mason stiffen protectively beside her. Or was that jealousy? Whatever the reason, she silently willed him not to do anything to ruin what she was building here.

Wanting to keep her safe was one thing, but messing up all her hard work was another. After everything he'd done to her, at the very least, he owed her not messing up the case that was going to make her career.

"We have much to talk about, my sweet angel child. I have many questions I need to ask to find out if you are the one," Genesis told her as his fingers stroked her temple. His touch sickened her because she knew what kind of man he was, but she kept her body relaxed and a smile pinned to her face. "I will return later and we will talk, but now I must go and meditate, seek the guidance of our Goddess."

Both she and Mason remained in place until Genesis and Exodus left the tent. As the flap closed behind the two men, Jessica finally let out a breath of relief. They were both safe, both alive, and as long as she continued to pull Genesis in then they would stay that way, and they'd take down one of the most dangerous domestic terrorists to ever make plans to attack their country.

She wasn't quite sure when things had changed from a she to a they, but for now, she was just going to roll with it. Truth was, if Mason hadn't been there tonight who knows if things would have worked out this well.

Retreating to the small space where Genesis had told them they would spend the night, Mason held up a fist. "You did it, you got in." His voice was sincere and there was admiration in his eyes.

Jessica felt a flush of pride. She didn't need Mason's praise, but somehow it felt nice. Lifting her own hand and curling her fingers into a fist, she bumped it against Mason's. "Maybe you and your intrusiveness actually paid off."

"Ha, see, told you it was a good thing I stuck around," he teased, amusement dancing in his eyes.

She chuckled. "Don't go getting an inflated ego, it's big enough as it is."

"Why did you do it?" he asked, sobering.

"Do what?"

"Save my life tonight. I was seconds away from being shot and you intervened. You didn't have to, they would have believed I'd dragged you out there to assault you, you were in the clear, but you put yourself in danger to save me."

"Contrary to what you seem to think of me, Mason, I do the right thing even if I don't particularly like the person." The *unlike you* part went without saying. The old Mason wouldn't have put his life on the line for her, but maybe the years had changed him, and he wasn't that man anymore.

"I feel like we got our wires crossed somewhere along the way." Studying her thoughtfully, he looked almost sad about that. When he held out his hand again, she couldn't help but notice how big it was and how strong those long fingers of his looked. Prominent veins lined his forearms and his shirt strained against his muscled biceps. "What about a truce? I'd like to stay and help you close this out. Not because I think you can't do it on your own," he added before she could remind him that this was in fact her job. "But because I like to finish what I start, and I'm here now, I'm involved, and I want to stay and help. Want to be your partner in this, but you're in charge and I'll defer to you."

Was that a fair deal?

Jessica sensed that this was the time to insist he leave and let her get back to focusing on her case. If she told him to go now, she knew he would, even without him saying it.

Thing was ... maybe she'd like him to stay.

Maybe having Mason work this with her wasn't as awful as she would have thought.

Slowly, she reached out until her palm touched his. Heat radiated between them, and she couldn't even say it was just a physical thing. It felt a whole lot more like burning attraction than she would like to admit.

When those long fingers curled around her hand, something fluttered inside her, and she was a little embarrassed to admit—even to herself—that her panties did indeed get a little wet when he focused that dark stare on her.

"Stay," she whispered because she seemed almost incapable of uttering more than a single word.

The smile he beamed on her proved she was no stronger than the average woman, no more immune to his charm than any other woman he aimed that smile at to get his way.

It should bother her, but she was riding the wave of the high of knowing she had a chance at positioning herself as Genesis' angel.

And just like that her wave crashed.

She wasn't there yet.

It was too early to be celebrating.

Too early to be getting distracted by the fact that her new partner was way too sexy for his own good.

Jessica sobered. "I'm nervous about his questions," she admitted. "If I don't give the answers he wants, not only am I out as a prospect for his angel, but there's a good chance he'll kill me. Both of us."

"Hey." Mason squeezed the hand he still held. "You've got this. I believe in you."

It shouldn't make a difference, shouldn't matter to her at all, not after the things he'd done to her, but for some reason Mason's words infused her with strength and confidence.

How he'd managed to worm himself into not only her case but also into her good graces she had no idea.

How to stop it from happening, she didn't know that either.

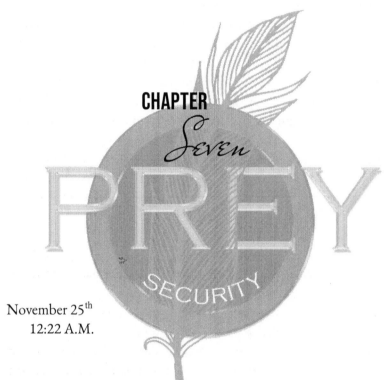

CHAPTER
Seven

November 25th
    12:22 A.M.

"We can't sleep, not now, we still have to prep," Jessica said.

The indignance and determination in her tone made Scorpion smile. How could he ever have thought this woman was immature and selfish?

Jessica was anything but. She was dedicated to her job, and willing to risk everything to catch a dangerous man and stop a terrorist plot. Never once had she wavered in her role in the days he'd been watching her, and she'd managed to save his life last night. He wanted to know why her brother had lied about her and how much of what David had told him was a lie, but this was hardly the time to revisit the past.

Genesis and his second in command had yet to return to the tent, which had given him and Jessica plenty of time to prepare her for the coming quiz Genesis would give her to determine if she was the woman he wanted. Scorpion had zero doubts about Jessica's ability to pull this off. The woman was good at what she did. She was able to read people and was able to adapt accordingly.

How could she fail?

It meant a whole lot more to him than it should that she had agreed to let him stay and work this with her. Because if she had told him one more time that she wanted him to leave, he would have done it.

This was where he wanted to be. Yes, he wanted to follow through on this case, but it ran deeper than that. Something had changed in the last few days, he felt something for this woman that he never would have suspected he could feel.

Respect and admiration. Seeing how hard she worked it was hard to feel anything else, but there was more there. He liked her, she was smart and sassy, gorgeous, and she had a big heart. A heart big enough to want to save his life even though she didn't like him.

A hint of tenderness was mixed in there, too.

"Jess, you need rest. You look like you haven't slept properly in weeks." Without thinking, he lifted his hand and trailed a fingertip across the dark smudge under one of her eyes.

Her pupils widened at the contact but she didn't pull away.

What was happening here?

For the last decade or more, he had thought she was nothing but a spoiled brat, yet in just a few short days his entire opinion of her had reversed. She was the complete opposite of spoiled, in fact, he'd garner a guess that she was one of the most selfless people he'd ever met. He knew that she hadn't done the things her brother had accused her of which meant he feared he owed her a whole lot more than an apology.

"Mason," she whispered his name in a soft, breathy voice, and his body began to stir.

"Hmm?" His gaze moved from her eyes, currently glowing an almost electric blue, to her plump, full lips.

He wanted to kiss her.

Bad idea?

Yep.

Especially with the suspicions he had tumbling around in his head about the real story of her childhood. Add to that the fact they were undercover, and currently sitting on the floor of the tent of the cult leader, and kissing should be the furthest thing from his mind.

But he couldn't seem to look away.

Scorpion had never felt a need this powerful. They weren't safe here. Genesis could return at any second and one wrong move would get them both killed and blow this case, meaning Genesis would remain free and able to carry out his plans.

Still, none of that seemed to matter as his head dipped and moved toward her, pausing just long enough to allow her to pull away if she didn't want this.

She didn't.

And when his lips touched hers, he got this weird feeling in his gut. It felt like home. Felt like something had been missing all his life, and it had suddenly clicked into place. Felt like something he could far too easily become addicted to.

Stop now while you still can, a small voice at the back of his mind called out.

He ignored it.

What was the worst thing that could happen?

So, he got addicted to her? Addictions were made to be broken, right? Wasn't like he was going to ask her to go out with him, date him, maybe even have a future with him. That would be stupid, they were too different, there was too much history between them, too much water under the bridge.

It would be crazy.

Yet when she gave a soft little moan and shifted onto her knees so she could get closer to him, he wondered why exactly it was so crazy.

Strip everything else away—the past, the fact that he'd thought she was stupid, might have aided in committing the crimes she'd accused him of even if he hadn't known it, that she might not hate him anymore but that didn't mean she liked him—and they did have some things in common. They both worked in protector jobs, they both cared about making the world safer, they both put their lives on the line, and no one could deny that attraction sizzled hot between them.

Was it enough?

For now? For more? Scorpion didn't even know what he was asking.

All he knew was that this was the kind of kiss you lost yourself in. It consumed you, drowned you in emotion, burned you up. It was everything.

Apparently, he wasn't the only one who felt that way because Jessica's fingers began to fumble with the buttons of his white shirt.

Stopping her would be the right thing to do. Emotions were flying high and adrenalin was pumping. How could he even know that Jessica was thinking clearly right now? The last thing he wanted was to give her another reason to hate him, because even though he had no idea what the future held, he did know one thing.

Having this woman hate him would hurt.

Giving her a reason to see him as a regret would feel like he had let her down all over again.

"Babe," he whispered, somehow finding the strength to catch her fingers and guide them away from his chest.

"You don't want this? You don't want me?" she asked. Any other time, he would have thought she was being coy, that she was a woman confident in her body and the effect it had on men. But he saw the rare hint of vulnerability and uncertainty hidden deep in the now sea-green depths of her eyes.

There was no way his assumptions that she went hunting for sugar daddies rather than support herself were even remotely correct.

Taking the fingers he still held, he brushed them against his crotch where his length was practically straining to get through the denim. They both watched as it twitched in response to her soft touch.

"Seem like in any way I don't want you?"

"If you don't want ... sex ... I can just get you off with my hand," she offered, sounding so sweetly unsure of herself that that protectiveness he'd been feeling earlier surged until it was overwhelming.

"I don't want," he said bluntly. "I want you so badly it hurts. I want to slide inside your tight, wet heat. I want to hear every sexy moan that's going to fall from those lips. I want to watch your face as you come, memorize your expression. I want to taste you, and touch you, but what I don't want is to be a regret."

Her face softened, and she blushed the prettiest shade of pink before gifting him with a smile so genuine, and so sweet, he could practically taste it. "You won't be a regret."

"Are you sure?" Scorpion wasn't used to feeling this way with the women he dated. Then again, there was nothing usual about this woman. He'd hurt her, that he knew for certain even if he wasn't sure of all the details, and he wanted to make up for that.

Not with sex.

But by showing her that she was special, and amazing, and someone worthy of all the goodness there was in the world.

"Positive. If I didn't want this I wouldn't have let you kiss me, I wouldn't have wanted more. Wouldn't want this." Her fingers still rested against the bulge in his pants and when she began to stroke him, he groaned as a ripple of pleasure started inside him.

Embarrassing himself like some horny kid who didn't know how to take care of his woman was not how he wanted this to play out. He wanted it to be as perfect as it could be, given they were undercover and in the tent of a terrorist who could return at any second.

Yeah, best to forget about that bit for now.

"We do this, I do it right," he told her as he picked her up and pulled her into his lap, then captured her lips in a kiss he hoped conveyed how sorry he was for hurting her in the past, and how much he respected and liked the woman she had become, and the girl she had been back then.

∾

November 25th
   12:38 A.M.

OMG did he just kiss me?

Jessica felt ridiculously girlish as his tongue swept between her lips, and excitement bubbled in her stomach, and tingled through her limbs.

When she was a teen there had been no time for boys. Between caring for her disabled father, her depressed and drug-addicted mother, and two little sisters, all while trying to put food on the table, keep the house running, and going to school, there had been no time for fun. Then there was college and working to help support her sisters. After graduation, she had thrown herself into work. If she couldn't be a lawyer then at least she could work her way up the ladder being the best cop she could be.

The odd time when she had bothered to date, she'd never been kissed like this.

Never felt anything as strong as the sensations currently assaulting every inch of her body.

It felt like Mason had somehow lit a match and set her on fire. Every sense was heightened. Beneath her fingertips, she could feel every definition in his pecs, the way they rippled beneath her palms as he kissed her with a hunger that rivaled her own. The smell of their arousals filled the air, combining into a scent that was intoxicating. It filled her with a desire that needed to be sated.

Mason's hands brushed across her breasts, and even through the simple white cotton dress her nipples immediately pebbled. It felt like more than just pleasure. It felt like joy, happiness, freedom.

"More," she whispered as his hands cupped her breasts.

"Jess, we shouldn't, Genesis could ..."

Crushing her lips to his to cut him off, she tangled her fingers in his hair, unwilling to let him pull away now that he'd started. For one moment she wanted to be free from responsibility. After eighteen years of having to take care of everything and everyone around her, she wanted one moment to do something just for herself. Jessica had never been selfish, she'd stepped up when no one else had, cared for her family, and taken a job where lives depended on her.

For once she wanted to put herself first.

Was that so wrong?

"Please," she whimpered. A pleasure she had never experienced before was building inside her and she wanted to let it out, wanted to experience it all.

"Aww, babe. You're messing me up inside. I can't think straight when I'm around you." Mason leaned forward, touching his forehead to hers. "I want to understand why I got you all wrong. You're not who I thought you were."

"Later," she promised. They needed to talk it out, she acknowledged that. Maybe with the air cleared she could finally move forward in all areas of her life. But not now. "First, please, give me this. I need it. I need you."

With a groan, Mason dragged her closer even though she was already in his lap. His hand shoved her dress up as his lips found hers again.

This was no sweet lovemaking as he shoved her plain cotton panties aside and dragged a finger across her center, it was pure passion and fire. She was already dripping wet and desperate to have him inside her, and she gasped as he pressed one finger just inside her entrance.

Not nearly enough.

If he thought he was going to take control and slow things down, do them on his timetable, then he was sorely mistaken.

For once she was going to just take what she wanted.

And what she wanted was this infuriating and yet protective man.

Sinking down until his finger was deep inside her, she unzipped him and claimed his hard length with her hand. It pulsed at her touch as she curled her fingers around him and began to stroke.

Knowing how she was affecting him felt good. While she wasn't shy with men, she wasn't usually this confident either. Always at the back of her mind was her past and the things she'd been made to do.

Not here and now with Mason though.

There was no past, no future, just this moment.

This exquisitely beautiful moment.

Mason slid another finger inside her, the slight sting as he stretched her even felt good because his thumb had found her bud, and he was working it mercilessly as his fingers hooked inside her to catch that place that had the whole world shimmering around her as indescribable pleasure began to build.

How had she not known that sensations like this existed, and she was almost thirty?

It seemed wrong, and yet there was no time to worry about it because those sensations kept building with each stroke of his fingers, each caress of his thumb.

She was getting close, but she didn't want to come until Mason was buried deep inside her, their bodies joined for one second of perfection before she would be forced to let the real world intrude on this special little bubble they had created.

Shifting her hips, she used her free hand to brush away Mason's when he tried to hold her still and instead guided his length to her entrance. Inch by delicious inch, she took him inside her, and when he was finally all inside her, it felt even better than she had been expecting.

When she rolled her hips, his length jerked inside her, and she could tell he was as close to coming as she was. Lifting her hips and then sinking down again, Jessica felt Mason groan against her lips as he still greedily kissed her, then his hands clamped around her hips. Those hands of his were so big that even holding onto her hips he could still reach her little bundle of nerves that was crying out for attention.

His lips, his hands, his hard length thrusting in and out of her, it was all suddenly too much as sensations continued to build inside her until she felt like she was a split second away from exploding. Only it was too late to turn back now, it was coming, this too-big explosion was coming whether she wanted it to or not.

The match had already been lit.

The spark already ignited.

When he thrust once more inside her, pressing the calloused pad of his thumb against her bud, that was it.

She was a goner.

Pleasure blasted off inside her, flying out through her bloodstream until it encompassed her entire body. She felt Mason come inside her and sharing this experience with him did funny things to her insides.

Softened them somehow.

Wave after wave of pleasure buffeted her, going on and on until she was sure she couldn't take a single second more of it. But by the time it finally ebbed and she sank down against Mason's chest, Jessica found that not only had she survived it, but it had been the single best moment of her life.

Almost.

Mason groaned.

Jessica stiffened.

"Don't tell me you regret that already," she said. Hadn't he been the one to say he didn't want her to regret this, yet he didn't seem to worry about regretting it himself. Kind of obnoxious of him given he was still buried inside her.

Arms closed around her, and his lips touched the top of her head. "No way I could regret that, babe. But I was reckless, not thinking straight. We didn't use protection."

Oh.

Was that all?

Snuggling closer, she touched a kiss to the bare skin of his chest, right above his heart. "I'm on birth control, got the implant right before I came." Now was not the time to tell him that it was because there had been a small chance that she would have to sleep with Genesis to keep her cover. She didn't want to do it, and her bosses said it wasn't required of her, but when she had committed to this case she had told herself she would do whatever it took.

No exceptions.

Besides, sex with men she despised wasn't something that was new to her.

Telling Mason that would definitely ruin the moment. All of a sudden, he seemed to have become protective of her, and knowing what she was prepared to do to bring down Genesis and Seeds of Life would not sit well with him.

"Good to know. Still, I was irresponsible, sorry about that. Won't happen again."

Them having sex wouldn't happen again, or them having sex without a condom wouldn't happen again?

Jessica was somewhat dismayed at the idea of them never sleeping together again. Not a good thing since there was no future for them. No matter the fact that he seemed to have softened, and didn't seem to be the man she'd known as a teenager who had stood by and allowed her to be abused, that would always stand between them.

How could it not?

Still, right now, she didn't want to think about that. She just wanted to bask in the afterglow of their lovemaking.

Everything was perfect.

Until it wasn't.

Like the rest of her life, nothing ever went in her favor.

A growl of anger sounded through the tent, and Genesis was there, pulling her away from Mason.

Her last thought before the world went dark and pain exploded in her head was that her one moment of selfishness had just gotten Mason killed.

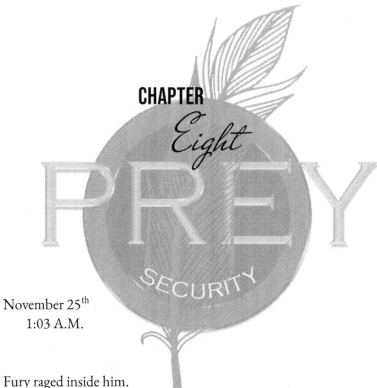

CHAPTER *Eight*

November 25th
1:03 A.M.

Fury raged inside him.

How could this be happening?

He'd thought he had finally found the one.

The one who would help him start the first generation of a whole new species of people. Part human, part star, part angel, the perfect combination to live in a perfect world.

Now it was ruined.

Rage clouded his vision and Genesis stormed across the room, grabbing the body of his pretty blonde angel and hauling her off the man she had been having sex with. He shook her and shook her and shook her as his anger grew with each loll of her limp head.

The blow Exodus had delivered when he and his second in command had entered the tent to find the lovers entwined in each other's arms had knocked the woman unconscious, and she hung like a ragdoll in his grip. He wanted her to wake up, wanted to demand that she give him answers.

What answer could she give, though, that would change what he'd seen?

His angel's brother—if, in fact, the man was her brother—had also been hit over the head, and although groggy, he wasn't completely unconscious.

"Who are you?" he growled as he tossed his angel's body to the ground. It landed with a thump that seemed to draw the brother out of his stupor, and he pushed up onto his hands and knees and crawled over to the woman. Placing his body protectively between her limp form and him and Exodus.

There was a vibe about this man Genesis wasn't liking.

At first, when he'd shown up here, with his military background and honed body he'd thought the man would make a perfect soldier. His plan had been to have him work the fields for a couple of weeks before promoting him from the general workforce to the army. Men like this didn't come along every day, and he had known that he would make a wonderful addition to the small but dedicated militia he was creating.

Now he wasn't so sure.

Genesis was sensing something powerful, something dangerous about the man who may or may not be his angel's brother.

No.

They couldn't be siblings.

They'd lied to him.

Siblings didn't have sex, it was against the laws of nature.

There was no doubt about what the two had been doing when he'd walked back in here expecting to find them both fast asleep. He had seen with his own two eyes, and that didn't lie.

How many times had Exodus cautioned him not to see things as he wanted them to be but as they were?

It was hard for him, especially when it came to his cause. This was important. More than important, it was everything. Life and death. For many years, he had been searching for his angel star and he'd thought this gorgeous woman with silky blonde locks and amazing eyes that seemed to change color each time he looked at her was the one.

But if he was wrong about her, he was wrong.

No use in pretending otherwise.

Wouldn't be the first time a couple had been caught hiding in the woods and making out. Perhaps these two were nothing more than lust-filled unbelievers who had no place here in the safe place he was creating for the chosen ones to move to the next plane of existence.

"I asked you a question," he snarled at the man who had moved onto his knees and was watching him with a calm and calculating expression. This man was *too* calm. *Too* calculating.

Genesis wanted to know what was going on inside the man's head, but he found he couldn't read him.

That angered him.

Normally, he could read anyone. It was one of his best skills and how he'd managed to build such a group of loyal followers. But this man seemed immune somehow and he didn't like it one bit.

"Answer me," he bellowed. When his angel flinched at the loud sound and began to move groggily, the man shot him a reproachful frown.

"You know who I am. I presented myself here, I went through the training, and I was approved to come and work here. This is where I want to be. If I didn't want to be here I wouldn't be," the man said like it was that simple.

Only it was far from simple.

There had been a few people who had managed to fool him. Some who had come here under false pretenses to undermine what he was doing. Was it possible that this man was one of them?

His angel had been here for months, he'd noticed her from the very beginning. Something about her, a mixture of sweetness and confidence, had captured his attention. She was a very beautiful woman, and he had been hoping for a sign that she might be the one he had been searching for since he was a young boy and the stars first talked to him. In all that time she had never set a foot wrong. She obeyed the rules, worked hard, and served the community in whatever task she was given.

She was perfect.

Until this man had shown up and interfered.

Or maybe ...

Was it possible that this man had forced himself on her? When they'd come into the room it looked like he was holding onto her.

Perhaps his angel had been an unwilling participant in what had gone on in his tent tonight.

If he found out this man was here as a spy or a tool of the devil, then he wouldn't hesitate to eliminate him. There had been a few who had tried to disrupt the order of things here, who had managed to fool him, and all of them had been dealt with swiftly, much in the same way as he'd had to deal with one tonight.

That woman's body would join the others in the mass grave outside the camp, and if Genesis found out this man was also lying to him then his body would be added to that grave.

Allowing anyone to destabilize things here was not an option.

This was too important.

Souls. That's what they were talking about. His soul and the souls of many. All who agreed with him, who submitted to him, and who followed his teachings, would live.

All who disobeyed would perish.

It was as simple as that.

"I think you're lying. I think you stole something that wasn't yours to take." The rage that had been planted inside him so long ago, that he had managed to get under control was now fighting against the bonds he'd used to contain it. If this man had touched his sweet angel star, stolen something from her that was supposed to be for him, then he wouldn't just pay with his life. Nope. Genesis would order him to be punished before he was slaughtered.

The woman slumped back down, passing out again, the blood from her head wound pooling around her pale face as it rested against the floor of the tent.

Shooting him another reprimanding frown, the man spoke slowly as though he thought Genesis was some sort of idiot. "You know who I am. I'm Mason Markson. Former military. Brother to Jessica. I came here because I finally woke up and realized that my sister knew what she was talking about. I've seen a lot of evil. Done my share of eliminating it when and where I could. It wasn't enough. I want to do more. That's why I'm here."

"You think most men have sex with their sister?" he sneered. He wasn't the idiot here. Mason was. If he thought Genesis was buying what he was selling, then he was more than stupid.

Pressing his lips together the man didn't answer.

Which was in and of itself answer enough.

"Have them taken to the reflection shed and kept there until I decide what to do with them," he ordered Exodus who immediately called out for some of their men to come and help.

Mason made no move to fight off the men who roughly grabbed his arms and dragged him to his feet. But when Exodus bent and scooped up the unresponsive form of Jessica, he shot the man a murderous glare. Whatever was going on between the two of them it was obvious that the man was protective of the woman.

Alone in his tent now, Genesis dropped to his knees. Before he could deal with the couple he needed to pray to his star for guidance.

It was the goddess of the moon who had first revealed to him his path in life, and he sought her wisdom whenever he was presented with a problem. He needed to know if the couple should be put to death or if there was some sort of logical explanation that at present eluded him.

Please, be a logical explanation.

He wanted to find his angel, his star, his other half. He wanted to finally be complete. He wanted to destroy everything and everyone who dared to go against him. He wanted to rule his world and he wanted his queen beside him as he did so.

Was Jessica his angel star or was she a false prophetess who needed to be eliminated?

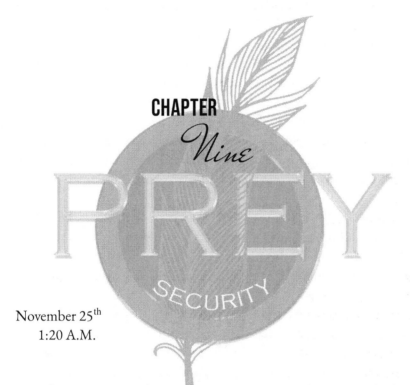

CHAPTER
Nine

November 25th
1:20 A.M.

It took every ounce of control Scorpion possessed not to unleash the anger storming inside him and kill every single person who had dared put their hands on his woman.

Okay, so Jessica wasn't *his* woman, but as long as she was his partner then in a way, she was his. And now that he knew the real Jessica, he liked her, respected her. Because he couldn't act like a responsible, intelligent, and well-trained operative, her life was now in danger.

He should have left when she asked him to.

He should have known the second he figured out she was an undercover cop that everything he'd thought about her was wrong, and she didn't need his help.

How many times had she made that more than clear?

But he'd had to push and keep challenging her because it was hard to reconcile the woman he saw here at Seeds of Life with the woman he had believed her to be this last decade and a half.

His arrogance and stubbornness were going to get them both killed.

It was only because he believed Jessica was a miracle worker and could talk herself out of death—Scorpion cared little for his own fate—that he didn't start killing Genesis' guards. They might have weapons and some training, but he was a walking, talking, deadly weapon. All he needed to take one of them out was his bare hands, and once he had a weapon the rest would be easy.

If he did that, though, he ruined any chance that Jessica had of bringing the cult down before they started enacting their plans to poison water sources. She more than deserved that chance, and the last thing he wanted was the blood of thousands of innocents on his hands.

So, he had to wait.

Be patient.

Trust the woman hanging limp and unconscious over the shoulder of Exodus.

A woman he should have trusted all along. If he had shown her even one iota of the respect he now felt for her when he first showed up here, they wouldn't be in this predicament.

Still, knowing it was the right thing to do and actually doing it wasn't easy, and by the time the reflection shed was thrown open and he was shoved inside, his hands were curled into fists so tight his fingers ached.

When Exodus literally threw Jessica's unconscious body into the shack, he would have lost it. Would have attacked. But more than that, he felt a driving need to protect Jessica from pain, so he had no choice but to lunge for her, catching her before she hit the ground.

The protectiveness he felt for this woman was unlike anything he had experienced before. He had a mom and two sisters, all of whom he was protective of. There had been times when they were growing up when he'd beat up boys who dared to break his sisters' hearts. He'd dated over the years, even thought he was in love once until he came home from an op to find his girlfriend in bed with her gynecologist. But nothing like this. This was a whole new level where he was almost blinded by the need to destroy anything that hurt her, regardless of the consequences.

Cradling Jessica in his arms, he knelt, ignoring the door being closed and locked behind him, and laid her out on the floor. They'd both been hit over the head when Genesis and Exodus found them together. Since Jessica had been hit first, he'd been able to move when Exodus swung at him, meaning the blow glanced off his head.

Having Jessica on his lap when the two men entered the room meant there hadn't been much he was able to do to protect either of them, but from here on out, he wasn't going to make selfish decisions. Nothing could come before Jessica and her safety. She was a good cop, but he'd stayed because he couldn't walk away knowing she was in danger, not because he wanted to put her in more danger than she was already in, infiltrating a cult.

It was almost pitch black in the shed, but he'd kept hold of his watch when he passed through the training and moved to the main commune with the others. Not only did it have a GPS tracker so Prey would be able to keep a check on his location, and the capability to monitor his vitals so Prey would know if he was killed, but it also had a flashlight.

That seemed the most important right now.

Switching the light on, he pressed his fingertips to Jessica's neck to check for her pulse. Even though she'd stirred briefly back in Genesis' tent, she'd passed out again. Blood was all over the side of her face and matted in her hair as it dried. The wound on her right temple was about two inches long, and there was already a good-sized lump.

No doubt she'd have a concussion.

Best he could hope for was it was a minor one because Seeds of Life didn't believe in leaving the commune to visit the nearest hospital. If the concussion was serious, there would be no way to scan her head to check for bleeds on her brain, and no way to monitor her condition beyond keeping a check on her vitals. He didn't even have painkillers he could give her.

Feeling useless, Scorpion cupped her chin, his other hand cradling the uninjured side of Jessica's face and angled it so he could get a better look at the wound. It really needed stitches, and if he had a suture kit on him, he could do it himself, but Seeds of Life didn't have even the absolute basics of a first aid kit. Pretty much if you got sick or injured out here you were on your own. The most the cult would do was pray to the stars for the return of your good health.

That wasn't going to help him right now.

"Come on, babe, wake up for me," he whispered, his fingertips stroking against petal soft skin. He was usually pretty calm and collected no matter what was going on around him, but right now, Scorpion couldn't seem to scrounge up an ounce of calm.

Silence met his plea.

Stillness as well.

"Jess, wake up, babe. Need to hear your sassy voice telling me how much I annoy you," he pleaded.

Leaning down to touch his forehead to hers, he shifted her so she was in his lap, and held her as tightly as he dared. Already, he had failed this woman big time in the past, and he was failing her all over again now.

"Won't let you down again, babe," he vowed.

"Going to hold you to that," a weak voice replied, and he grinned.

"Trust you to wake up right when I'm making you a promise," he teased.

"I have impeccable timing." She tried to sit up, but he held her right where she was, not quite willing to let her go until his heart rate slowed some. "You going to let me up, or cuddle me like I'm your favorite childhood teddy bear?"

His grin grew bigger. "I'm going to kiss you till you forget all about sassing me."

Jessica laughed, but it turned into a groan, and he had to remind himself that she might be awake and talking to him, but she was far from okay.

"Head injuries hurt." She moaned. "Maybe I'll stay right where I am for a while longer."

Yeah, a while longer.

The thought came out of nowhere and was as unsettling as it was unexpected. There was no future for the two of them, and he didn't want there to be. Only he really liked this smart, sassy, strong woman with the incredible acting skills.

"I'm sorry," he said as he smoothed away a lock of hair that had gotten stuck in the tacky blood drying on her cheek. "Shouldn't have lost control like that, forgotten where we are and the danger surrounding us. Shouldn't have let you get hurt."

In the thin light from his watch, he could see tenderness in her expression. It was a nice change from the anger and hostility he was used to getting from her. "Do you regret it?"

"No." The answer was completely truthful. Scorpion regretted not being more aware and realizing Genesis was coming before they were caught, but he didn't regret sleeping with this amazing woman.

"Good. Me either. Do regret the blinding headache though." Her eyes closed and when she rested her head against his chest something shifted inside him. Softened somehow. Warmed like she'd shone a ray of sunlight directly into his chest.

"You need to promise me something."

"What?" she asked somewhat dubiously.

"That you will do whatever you have to do to save yourself and not worry about me."

Lifting her head to shoot him a glare, the effect was ruined by her wince and the eerie glow of the drying blood in the shadowy light. "I'll save us both."

As he tucked her head back against his chest, he let out a sigh. That was exactly what he was afraid of. That Jessica was going to get herself killed by trying to save them both.

$\sim$

November 25th
    3:44 P.M.

"How long do you think we've been in here?" Jessica asked, not because she really cared about the answer, but because she was bored, hurting, hungry, thirsty, cold too, and wanted to say something to fill the silence.

She was sitting on the floor of the reflection shed with Mason behind her. She was sitting between his legs, with his knees bent and his arms wrapped across her stomach, and his chest at her back so she felt cocooned in a little bubble of safety. They hadn't spoken in a while, but the silence was companionable and comfortable, and even though she knew they were both in a precarious situation, Jessica wasn't afraid.

Either she was way too confident in her abilities to talk their way out of this, or her head injury was messing with her, lulling her into a false sense of security. Or maybe it was that she was way too confident in Mason's abilities.

The man oozed confidence.

Before—when she'd hated him—she'd found his arrogance infuriating, but now that she didn't hate him so much—okay, so she actually liked him—it was definitely comforting. It had turned out to be a good thing that he hung around.

A pinch on her chin drew her attention, and she turned her head to see Mason looking down at her with a bemused expression on his face.

"Why ask a question if you're not going to listen to the answer?" he teased, but she could see the worry in his dark eyes. It had been there ever since she woke up to find him holding her both tightly and gently —if that was even a thing—and she knew he was concerned about her having a concussion and how it was going to affect her when they were both trapped out here.

Her dream case to show her bosses what she was capable of and take down a dangerous domestic terrorist had gone up in smoke.

There was every chance both she and Mason would be killed and their bodies buried with the others she knew were out here. She definitely should be more worried about that. Concussion was messing with her for sure because she shouldn't be focused on this warm kind of soft feeling she had inside her every time Mason touched her, or kissed her, or looked at her with that concern in his eyes.

It was nice to have someone care.

Jessica knew she and her sisters had been lucky to have the foster parents they got. They'd been well looked after, cared for, encouraged to work hard, and plan out their futures, but it wasn't the same as having someone love you.

Not that she was saying Mason loved her, but maybe ... he liked her.

At least a little.

"Honey, you not responding is worrying me."

She smiled at the endearment. Before her dad's accident and her mom's addiction problems, she'd had good parents. There'd been lots of love and plenty of endearments. But that was a long time ago, and ever since then, she'd had to be the responsible one, the one who took charge, who looked after everyone. It was so nice to have someone take care of her for a change, and Mason had been so sweet and attentive with her.

"Didn't mean to worry you," she said. "Guess I zoned out a little, busy thinking. How long *did* you think we've been in here?"

"Fourteen hours and thirty-one minutes."

"Wow, that's a very specific guess."

Furrowed brows looked down at her. "Wearing a watch, remember, babe?"

"Oh. Guess I forgot. I'm fine," she added quickly because she could see how worried Mason was about her.

"You're not fine. You're nauseous and dizzy, you keep zoning out and forgetting things, you have a concussion, and instead of being in a hospital where you can be monitored. Or a house with a bed where you can get proper rest," he added, looking around their tiny, dark, dirty shack.

"I'm going to be okay. It's just a concussion. Not even my first. Besides, I've been resting in here for over fourteen hours."

"It's not proper rest if you're on the floor," he muttered under his breath, making her smile and then wince.

Before she could offer him more reassurances—because it was in her nature to take care of anyone around her no matter how she was feeling, and she wasn't feeling great right now—there was the sound of footsteps and then the lock being turned.

Mason moved quickly to stand, moving her back so she was resting against the wall—always taking care of her—and stood in front of her. A barrier between her and whoever was coming. Not a very useful one since there wasn't anything he could really do to protect them given they were outgunned and outmanned, but it was still sweet that he wanted to try.

When light flooded the room, Jessica immediately slammed her eyes shut. Pain sliced through her head as the too-bright light aggravated her concussion. The only reason she didn't moan out loud was because she knew it would upset Mason, and that was the last thing he needed right now.

"Genesis is ready to speak with you," Exodus announced.

There were four armed guards with him, and two of them immediately moved to grab Mason. Jessica could tell that he was restraining himself because she didn't doubt he could take out both of them without breaking a sweat.

The other two men reached down and grabbed her, hauling her to her feet.

It was a miracle she didn't throw up at the sudden and way too fast movement.

You'd have to be blind not to notice the way Mason's entire body went completely tense, but there was nothing he could do. Any move they made would only put them in more danger. As skilled as the two of them were, a stray bullet could still take them out, and to do any real damage they needed to get their hands on a few of those guns.

Marched through the camp and back to the tent where they had been caught making out last night, as they were dragged inside and shoved into chairs, her cheeks heated as she saw the room where she and Mason had had sex.

It shouldn't be what she was thinking about right now, but her mind was a little messed up.

Not a good thing.

Their best bet at walking out of here alive was her.

Her ability to talk her way out of anything, play whatever role she needed for the situation she was in was their only chance.

Once they were both seated with guards on either side of them, Genesis came strolling into the room. Jessica did her best to evaluate his body language and figure out if this was already a lost cause or if she at least stood a chance.

Genesis shot her a look, part anger, part confusion, part longing.

Perfect.

He still wanted to care for her, wanted to see her as the weak, fragile woman he needed her to be.

Lowering her gaze, she allowed tears to tumble down her cheeks.

"I'm so sorry," she said, allowing a sob to escape. The crying made her head thump painfully, but she had no time to worry about it.

"You betrayed me," Genesis growled. "And with your brother."

"It's not what you think," she wept, wondering how she was going to get herself—and Mason—out of this mess. No way was she going to do what Mason wanted and only think about herself.

What kind of person would that make her?

It would be easy enough to let him take the fall. Claim he'd touched her against her will and let whatever happened to him happen. But even if she still hated him, she wouldn't do that, and now that she liked him ... well, she had to make sure they both survived.

"We're not biologically related, we were all adopted. Me, Mason, and our sister. We were teenagers when we met, and ... there were feelings there. At least there used to be. But then I started hearing this singing. At first, I thought I was losing my mind, but then I realized it always got louder at night. I started seeing the stars blinking at me, and ... I knew it was them."

This was pure gibberish, she was making it up as she went along, but it seemed to be working. Genesis looked intrigued and that was about the best she could hope for.

Drawing on every ounce of knowledge she had about the man and his beliefs, she forged on. "That's how I found out about Seeds of Life, and I knew this was where I was supposed to be. I ended things with Mason, I knew there was something more important I had to do with my life. I tried to convince him to come, but he didn't want to. Then he realized I had been telling the truth about having a higher purpose, so he came to join our cause. Last night, what you saw, was goodbye. This feeling inside me is growing. I feel its glow getting stronger, consuming me. Do you know what that means?" she asked hopefully, giving him her best fragile look of hope.

"I know, child."

So, he didn't call her angel, but at least he didn't order her death.

Better than nothing.

"I don't know if you're telling me the truth, child, you are harder to read than most. But I will give you a chance to prove your loyalty to me.

Both of you a chance," Genesis added, looking to Mason. "But you two will not see each other again. I will not be made a fool out of."

As two of the guards grabbed Mason and dragged him out of the tent, Jessica watched him go. When he disappeared from sight, she felt a weird kind of emptiness inside.

She hadn't wanted a partner, but now that she had one, she didn't like the idea of not being there to watch his back.

And have him watch hers.

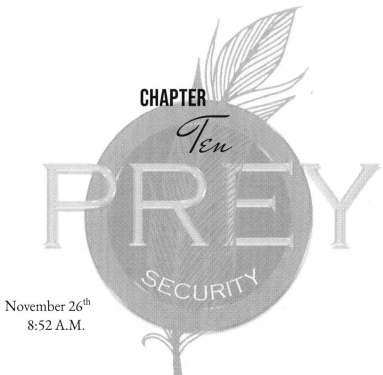

CHAPTER

Ten

PREY

SECURITY

November 26th
8:52 A.M.

Time seemed to go so much slower this time in the reflection shed.

Scorpion sat there and stared at the locked door and wondered how Jessica was doing.

Had her concussion gotten worse? Had she been given rest and at least something to help with the pain he knew she was in? She hadn't complained, and he knew it was for his benefit. The selfish woman he'd always thought her to be was actually the complete opposite.

Jessica Bowen didn't have a selfish bone in her body.

Everything she did was with somebody else in mind.

What possible reason David had for lying about his little sister and painting her out to be this awful, spoiled brat he couldn't fathom. But he intended to find out.

When he got back home—assuming he survived and convinced the cult he was on their side—he was going to have a sit down with his old friend. And if Scorpion found out that David was responsible in any way for what Jessica had done as a child, he would make sure the man was punished to the full extent of the law.

As well as receiving Scorpion's own personal punishment.

Tapping his fingers on his knee, he did another sweep of the small room. Now that it was light again outside, he was able to see as light filtered through the cracks between the walls. This shack wasn't well built, if he wanted to break out of here, he could. Wouldn't even take him all that long. But that wasn't the point. The point was to play along, pretend he was as invested in this plot as the rest of these people, and if he broke out of here, he wouldn't be doing that.

Still, it was hard to sit in here twiddling his thumbs, knowing Jessica was somewhere close by.

Worrying about her had become almost an obsession. Holding her all those hours they were locked in here together as she zoned in and out of consciousness had given him lots of time to think.

Every thought he'd had led him to the same place.

He liked this woman but knew a future with her was unlikely. Given they both worked demanding jobs that required them to disappear for periods of time, sometimes long periods of time, meant working out a relationship would be difficult. Then there was the fact that Jessica believed him to have committed a crime and had spent the last decade hating him.

Scorpion wasn't sure what exactly it was that he wanted, but he knew for sure he didn't want her to hate him. And he wanted to know what he'd done exactly so he knew how to fix it. Because if it meant Jessica no longer hated him, he was prepared to go to the cops and confess whatever crimes he'd committed against her.

Approaching footsteps had him straightening, preparing for whatever was coming. He had assumed he might be beaten or publicly flogged as was the custom here, but after being taken out of Genesis' tent, he'd just been returned here and left. The lack of food wasn't bothering him, he'd trained his body to be able to endure long periods of time without food, but the lack of water was taking a toll.

The door opened and Exodus stood there, two armed guards behind him. Something about this man rubbed him the wrong way. Genesis was delusional. He appeared to believe all of his star mumbo-jumbo, which, of course, made him dangerous, but he didn't seem to enjoy violence per se.

Exodus, on the other hand, looked like he enjoyed inflicting pain on others. An arrogance and darkness about him, told Scorpion this was one dangerous man. Cross him and it wouldn't go well for you.

"Get up," Exodus ordered.

Like the obedient would be soldier he was pretending to be, Scorpion immediately jumped to his feet, standing straight and tall before the man who could end him this second if he wished.

There was a hint of approval in Exodus' dark eyes, but his face remained stern and unmoving. The men behind him watched him almost with curiosity. He had no doubt that gossip was running rampant through the commune regardless of the rules about talking during working hours, and during sleeping hours.

"Follow me," Exodus said as he turned and began walking away from the main commune area.

While the guards flanked him, they didn't take hold of him, nor did they seem to be paying all that much attention to him as they walked through the camp.

As they walked, Scorpion scanned the workers in the fields, both hoping to spot a glimpse of Jessica and hoping he didn't. She needed to rest to recover from her concussion, so he hoped she was tucked away in a bed somewhere. But he needed to see her to reassure himself that she was okay.

Head injuries could turn real serious real quick. And out here with no doctor, no medical equipment, and no chance of being taken to a hospital, it would mean either death or permanent damage.

Passing the fields, and then the place where he'd been brought when he first arrived, Scorpion began to wonder if he was being taken out into the woods to be killed, his body disposed of. Since he didn't get that vibe from Exodus or the goons, he pushed the fear away. While he certainly didn't want to die today, it wasn't so much fear for himself as it was for leaving Jessica alone and unprotected.

Although, she seemed to be doing a better job of protecting him than he was doing protecting her.

The way she was able to adapt to any situation and still maneuver herself to the top was a thing to behold.

Up ahead of them appeared another smaller camp, hidden deep in the woods. He felt the guards relax even though there was no outward change to their demeanor and assumed this was the camp where the guards lived.

Looked like he was being given a chance to join them.

Thank you, Jess.

There wasn't a doubt in his mind that if Jessica hadn't come up with her crazy story and somehow managed to play on Genesis' weaknesses he would be dead right now, his body being buried alongside whoever had been killed the night they'd been caught in the woods.

Led inside a large open room, kind of like a crude gym, the four of them were joined by a dozen other men. Placed up the front of the group, Scorpion kept his body relaxed and fought against his desire to take out every single one of these men because he knew the threat they represented.

Once the other men had all fallen into line, Exodus came and stood in front of him, giving him a long, lazy onceover.

When their gazes finally met, he saw the darkness swirling in the man's eyes. Exodus might be the second in command officially, but this man was the one who was really in charge, who was really running things.

"I wasn't in favor of giving you a second chance," Exodus informed him. "I don't trust you. There's something ... unsettling about you. But Genesis believes the woman, and she has been a loyal and hard worker for several months now. So, you are being given a chance to prove your loyalty."

"Permission to speak, sir," Scorpion said, pretending he was back in boot camp addressing a superior.

From the smile Exodus gave, he knew he'd earned himself a few brownie points. From what he knew about Exodus, the man had been dishonorably discharged from the Marines and had likely had big plans on working his way up the ladder. Now he was in charge of his own little army, he could do whatever he wanted, and be the General with everybody looking up to him.

"Permission granted."

"How can I prove my loyalty, sir? I am prepared to do whatever it takes." More than that, he was hoping for an opportunity to gather intel that could and would be used to dismantle Seeds of Life before they were able to follow through on any of their plans.

"The time has come for us to begin our work. Wickedness has been allowed to run rampant across the globe for far too long, and it is finally time for us to stand up and do something about it. The first strike is being prepared, and you will help. You will be part of it, part of history, part of ushering in what is soon to be a new age filled only with those who are ready and willing to serve our Goddess the Moon and her children the stars."

While it was clear Exodus cared little about Seeds of Life's so-called goddess, there was excitement and purpose in his tone. He liked the idea of being the leader of an army who was going to decimate the world, killing thousands of people in the process.

But this was the chance Scorpion needed. A chance to learn the cult's plans so they could be stopped, and proof that would have everyone involved convicted. A chance to help Jessica close out her case and maybe earn himself enough goodwill that he could make up for hurting her in the past.

Assuming he could pass the test.

Because if he couldn't, then he would be executed.

~

November 26th
2:13 P.M.

The worst part about this was absolutely not knowing where Mason was and if he was okay.

Every time Genesis woke her up, Jessica longed to ask about Mason, to find out what was going on with him, and whether he'd been killed, punished somehow, or was being given a second chance. Even though Genesis had said he would give them both a chance, she was under no illusions. Their positions were precarious, both balancing on a tightrope and one teeny wobble would be all it took to have them falling.

Falling to their deaths.

So, she refrained from asking even though she was desperate for an answer, some reassurance that he was doing okay, and instead just prayed that he was.

Shifting slightly, she burrowed deeper into the blankets. The cot she had been put on to rest and recover wasn't uncomfortable, but it wasn't comfortable either. Ever since Mason had been dragged away, she'd been cold. A deep chill had taken up residence inside her, and she couldn't seem to shake it. The effects of the concussion or a manifestation of her fear for Mason, she wasn't quite sure, and in the end it didn't matter. She wasn't getting treatment beyond being left alone to rest, and she wasn't getting answers, so she just had to suck it up and recover as quickly as possible so she could do what she'd been sent to do.

When she heard the shuffle of footsteps, Jessica wanted to close her eyes, curl onto her side, burrow beneath the blankets, and pretend she was asleep so she didn't have to interact with Genesis in any way.

But that would negate the entire purpose for her joining the cult.

This was what she wanted, after all. An in with Genesis, a way to gather intel that would help her bosses dismantle Seeds of Life. Wasting it would be both counter-productive and stupid.

Forget about Mason.

He can take care of himself.

He didn't care about you when you were a kid being abused.

Although that no longer felt right. It was what she had believed for a lifetime, but the man she had been getting to know these last few weeks didn't seem like the kind to stand by and allow a thirteen-year-old girl to be forced into prostitution or uphold a friendship with the man who had abused a kid.

Whatever she thought she had known about Mason Markson was wrong.

At least she prayed that it was.

Because this man ...

This man she could fall for if she let herself. And falling for him when she still didn't know the truth about the past would definitely be the stupidest thing she had ever done.

As much as she wanted answers about the past, and how Mason was doing now, she had to shove it all away. Focus on the here and now.

Genesis stood beside her cot, a bowl of soup in his hands. So far, she was yet to keep any food down and hadn't even been able to put anything in her mouth without gagging. Given the lingering nausea she wasn't even hungry.

But there was a stubbornness this time in Genesis' eyes, and she knew she was going to have to eat what he'd brought for her if she wanted to keep herself on his good side. Keeping on the cult leader's good side was the only way to keep herself and Mason alive, so she pasted on a wobbly smile.

She'd figured out that he liked her to be fragile and helpless. He wanted his angel star to be someone he could take care of. A partner, yes, but not in the traditional sense. Genesis didn't see her as a possession, but he didn't see her as a real person either. It was kind of like she was a pet, but more a working pet, like a K9 or a sheepdog or something. She would perform a role he was unable to, but he was still the dominant one in the relationship.

Thinking of a relationship and Genesis in the same sentence didn't help her nausea, and she pressed a hand to her stomach in an attempt to control it.

"You are still feeling sick, my child?" Genesis asked. He hadn't called her his angel since he'd caught her and Mason together, but at least he wasn't willing to count out the possibility that she was who he had been searching for.

Yet.

"Yes," she replied in a trembly voice. Not hard to fake since she felt weak as a kitten right now.

"You need to eat something, keep your strength up."

As much as she wanted to refuse, Jessica forced another smile and reached out hands that shook to take the bowl.

"No, my child, I shall feed you." Genesis pulled over a chair and sat beside her cot.

Even more than she didn't want to eat, she didn't want this man feeding her like she was a helpless child. If it was Mason sitting beside her, taking care of her, that would be a whole different thing.

"Open, child," he said as he scooped up a spoonful of soup and guided it toward her lips.

Playing this role wasn't turning out to be as easy as Jessica had thought it would be. Acting was easy for her, she knew how to read people and adjust her own behavior and attitude accordingly. She knew what to do now, too, that wasn't the problem, it was actually doing it.

Concussion or Mason?

Which was messing with her?

Opening her lips, she allowed Genesis to tip the soup onto her tongue, and even though it tasted sour going down her throat she managed to swallow it. Now she just had to pray she could keep it down.

Genesis beamed at her as he dipped the spoon into the bowl again and fed her another mouthful. "After you eat you shall take a bath. I have one of the women preparing one for you. After that, you can get some fresh air. That's what you need."

What she needed was painkillers and proper rest where she wasn't constantly being woken by this man.

Still, she gave him another tremulous smile. "Whatever you think is best, Prophet."

That was the right thing to say if his approving nod was anything to go by. "I want the best for you, my child."

"I know. I believe that."

As he fed her another spoonful, he rested the bowl on his lap, and with his other hand, brushed his knuckles across her cheek.

It took all of Jessica's energy not to flinch at the touch. Instead, she made herself lean into it as though it were what she sought.

His smile never left his face, his thoughtful eyes studying her as he fed her the rest of the bowl of soup. Hard as it was to keep down, somehow, she managed it, and by the time he set the empty bowl on the floor beside his chair, she realized that while she might not have enjoyed the meal, it had invigorated her a little and she could feel her strength returning.

"Come, my child. I will help you bathe."

Jessica froze.

Momentarily losing control of her façade.

He wanted to *help* her bathe?

She'd assumed he just meant he would leave her to take her bath and come back for her when she was done to give her the fresh air he believed she needed.

It meant that he was seeing her as the angel he wanted her to be, but the thought of being naked and vulnerable before this man filled her with icy dread. Her bosses hadn't given her specific instructions on how far they wanted her to take things, they'd left it in her hands. Because of her past, she had believed there wasn't anything she wouldn't be able to handle, and she had been prepared to go beyond a simple bath if that was what it took to bring Genesis and Seeds of Life down.

But now that she was here and had to follow through, it was a lot harder than she had thought it would be.

A *whole* lot harder.

"Th-thank you, Prophet," she murmured as she pushed off the pillows plumped behind her head and swung her legs over the side of the bed.

She hated that she was weak and wobbly and needed Genesis' help to stand, but she did. His arm around her waist didn't appear to be anything sexual on his part. He didn't try to touch her breasts or even hook his hand around her hip and hold her tight against him. Still, he was touching her, and she didn't want him to be touching her.

"You're welcome, my child. We have much to talk about once you are well." His gaze moved to the wound on her temple he had cleaned earlier. "I am sorry you were hurt. But you should have been truthful with me, yes?"

"Yes, Prophet," she whispered.

Her acquiescence obviously pleased him because he couldn't stop smiling as he led her out of the small room and into his personal room. Other than having a real bed, it wasn't really any different than the tent she had shared with a dozen other women. At least he didn't treat himself to a lavish lifestyle while his followers lived in poverty.

In the center of the room was a large wooden tub. Her body wanted to rebel at the sight of it. As nice as it would be to soak in the warm water, especially given you were only allowed to bathe properly once a week on the commune, she didn't want to do it with an audience. At least not this audience.

But if she refused, she could kiss any chance of convincing Genesis she was his angel goodbye. That meant she and Mason would likely be killed.

She couldn't let that happen.

So, she stood still while Genesis removed her blood-stained white cotton dress, then helped her step out of the white cotton panties, leaving her naked before him.

Wasn't the first time she had been naked in front of a man against her will.

She did it only because she felt backed into a corner.

As he scooped her up and set her down in the tub, then picked up a loofah and began to wash her, she fought back tears. This also wasn't the first time she had cried on the inside because nobody cared enough to hear the outpouring of her pain.

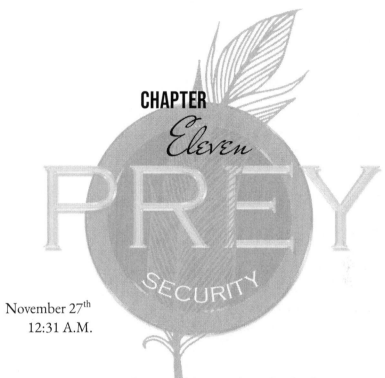

CHAPTER
Eleven

November 27th
12:31 A.M.

He was never supposed to spend long with Seeds of Life.

Just as long as it took to get through orientation and locate Jessica. Then Scorpion was supposed to grab the woman and get her out of there. While it had only been two weeks since he arrived at the Seeds of Life commune, it felt like so much longer.

A lot had changed in those two weeks.

Everything he believed about the woman he had come to rescue, and a lot about himself as well. Knowing that Jessica believed him to have committed a crime made him re-evaluate everything he had thought he knew about himself.

Leaving now felt wrong on so many levels.

Leaving Jessica behind felt worse.

She was still back there on the commune, but he'd had no contact with her since being dragged out of Genesis' tent. Although he had been brought to the guards' camp, he was kept isolated from everyone else, alone in a tiny tent, always with an armed man standing at the door.

They didn't trust him yet and the only way he was going to garner any trust was to pass this test.

So far, all he had done since he got here was put Jessica in more danger than she had already been in.

Now it was time for him to pull his weight.

Whatever this test was, he was going to ace it.

Forcing his gaze to remain fixed on the front of the vehicle, and not turn to look over his shoulder at the commune that was already quickly disappearing from sight, took more effort than it should have. How a woman he had disliked when he'd thought of her at all over the last decade had managed to make such an impact on him in such a short amount of time made zero sense.

But she had.

More than she knew.

Probably more than he even realized yet.

I'm coming back for you, Jess.

At least he prayed he was.

Failing the test would mean he was a liability to the cult, and he would be eliminated. If it came down to fighting for his life, he would do it. Dying to protect Jessica was one thing, but if he didn't prove his loyalty to Seeds of Life it would work against Jessica. Which meant he would have to kill the other guards who had come with him tonight, Exodus included, and find a way to try to set it up like it hadn't been him who had killed them.

It wouldn't be easy, but Scorpion had already figured out his priority.

Jessica.

Her life, her safety, her case.

Whatever it took he would do.

If need be, he could call in every favor he had to make sure this worked, and there would be no blowback on Jessica. Strong, brave, loyal Jessica who wouldn't like to know he could see through her shields to the vulnerabilities she hid beneath.

Vulnerabilities he wanted to explore, wanted to understand, wanted to heal.

Damn woman had him so messed up he couldn't think of anything else.

Thing was, he didn't even care. For some strange reason, he liked being messed up by his crazy woman.

For now, though, he had to focus on this job and doing what he needed to in order to ensure her safety. That was what was important.

Although he had a million questions about what this test was going to entail, he hadn't asked any of them. Playing the role of loyal soldier meant doing what you were told, when you were told to do it, without questioning those orders.

So, when Exodus himself had appeared in Scorpion's tent telling him to get up, get dressed, and join the others in the SUV, that was exactly what he had done. He could tell that the man was pleased with his attitude, so it was one mark in his favor. He still had to earn a whole lot more before he gained Exodus' trust though.

No one had spoken as the SUV took off, driving through the commune and now out onto the roads that would lead them out of the West Virginian forests to wherever it was they were going.

At least thirty minutes passed in silence.

Not a single one of Exodus' men made a sound, asked a question, or did anything at all other than sit there. Maybe it was because they already knew where they were going and what they would be doing when they got there, or maybe it was because they feared their leader and didn't want to do anything to incur his wrath.

"Pull over," Exodus ordered.

Immediately, the driver pulled the vehicle over to the side of the road. He did no more or no less, leaving the lights on and the engine running.

Scorpion had to hand it to Exodus, he had the absolute and complete loyalty and devotion of the men who worked for him. It was what you needed to wage a successful war, and that was exactly how Seeds of Life saw it. They were at war with everyone who didn't believe the same things they did, and they were ready and willing to fight for their beliefs and kill innocent people to do it.

"Markson, out," Exodus ordered.

The man beside him moved so Scorpion, who was in the back sandwiched between two of Exodus' men, could exit the car. Once he was out, the other man slid back in and closed the door behind him.

With the car engine still running and the other three men still inside, he wondered for a moment if Exodus planned to just dump him there and return to the commune without him. If that was the case, he would figure out a way to get back there and get to Jessica because he wasn't leaving her to face down the entire cult on her own.

Turned out, he didn't have to worry about being left out there like an unwanted dog.

"I want you to wave down the first car that approaches," Exodus informed him. "Once they stop to render assistance, I want you to execute everyone inside the vehicle."

His stomach turned.

In order to prove his loyalty to the cult, Exodus wanted to ensure that not only would he follow all commands issued, but that he was willing to go so far as shedding blood for the cult if that was what was required of him.

No way could he kill innocents.

"You are a military man. You have killed before, yes?" Exodus asked, a mocking brow arched. "I can assume you are not going to be too queasy to get the job done."

"Done two tours overseas," he replied. Not true. He'd worked a lot of missions in his years in Delta, even more at Prey. But the background the cult would have seen when they looked him up would show he had served two tours before being honorably discharged. "Killed my share of the enemy. I won't let you down." Scorpion even threw in a salute to accompany his words.

Exodus smiled and then held out a weapon. "You'll need this."

As Scorpion took the automatic rifle, he longed to use it to eliminate these four men. It would be so easy, over and done with before any of them even knew what was happening, but in the end, killing these men wouldn't change the cult's plans.

Instead, he had no choice but to hold onto the weapon and wait.

Wait for a vehicle to come.

Wait for an innocent good Samaritan to stop to offer assistance to what appeared to be a car that had broken down on the side of the remote road.

He hoped the road was remote enough that there would be no other cars, but of course, that hope was short-lived.

A mere fifteen minutes after he was given his orders, he saw the glow of approaching headlights.

Now or never.

It was either go through with this or blow his cover.

Stepping into the middle of the road he held the weapon behind his back and waved his free arm in the air to catch the driver's attention. Part of him hoped the driver wouldn't see him in time and knock him down. At least then he wouldn't be forced to choose between Jessica and stopping Seeds of Life plans, and killing whichever innocent motorist happened to be on this road tonight.

But that didn't happen.

The driver slowed to a stop, and Scorpion approached.

"Need some help?" the driver asked as he lowered his window.

Inside the vehicle was the driver, a young man, probably in his mid-twenties, and a woman about the same age asleep in the passenger seat. Since they both wore gold wedding bands, he assumed the couple were husband and wife. And in the backseat was a small infant, no more than a couple of weeks old, asleep in its car seat.

Could he kill a couple and their newborn child?

Even for a cause as good as the one that had brought him here tonight?

Scorpion had been prepared to steal, even been prepared to hold someone up at gunpoint or beat someone up.

But not this.

This he couldn't do.

Only Exodus and three of his goons were waiting in the vehicle for him to do this. If he didn't, he would either be killed here or returned to the commune and executed there. Even if he didn't kill this little family one of Exodus' men would. They were witnesses now. They weren't leaving whether Scorpion was the one to pull the trigger or not.

"Yeah, I need some help," he muttered, just not the kind of help the man was offering.

With no other choices and no way out that he could see, he stepped closer to the open car window, lifted his weapon, and fired off three shots.

~

November 27th
10:10 A.M.

The better she felt the worse she worried.

Jessica could feel her strength returning. A couple of days had passed since she and Mason were caught making out, and while she couldn't say she was at one hundred percent yet, she was definitely improving a little at a time. The dizziness was mostly gone, it was only if she stood too quickly that it caught her. The headache had faded until it was more a dull annoyance than the raging agony it had been at first. Nausea still lingered a little, caused by the thought of food more than actually eating it, and as much as she hated Genesis feeding her like she was a baby, she went along with it because she knew her body needed fuel.

Now more than ever.

There was a shift in the air at the commune. It hinted that something was coming, something was about to change, and she hated not knowing what it was.

Made her antsy.

Only there was no way to work out her pent-uppent-up frustration. Mason wasn't here so she couldn't verbally spar with him or physically spar if he was up for taking her on. Not having seen him in days added to her nervous energy and worrying about him had become her new hobby. Since she was still weak and got tired easily, she was still spending a lot of time in bed sleeping, and even when she was up Genesis wouldn't allow her to do much.

They hadn't been back to the main commune area, so there had been no opportunity to get a glimpse of Mason, assuming he was there and okay. The fresh air Genesis claimed she needed consisted only of walking around the small garden surrounding his tent. There were a few young women who tended to him and his needs, and any time they saw her she could see their curiosity.

Since there were only a few hundred people here and it had been six months since she joined the commune, Jessica knew most of the people by sight, a lot of them by name. While she followed the rules and didn't talk to the others much, there were times when they were allowed to talk amongst themselves, and she had made a point of meeting all the women here. It was likely the men would be more in the know of what was going on, but the commune liked traditional gender roles and segregation. Unless married or paired up, single females weren't allowed to interact with single males.

Still, she knew most of the people here by name and a little about their backgrounds, and she could see the young women—because apparently the only ones fit to serve Genesis personally were teenage girls—wondering if she was the chosen one.

It didn't feel anywhere near as great as she had thought it would to be convincing Genesis that she was indeed his chosen one.

When she'd taken on this case, she'd been so excited. Her big break. A chance to move from working VICE—not that anything was wrong with that, she was good at dealing with the women because they had a lot in common—to homicide or major crime. She'd make a huge impression on her bosses, show them how talented she was and what she could bring to any team, and get a huge promotion.

Now that felt so hollow.

Her focus should have been on this case, on the mission itself. Infiltrating the cult, gathering enough intel to have them raided, and the leaders arrested before they could carry out their plans. *That* was what was important, not herself and her ego.

Maybe she didn't deserve those big promotions she thought she was ready for.

She should know better than to let her ego creep in. Look what it had done to her brother. David had gone from the sweet, kind of geeky big brother she remembered from when she was very small, to the egotistical, arrogant man who instead of stepping up and helping to take care of their family when their parents couldn't, spent his money on himself and made her work as a prostitute to pay the bills.

No way did she want to be like him.

Not in any way, shape, or form.

Movement at the tent door caught her attention, and she prepared herself. It could be Genesis returning to feed or bathe her, but it could also be someone else. Exodus had been hanging around this morning when Genesis took her outside to sit in his garden and get some fresh air.

The way he'd been watching her had creeped her out a little.

Gone was his usual hostility. It looked like he had decided to accept her, not just as part of the cult but as part of the inner circle, but she had no idea why. No idea what had changed.

Was it something to do with Mason?

Had he been hurt? Or had he been able to prove his loyalty to the cult which in turn had helped cement her loyalty?

Both Genesis and Exodus walked through the tent door, and from the expressions on their faces, they were here for a reason, not just to see if she was recovering well.

Straightening in her chair, she kept her expression mild, meek, submissive, just the way both men liked their women.

Playing this role was supposed to be easy, yet it kept getting harder by the day.

"How are you feeling, my child?" Genesis asked as he passed her a glass of water.

"Better, thank you, Prophet. You've been taking such good care of me, I am so very grateful, especially since I am so very unworthy."

Genesis looked to his second in command and arched a brow. Exodus responded by nodding, then both men pulled up chairs to the table where she was sitting and looked at her.

It took all her effort not to squirm.

"I believe you are well enough now, my child, to answer a few questions," Genesis started.

So, it was time.

Make it or break it time.

If she gave the answers he wanted, she would cement herself in the role of Genesis' angel star. But if she didn't, it would all be over. At best, she would just be sent back to be a worker bee, but the worst case was they would just be done with her, kill her and move on.

It didn't escape her notice that a part of her—a bigger part than she would have liked—wished Mason was here. There was nothing he could do for her, but just having him here as moral support would help.

"Of course, Prophet. I'm here to serve," she said, and relaxed a little when Genesis nodded approvingly.

"Very good, child. Can you tell me when you first heard the stars?"

"I was a little girl. My family ... they weren't ..." It wasn't hard to let tears fill her eyes as she said the words. While this was part of the cover story she had made up before coming to the cult, there were parts of it that were true. "They ... hurt me. One night I ran away, out into the woods. It was dark and I got lost. I was scared. Of being alone, of getting in trouble, I was panicking, but then ..."

"Then what, my child?"

"Then I heard this sound. It was so dark I couldn't see where I was going, but all of a sudden, there was light. Starlight," she allowed a note of wonder into her tone. "It was so beautiful. Magical. Special. Warm. It showed me a path through the woods, but not back home. It took me to a house. A couple. It turns out the man was a police officer. I told him about my home and he and his wife ended up adopting me. If it hadn't been for the light I would have been lost out there for days, weeks, maybe forever. The stars ... I believe they saved me for a reason. I just never knew what that reason was. But then I heard about you. About Seeds of Life, and I just ... I can't explain it. I just had to be here. When I arrived that warmth that has been inside me since that night grew." She gave a helpless shrug and looked anxiously at Genesis. The anxiety wasn't faked. "Does that make sense, Prophet?"

For a long moment he just stared at her.

She couldn't read his expression.

Despite her best efforts not to show any weaknesses and to remain calm, if a little anxious, her hands twisted together.

Had she got it all wrong?

The story was supposed to show a connection to the stars that went back to childhood, as well as leading her here. But maybe she had read the man's profile all wrong, maybe that wasn't what he was looking for in his angel star at all.

I'm sorry, Mason.

I failed.

CHAPTER

Twelve

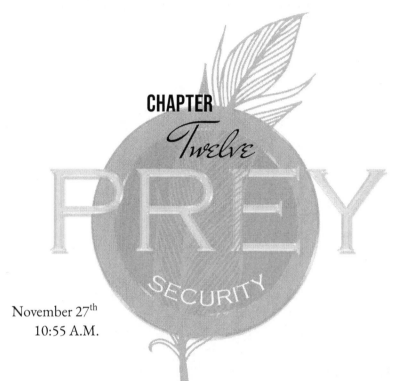

November 27th
10:55 A.M.

If he had to sit alone in here for another second, he was going to lose his mind.

Only of course Scorpion knew that wasn't true.

He had been trained to withstand all manner of torture. From physical to psychological, he'd mastered it. His naturally calm persona worked for him because he was already someone not prone to panicking in any and all situations. Add in training, and years of implementing control over his body and his surroundings in Delta and then Bravo Team, plus a couple of times when he and his team had actually been captured and tortured, and this should be a piece of cake.

Roof over his head, even if it was just a tent, a bed to sleep on, and a table and chairs to sit at. Clothes to wear, meals that were simple but nutritious and tasted fine, fresh water to drink, and a toilet, a composting toilet but definitely better than nothing.

There was nothing really to complain about.

Except the endless hours of boredom as he sat alone in the tent with nothing to do and no one to talk to.

That wasn't entirely true.

There was something to do all right.

Worry over Jessica.

Guilt over what he'd done this morning.

Both weighed on him with a heaviness that was slowly starting to crush him.

While he might not have come here with the best of intentions, when he had realized he'd made a mistake in judging Jessica without having all the information, he'd wanted to stay and make things right. And this morning he hadn't had a choice. He'd done what he had to. The greater good and all that.

Didn't help.

Nothing helped.

Normally, if he was on edge because of a mission or the mess that was going on with Axe and Beth, or any of his other teammates, he'd work out. Run, weights, it didn't matter what he was doing because he was doing something and that helped contain the thoughts and memories of the things he'd done, the things he's seen, and the times he hadn't done enough.

Other than a few reps of sit-ups and push-ups there was nothing else for him to do but think.

A sudden commotion outside caught his attention and he stood and walked over to the door to his tent. A guard was no longer outside, but Exodus had ordered him to stay inside and not come out until he was given permission. It wasn't because the man still didn't trust him, it was just to exert dominance and control, and while it was annoying, Scorpion went along with it because he wasn't going to bust Jessica's case wide open just to prove to Exodus that he had no real power.

So, he'd sat in there like a good boy, proving once again that he could be a loyal soldier who followed the rules, who could be trusted to follow an order without complaint and without discussion.

Now, though, he wanted to know what was going on.

Since he wasn't going to outright disobey and set back the progress he'd made—especially given what he'd been ordered to do this morning

—Scorpion got down on his stomach and lifted up the bottom of the door flap just enough that he could see out.

It looked like the rest of the guards were gathering together in the small open space between the tents. There was a large firepit out there, although currently no fire burned, and several wooden benches grouped around it. Although he hadn't been invited to join since Exodus seemed determined to keep him alone a while longer, he'd heard them laughing and talking out there at night after the evening stargazing ritual.

From here, Scorpion couldn't make out the words the men were saying, but it was clear they were all excited. Men talked over the top of one another, and even the couple of women who tended to the camp had joined in.

Whatever was going on was big.

Really big.

Jessica.

Immediately his thoughts went to her. No one had given him any updates on her, so for all he knew she'd had a bleed on her brain and died in the couple of days since he'd last seen her. Didn't seem to matter to his imagination that it wasn't particularly likely she would have succumbed to the head injury, his concern for her was all-consuming.

Even if she hadn't died, she was in as much danger as he was until they fully convinced Genesis and Exodus that both of them were loyal, true believers, who would back up Seeds of Life's cause with everything they had to give.

If something was going on it had to do with her.

He was sure of it.

Don't ask him how he knew because there was no answer he could give, it was just a gut feeling. Gut feelings had saved his life and the lives of his teammates several times over the years, so he had learned to trust them.

So, trust it he did.

Exodus appeared amongst the crowd and Scorpion didn't hesitate to get back to the chair at his table. The man couldn't see through the tent and know that he was lying on the floor watching, but sooner or later, Exodus would come to check on him, and when that happened, he wanted to be seen to be doing the right thing.

If he wanted answers on what was going on and access to Jessica, even if it was only from a distance, then he had to keep up his act and be on his best behavior. Besides, he couldn't even hear what the men were saying so no information could be gleaned from staying where he was.

No sooner had he gotten himself settled back in his chair at the table than his tent door was opened, and Exodus strolled in like he owned the place. A hint of surprise flickered in the man's eyes, no doubt he had expected Scorpion to be trying to figure out what was going on, what had the camp in an uproar.

"Stand, soldier," Exodus ordered.

Scorpion did so, feet spread, hands clasped behind his back, shoulders squared, ready and awaiting his next order.

"I'm sure you can hear from what's going on outside that something has happened," Exodus said.

Of course he could.

Wasn't like he was stupid.

Keeping his cool, he merely gave a single nod of his head.

"It is a day to be remembered," Exodus continued, clearly enjoying prolonging Scorpion's suffering by not just coming right out and telling him what was happening. "It has happened."

It was on the tip of his tongue to ask what had happened, but he resisted the impulse and waited.

Sooner or later—preferably sooner—Exodus would just spit it out. And each time he showed his restraint and ability to submit to the chain of command, he earned another piece of trust. Sooner or later he would have enough pieces to put together to earn access to everything that Seeds of Life was planning.

Big picture.

"Genesis has found his angel star," Exodus announced.

Jessica.

It didn't need to be said for him to know who the man was talking about.

She'd done it. Done exactly what she'd been sent here to do even with his interference.

Pride for her flooded through him and he wanted to break into a grin and cheer her successes. She deserved them. For her perseverance, her sacrifice, her dedication, and her ability to adapt to whatever was thrown her way.

I knew you could do it, Jess.

"Do you want to know who it is?" Exodus asked, obviously enjoying himself. The man was a sadist if ever there was one.

"Only when you're ready to tell me, sir," he replied in his best cadet voice. It had been a long time since he'd been that young and inexperienced, but he still knew how to play the game.

It was obvious Exodus was impressed and Scorpion inwardly smirked.

"Your sister is the chosen one," Exodus told him what he had already been expecting to hear. No one other than Jessica was capable of convincing the cult leader that she was exactly what he had been looking for. "Are you jealous?"

"No, sir. Of course not. I said my goodbyes to my sister. I am here to serve as is she."

"You know that she will belong to the prophet in every way," Exodus taunted, not willing to leave it at that.

Oh yeah, he knew that.

Didn't like it either.

Because if he had learned one thing about Jessica in the short time they had spent together, it was that once she made up her mind she committed one hundred percent.

There was nothing she wouldn't be prepared to do to bring Genesis and Seeds of Life down.

Nothing.

Which utterly terrified him.

∽

November 27th
   6:52 P.M.

Apparently, being the chosen one was a whole lot more work than she had realized it would be.

Jessica supposed she should have known there was going to be more to it than just being privy to Seeds of Life's plans, but honestly, she hadn't thought past winning Genesis' trust. That was all that had seemed important, but now that she had been accepted as the woman Genesis had been looking for a whole lot more was needed to be prepared for.

After proclaiming her the angel star, Genesis began the first in a series of rituals.

First had been a long soak in cold water. That had not been a fun experience. It wasn't the first time she'd had to clean herself in cold water. There had been times as a kid where they hadn't had enough money to pay the gas bill and with no hot water there had been no choice but to clean in a freezing cold shower.

But that had been a long time ago and that first second when the cold water covered her bare skin had been a shock to her system.

Still, if given a choice between sitting in cold water for hours or having a creepy, delusional, and violent man with a god complex sitting there watching her she would choose the cold bath every single time.

There hadn't been a single second since pronouncing her his chosen one that Genesis had left her alone.

He'd watched her while she took the cold bath, then fed her lunch. Next was hours soaking in a milk bath. Given how precious resources were when you were living off the land and didn't have the luxury of just popping down to the grocery store to grab something you needed, she had been surprised when she was guided to the metal tub filled with milk.

Apparently, it was most important that she soak in it for hours, and Genesis had sat and stared at her the entire time.

Creepy.

Way past creepy.

The man was as crazy as he was dangerous. The more time she spent around him the more she came to understand just how unhinged he was.

After her milk bath she had been fed dinner and then sent straight off to bed. While he hadn't slept in the bed with her, Genesis had made her sleep in his room in his bed while he slept on the floor beside her. Every time she woke, he wasn't asleep, he was standing staring at her.

Super creepy.

Fed breakfast, by then she was getting used to the idea of Genesis feeding her. Didn't mean she liked it. She absolutely did not. Hated it in fact. But it had become part of their routine and she no longer even bothered to attempt to pick up her own spoon or fork. Today's routine had included being measured for a specially made gown, and hours and hours of meditation.

All leading up to this moment.

Dressed in the gown which had somehow been finished in just hours—Jessica assumed because Genesis had dozens of women working on it simultaneously to get it done in time—her hair brushed and brushed until it shimmered and shone like spun gold, she was being led through the woods, Genesis' hand holding hers.

"Do you know how I knew you were the one, my sweet angel star?" he asked.

"No, Prophet." Actually, she did, but anything he told her could be helpful information. Sometimes it was the tiniest of details that turned out to be the most important. And while she assumed it was partly the story she'd told him, and her ability to present as meek and mild, if there was more to it then she wanted to know.

"I told you, my angel star, that it was not necessary for you to continue to call me Prophet. We are partners now."

Even though the smile he gave her made her want to go and take a scalding shower to wash off the dirtiness it left her with, instead, she allowed a small blush and an answering smile. "Sorry, Pr ... I mean, Genesis."

His free hand patted her head like she was the opposite of his partner and instead was more like his favorite new pet. "Very good. Now come here and you will see why I knew it was you the moment I found you in the woods with your brother. When you see you'll understand how I was able to forgive your transgressions."

They started walking again, and a couple of minutes later, they walked out into a clearing. Ringed almost perfectly by trees, there was a definite air of fairy magic. Or she supposed star magic since that's what Genesis was obsessed with.

Right in the middle of the ring was a large stone. Like the clearing itself, the stone was almost perfectly round, and the moon was shining down on it like a spotlight. She got it. The time of year had lined up, and he was associating her arrival, him finding her out in the woods just days before the moon was going to shine perfectly on the perfectly round stone in the perfectly ringed clearing, all linked in his mind and all centered on her.

"The moonlight," she said, adding a hint of awe to her tone that didn't completely have to be faked. This was a beautiful spot with magic in the air. Jessica just prayed it was magic for the good guys and not for the bad guys. "The goddess shines on this place."

"The goddess shines on you," he corrected. "When I saw you in the woods a few nights ago, she was shining down on you then, too. Telling me there was something special about you. That I shouldn't just walk away. Tonight, she will tell the entire community that you are the chosen one."

"I am eager to fulfill the goddess' wishes," she said so sweetly she was surprised she didn't give herself a cavity.

"I know you are." Leaning in, he touched a kiss to her forehead and the only way she could keep her composure was to pretend that it was Mason who had just kissed her so tenderly.

With hours of just sitting around with nothing to do and no one to talk to, he had been constantly on her mind. As badly as she wanted to know that he was okay, she was afraid to ask. So, she did her best to pretend that he was there with her, backing her up, offering his support, and cheering her on.

Hopefully, that wasn't wishful thinking.

"Take your place, my angel star." Genesis' hands spanned her waist and he lifted her, setting her on the round stone in the middle of the clearing. "Come, meet your chosen one," he called out and immediately people began to flood into the clearing.

They were all people she recognized, but the expressions on their faces weren't the ones she was used to seeing. There was wonder and awe. They looked at her like she really was some sort of god. With the white flowing gown and her hair shimmering in the moonlight, she probably did look like an angel.

But she wasn't.

She was the same woman she had always been, and Jessica realized she felt a little guilty. Some of these people truly believed Genesis and his crazy claims about star twins and eliminating everyone who didn't believe what they did. She had come here under false pretenses, and she was pretending right now to be their chosen one, the one they were waiting for, the one they looked up to. There wasn't anything wrong in what she was doing, but in this moment it felt like there was.

Genesis stood beside her, and while she kept still, her gaze was constantly roaming the crowd, scanning it for a glimpse of the only person she wanted to see.

Only she didn't see him.

Where are you, Mason?

Why wasn't he here with everyone else?

Panic bubbled inside her. If he wasn't here when every other member of the cult was, then that couldn't be good. Had he been hurt? Killed?

When the clearing was packed with the cult members, Genesis stepped up on the stone alongside her. Since it was really only big enough for one person to stand on, his body was close to hers. He stood at her back and pulled her to lean against his chest. His arms crossed her body, one across her chest, the other across her stomach as though he were holding her to him.

Don't fight him.

Somehow, she managed not to, probably because she was more preoccupied with her fear for Mason and his safety.

"This is the angel star we have all been waiting for. I have spoken with her, and the goddess has spoken to me. She is the one. She has arrived, and you all know what that means."

Jessica didn't but she could guess.

Everyone else must because a round of cheers went up.

"The time has come for the first stage of our war to begin," Genesis continued. "We will rise up. We will eliminate the unbelievers. They are either for us or they are against us, and what will happen to those against us?"

"They will fall," was yelled out by dozens of the cult members.

Not if I have anything to say about it.

The fate of the world felt like it was resting on her shoulders, and nobody was there to help her carry the load.

There was never anybody there when she needed them.

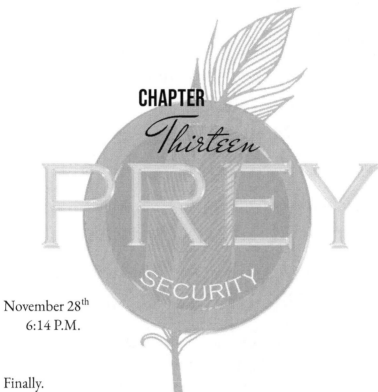

CHAPTER
Thirteen

November 28th
6:14 P.M.

Finally.

Scorpion would have lost his mind if he had to spend another second alone in this tent.

The fresh air felt good on his face, and his muscles rejoiced to be able to do more than pace like a caged tiger around his small eight-by-eight tent.

Not that moving freely was what he really cared about.

What he really wanted was a chance to spot Jessica.

Three days had passed since they'd had sex and gotten caught, and barring any complications, she should be starting to feel better as she recovered from her concussion. It would take another week at least for her to completely recover, but if Genesis had allowed her the rest she needed, she should be doing better than when he'd last seen her.

At least he hoped she was.

Wouldn't believe it though until he saw her with his own two eyes.

Which, hopefully, he would any moment now.

It wasn't Exodus who had come to his tent to tell him he would be joining everyone for the nightly stargazing, although he knew it was the man who had given the command. He hadn't seen Exodus since the day before when he came to share the news that Jessica had been crowned the chosen one. Not getting the reaction he hoped for had cemented in Genesis' second in-command that Scorpion was a loyal believer who wasn't going to cause problems for the cult leader or anyone else.

About time.

The guards who had come to let him out talked amongst themselves, basically ignoring him. It made him feel like the new kid in school, not that he cared, he wasn't there to make friends he was there to gather intel, and to do that all he needed to do was listen.

As they walked, the four other men were chattering away in excited tones about how glad they were the beginning had come.

Didn't take a genius to figure out what they were talking about.

With the crowning of Jessica as Genesis' angel star, the man was likely ready to begin waging his war.

Good thing he'd come when he had. Not that Jessica couldn't have handled this on her own. Scorpion had every confidence that she could, but two sets of hands were always better than one, and now he could gather intel from Exodus, and she could gather it from Genesis.

As they approached what looked to be a clearing, he could hear the sound of chattering voices. This wasn't the usual space where they met for their nightly stargazing meetings, and when he stepped out of the trees he could see why.

In the middle of a nearly perfectly ringed clearing was a large round stone.

On the stone stood Jessica.

Dressed in a flowing white gown, with her hair cascading down her back in golden waves, she was a stunning sight.

Actually, she looked like an angel or a star.

Like their brains were linked on the same wavelength, and she registered his presence, her head turned, and despite the yards between them and the mass of people in between, their eyes met. It was dark, and he couldn't even really see her eyes, they were just black holes in her pale face, but he knew she was looking right at him.

Could feel it.

Relief hit him a lot harder than he thought it would.

Of course, he'd known he would be relieved to see that she was okay. Had spent the last couple of days thinking of nothing but Jessica and how she was doing.

But he hadn't known it would feel like this.

What was this woman doing to him?

She occupied his thoughts, she occupied his dreams, and she made him feel things he hadn't with any other woman he'd dated. She made him think about the future and what he wanted out of it.

Three of his teammates were involved with women now. He was used to it just being Axe and Beth, but now there was Tank and Tillie, and Rock and Ariel. It changed things having the women around. Not in a bad way, things were just different. Instead of the six of them hanging out together when they weren't on an op, now the guys wanted to spend that time with the women in their lives.

They still did things together, worked PT every day, worked Beth's case every free second they had, plus working Tillie and then Ariel's in between, but he couldn't deny something had felt a little off with him since he'd seen the relief in Rock after finally making things right with the only woman he'd ever loved. It was different for Panther, he had his eight-year-old son Andy to focus on, and Trick seemed to enjoy keeping things with the women who entered in and out of his life as casual as they got.

Had he gotten to the point where he wanted more than casual?

As he watched Jessica relax just knowing that he was there, he had to wonder if maybe he was ready to have something deeper. Marriage and kids had always been on his plan, but his plan had never had a specific timeline. It would just happen when it happened and if it didn't he was content being Uncle Mason to his sister's kid, and Andy, and any other kids his teammates had.

While he'd known Jessica since he was eighteen, he'd never really known her. Not the real her anyway, just the version her brother had created. If someone had told him she would be the woman to get him thinking about what he wanted his future to look like he would have laughed in their face.

Yet ...

She was making him think about the future and what he wanted it to look like.

And she wasn't even trying to.

The five-year age gap between them and the fact she was just trying to build a career where he and Bravo Team were able to take time to focus on the cases personal to them with the blessing of their boss meant they were in different places in their lives. Plus, he'd never even talked to her about what she wanted her future to look like.

Maybe she didn't even want marriage and kids.

If she did, it didn't mean she wanted them with him.

Why would she want them with him?

"It is time, my children," Genesis called out, stepping up onto the stone behind Jessica. Since there was barely space for two people to stand there, he had to pull her up against his body, his arms wrapped possessively around her.

Before he could stop himself, Scorpion found his breathing had increased and his hands had curled into fists.

He didn't like seeing someone touch his woman ... partner.

Had to stop thinking of her as his. Yes, they'd had sex, one time. That was it. There were some sort of feelings developing, on his side at least, but that was as far as it went. Maybe when this was over, he could ask her out. If he thought there was any chance of her saying yes.

Like she knew that he wouldn't like seeing Genesis' hands on her, he felt the intensity of Jessica's stare. She may as well be yelling at him not to do anything stupid and mess up her case.

Scorpion smiled despite himself. She was a firecracker of a woman, all spark and sass and strength, a whole lot of determination, too, and she cared about people in a way that was usually so rare. Jessica Bowen was a good person with a good heart, and he hated that he hadn't seen that before.

But he saw it now, and he was prepared to do whatever it took to help her with this case.

Nodding, he forced his body to relax and was sure that in the moon-light he saw the ghost of a smile light her lips. Just for a moment and then it was gone. Replaced by an expression of serenity that was almost unnerving.

Playing her part so convincingly, she looked like she believed she was some angel star sent from the moon to help guide Genesis and the members of Seeds of Life into a new world. It was creepy in its sincerity even as he knew she didn't believe a word about it.

"The stars have come out to bathe us with their glory, and with our angel standing here before us, we can start to prepare for the beginning of the end," Genesis continued.

There were several chants of affirmation from amongst the gathered crowd, mostly from the men as the women were supposed to be seen and not heard. The other guards, in particular, seemed excited at the idea of killing innocent people. Had any of them even taken a life before? It was one thing to be all valiant and proud to protect what you believed in, but it was another to actually take a life.

He knew that, he'd taken lives before, and while he wouldn't hesi-tate to do it again to protect the people he loved and cared about, and the innocent, it didn't come without a cost.

A cost that in this moment felt much too high.

There were too many innocents and too many evil men and women wanting to hurt them.

His gaze locked with Jessica's, and he felt something pass between them. A deep understanding that whatever it took they were going to bring Seeds of Life down, and they were going to do it together.

Partners.

For now at least.

What the future held he would have to wait and see.

∿

November 28th
9:39 P.M.

. . .

Jessica was sick of this stupid stone.

Ever since Genesis had brought her out there the day after he had pronounced her his angel star, he'd told her she had to stay there. Always.

Bathroom breaks were all she was allowed, and because he had decided she was an angel of the stars, she didn't get to use the inside composting toilets anymore. Not that they had been awesome by any stretch of the imagination, she much preferred to flush away her business, but at least they were a toilet.

Infinitely better than a hole in the ground.

It sucked.

Big time.

Camping had never been her thing. The idea of sleeping outdoors on the ground, even if it was inside a sleeping bag, was not a fun one for her. Sleeping in the tents these last several months had been bad enough, but at least they had a cot to sleep on and blankets.

Out here she had nothing.

Genesis decided she didn't need anything more than this special stone that, to him, was a sacred place. When she wasn't sitting out here "speaking" to the moon and the stars, she was giving speeches to those going through orientation or reprimanding those who had been found to have broken a rule.

Really, she had no idea what she should be saying, but like she always did, she went with her gut and so far it seemed to be paying off. Now she just needed Genesis to start telling her specifics about his plans, so she had something concrete to give her boss.

Tonight wasn't about her job though.

Tonight was personal.

Nothing moved in the quiet clearing. Stargazing time was over, and everyone had gone back to the camp. Genesis had returned to his tent, and she was hoping that, like last night, he wouldn't return again until the morning when he came to bring her breakfast.

Slipping off the stone, she stretched her aching muscles. Sitting out in the cold night with nothing but a fairly thin woolen gown was not the best when you were trying to recover from a concussion. But, apparently, Genesis didn't believe that angels got cold so he hadn't given her anything to keep her warm. He better hope the temperatures didn't drop much lower because even at her healthiest, she couldn't survive overnight without a source of warmth, and he could easily return one morning to find she had succumbed to hypothermia.

If she was caught anywhere but on the stone, it wasn't going to be good for her.

But this whole case was about taking risks.

No gain without pain.

And this was a risk she couldn't not take.

Just as she started creeping toward the trees—not entirely sure Genesis hadn't left some of his men to watch over her—the heavens opened, and a downpour of rain dumped down upon her.

Great.

Ducking her head didn't do much, but at least it kept the water a little out of her eyes as she ran through the dark and into the cover of the trees. That, too, didn't provide a whole lot of protection from the rain, but at least it kept the worst of it off her as she ran as fast as she dared. Her balance wasn't back to one hundred percent yet, and the last thing she needed was to fall and injure herself.

From what she had been able to gather, the men who served as both guards at the main camp and as Genesis' soldiers lived in a separate camp a little way away from the rest of the commune. That had to be where Mason was staying.

At least she was praying that it was.

Because she needed to talk to him.

It was crazy because she'd come here knowing this was going to be a case she would work on her own. She hadn't wanted backup and hadn't believed she needed it. When Mason first appeared, all she'd wanted was for him to leave her alone, but now things had changed.

Now she found herself needing the reassurance of knowing he was working this with her. That she wasn't in it alone.

Jessica was so very tired of handling everything alone.

For once it would be so nice to have someone there to help her share the load.

Maybe that was why she had shifted in her attitude toward the man she had loathed for so many years. Once he stopped being so arrogant and looking down his nose at her like she was mud on his shoe, he made her feel like he wanted to do this with her. That he wanted to have her back, support her, and not take over and do it for her, but be there with her.

A bright glow ahead told her she had reached the guards' camp, and Jessica slowed her speed and began to creep through the trees, making sure she didn't alert anyone to her presence.

When she got close enough, she could see a large bonfire burning in the middle of the camp. Men hurried around trying to set up a cover over it so the pouring rain didn't put it out. She might not know much about camping, but she was pretty sure that nothing short of a proper roof was going to keep the fire going in rain like this.

Still, if they wanted to try, it kept them occupied so they wouldn't notice her.

Her gaze scanned the group searching for the only man she cared about.

Mason.

There he was.

Relief at seeing him alive and in one piece—even if it had been only an hour ago she'd seen him at stargazing—was a whole lot stronger than she would have thought.

Than it should be.

Just because she was starting to feel ... things ... for the man, it didn't mean it was a good idea. He was still the same man he'd been when she was a teenager and he'd stood by and allowed her to be hurt. Until she knew the truth about why, feeling anything for him was dangerous.

Like something joined them together, a thread of something that couldn't be seen or understood, he looked right at her, and she could tell from the way he stiffened that he'd seen her despite the fact she thought she'd hidden herself away behind the tree trunks.

Saying something to the other men she couldn't hear over the drumming of the rain, he disappeared inside a small tent a little way off from the others.

Perfect.

They could be alone together in there.

By the time she crept around the outside of the camp and up to the back of his tent to find he'd lifted the back wall a little so she could crawl inside, she was shaking all over from the cold, her teeth chattering. It was a good thing that Mason's tent was a short distance from the others because she was sure that chattering could be heard over the pouring rain.

"You're ice cold," Mason muttered as he grabbed her elbows and guided her up to her feet. Then without hesitating, he leaned down, took hold of the hem of her dress, and pulled it up and over her head, dropping the soaked material at their feet. His own shirt joined it and then the next thing she knew, he had picked her up and was carrying her over to his cot, where he sat down with her snuggled on his lap and tucked the blanket around them both.

Jessica didn't even care that the wool felt scratchy against her bare skin, or that she was still trembling violently, or that her jaw ached from trying to clamp her teeth together to stop the chattering.

This was nice.

Curled up like this in Mason's arms, he hadn't even hesitated to step up and take care of her, just done it like it was the most natural thing in the world.

Tears stung the backs of her eyes, but she fought them. She didn't cry, learning so long ago that it didn't help. If anything, it tended to make things worse. Besides, Mason already thought she was weak, pathetic, selfish, and spoiled, she didn't want to add crybaby to that list.

Only as he held her tucked close against his bare chest, not seeming to care in the least that she was wet and freezing and must be making him wet and freezing, it didn't feel like he thought she was weak, pathetic, selfish, and spoiled.

In fact, the way he was rubbing a hand up and down her arms and her back, while his other hand cradled her head keeping it tucked underneath his chin, it felt like he cared about her.

But that was crazy.

Wasn't it?

Truth was, she didn't know anymore.

She wasn't sure if the man she'd known him to be back then was the real Mason or if this man who had shown up at the cult and stayed to watch her back was the real Mason. Or if she was only seeing what she wanted to see, and this man really was the same old Mason she'd always loathed.

Before she could stop herself, the question came bursting out. "Why did you stand by and let David pimp me out?"

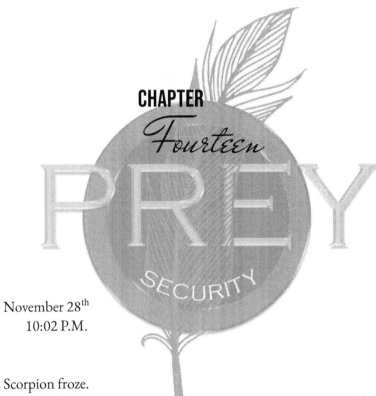

CHAPTER

Fourteen

November 28th
10:02 P.M.

Scorpion froze.

His blood stopped flowing, heart stopped pumping, and his lungs stopped breathing. At least that's what it felt like.

"What did you just say?" he demanded, the words falling from his lips in a low, dangerous growl.

Jessica heard it to because her head jerked up and she tried to pull away from his embrace. He tightened his hold on her but gentled his voice a little. It wasn't her he was angry with right now.

It was himself.

How had he not known what was really going on?

While maybe he hadn't quite believed David's story that Jessica was doing it to buy herself clothes, shoes, and makeup, he had thought she was doing it of her own free will. He'd just thought that it was maybe to help cover the cost of the bills since neither of her parents were working and her dad had a ton of medical bills with his accident and resulting injuries.

But to learn the truth ...

He was gutted.

"I know you knew," she said softly, eyes downcast. For the first time since he'd found her here, the confident, self-assured woman who didn't hesitate to tell him what she thought had disappeared.

In her place was an insecure shell of that woman.

Taking her chin between his thumb and forefinger, his heart cracked a little when she flinched as though afraid he was going to hurt her. Now knowing the truth about the past, he realized how badly he *had* hurt her.

Nudging her chin up until she was forced to meet his eye or close her own, he felt a spark of pride when she didn't back down and met his gaze squarely even if he could see the pain and fear swirling in her now gray eyes.

"I didn't know everything," he told her honestly.

"But you knew I wasn't safe," she whispered.

It was him who wound up closing his eyes, unable to bear looking into those pained gray depths a moment longer. "I knew you weren't safe," he echoed.

"I don't understand," she said helplessly. "The man I've gotten to know these last couple of weeks wouldn't stand by and let a thirteen-year-old girl be pimped out."

"I didn't know it wasn't your choice."

"I was *thirteen*. Why would it be my choice? I didn't even really get what sex was exactly until David let one of his friends sleep with me for fifty dollars. Not that I ever saw a cent of that money." Anger and bitter-ness—both well deserved—were in her tone, but there was also a pleading quality. She didn't want him to be the bad guy.

"David said you blew all the money he sent home to pay the bills and still wanted more so you could buy things for yourself," he said in his own defense, but was quickly realizing there was no defense for what he had done, or at least acquiesced in.

A bitter laugh fell from her lips. "David didn't send money home. David didn't do anything that wasn't in David's own best interest. He didn't help take care of the house, the laundry, the cooking, or the clean-ing. He didn't help try to get our mom out of bed when all she wanted to do was lie there, take her pills, and stare at the ceiling. He didn't help with our younger sisters. He didn't do anything. Whatever money he made, he kept for himself, along with what he made pimping me out. I didn't care about makeup and clothes, the clothes I wore were from a thrift store, and I fixed them over and over again until they were no longer patchable. He didn't pay a dime toward our mother's funeral, he didn't even come home to see if I needed help with anything. And he certainly doesn't contribute to paying the bills at our father's nursing home."

Jessica was breathing so hard that she was no longer shaking from the cold but from anger.

"I struggled to keep everything together. I was ten years old. *Ten*. But I stepped up. I took care of everything. David did nothing. My mom did nothing but get herself addicted to drugs and then kill herself. I did it all. I gave up my dreams of being a lawyer because no way could I afford college and Dad's medical bills. I did it all with zero help. I cannot believe you are admitting that you knew a young girl was being forced to prostitute herself and you did absolutely nothing to stop it from happening."

When she shoved at him, Scorpion reluctantly let her go. He knew it was only because there were the rest of the guards around that she wasn't screaming and yelling at him.

"I didn't do nothing to stop it," he told her quietly.

Jessica froze. "What?"

"I didn't think it was okay for a kid your age to be prostituting herself. I didn't know David was forcing you, I thought either your mom was, or you were doing it to try to earn extra money to pay the bills. Either way, it wasn't okay. I followed you, knew where you were, and called in an anonymous tip that a teenager was being abused. I waited till the cops and CPS showed up to make sure you were safe. After that, I let the friendship with David start to fade. I didn't under-stand how he could let you do that and not put a stop to it."

"That day I was so scared. I thought I was going to jail. If I did there would be no one to take care of my sisters. They'd be so scared without me. But the cop who was there was so nice to me. She asked me if I was being forced to do that and I told her I was. I was scared to tell her it was

David, I thought if I got him in trouble, he might kill me. Everything changed that day. My mom didn't fight CPS taking me and my sisters. I refused to leave them, and that same cop told me I didn't have to. She took all three of us into her home. It was the first time in five years I felt safe." Her gaze met his. "You did that for me, and I never even knew it. Thank you."

"Don't thank me, Jess," he said fiercely. "I didn't do enough. If I had found out earlier I would have put a stop to it. Damn." Scorpion raked his fingers through his hair, needing the sting of pain in his scalp to ground him. "I'm so sorry. All this time I never knew David did that to you. I thought you were this spoiled princess who didn't step up when her family needed her. He made it sound like he did everything. I should have known."

Walking toward him on trembling legs, she stopped close enough for him to touch, but he didn't. He wasn't sure she'd want him to. "I'm glad you didn't know. I don't think I could have handled it if you'd known what was happening to me and stood by and did nothing."

Tentatively, he reached out to rest his hands on her hips. "I want to kill him."

"I've wanted to a thousand times before but I didn't. You won't either, because you're a good man. You saved me and my sisters. If you hadn't done what you did, David would have done the same to them when they were older, I'm sure of it. You gave all of us a chance to have a life."

It hadn't been enough.

Jessica had been forced to give up her dream of law school because of her father's medical bills, and he would bet every spare cent she made went to pay those bills and take care of her two little sisters.

But who was taking care of her?

Scorpion didn't like that he knew the answer to that question was nobody. Jessica was always the giver of care never the receiver of it.

Until now.

When they got out of there, he was going to make sure she never had to worry about anything again.

Leaning forward, he touched his forehead to her chest. "I'm sorry I didn't do more."

"You did enough." Her hands lifted to circle his shoulders and she held him to her. "I'm ... scared about what comes next," she admitted. "When I took this job, I was prepared to do whatever it took to bring down Seeds of Life. Nothing was off the table. Genesis wants an angel star baby, I was prepared to keep cover and have sex with him if that was what it took." When his body went stiff at her selfless words, she began to stroke his spine, soothing him, again taking care of those around her with no thought for herself and her own needs. "I thought with my past that sex with a man who repulses me would be something I could do. I've done it before. I'm on birth control so I know the chances of me getting pregnant are slim. But what if I do? What if I can't go through with sex with Genesis if he wants it and I ruin everything? So many people are counting on me, and the stakes are so high. I'm scared I'm going to fail, and I'm so ... tired."

With her admission, she sank down against him and as he cradled this strong woman to him, Scorpion was filled with a need to be the one to step up and show Jessica what it was like to have someone be there by her side to help her carry her loads.

If she'd let him.

~

November 28th
    10:22 P.M.

If she had to guess, Jessica would have thought admitting her weakness to anyone—let alone this man who confused her in so many ways—would have made her feel uncomfortable, like she had shown him a glimpse of an easy way to destroy her if he chose to.

Instead, what she felt was relief.

For so long, she had been struggling, holding it all together for other people's benefit, and not allowing anyone to see how much the burdens she had been forced to carry from such a young age had worn her down.

Now she had thrown them out there, and it felt good.

She felt good.

Lighter somehow.

Especially since Mason's sturdy chest was beneath her and his strong arms wrapped around her, holding her up. He was real and solid, and more than that, he seemed to *want* to help her. It had been so long since someone had been there for her like that, it was almost impossible to believe it was real.

But Mason made it feel real and made her believe that a different future was possible. A future where she wasn't fighting through life alone but had a partner by her side. One who supported her, encouraged her, knew when to let her handle something alone, and when she needed them to step up and help.

Could Mason be that man?

"Did your boss tell you that you had to have sex with Genesis if he asked for it?" Mason asked. There was such an alpha male possessiveness to his tone that it made her laugh, and she lifted her head.

"No. Of course not. It was something I was prepared to do on my own." It had all seemed so simple until Mason came barreling into her life and changed everything.

"You're not going to fail, Jessica. You don't have it in you. You're too smart, too aware of yourself and others and how to best adapt to get what you want out of them. Having sex with Genesis isn't something you have to do."

It was nice of him to say that, only ...

It felt like it was.

The pressure to get the intel needed to stop Seeds of Life before they enacted their plans was almost more than she could handle.

"Your ... I can't even say the word because he didn't act like it ... *David* made you feel like you're not worth anything, that your only value is what you can bring to someone else. It's not true, baby. You have value all on your own." Large hands lifted to frame her face, and when his calloused fingertips caressed her temples, his touch was so gentle it made her eyes sting. "How do I convince you of that?"

You can't.

That was her immediate reaction, but she didn't speak the words aloud. After spending close to two-thirds of her life having to play mommy to her younger sisters, taking care of a depressed mom and an

entire house, and being the one who had to be responsible for everything, you couldn't just undo that thinking in a day. Or a week. Or a
month, or a year. Or maybe ever.

Time was ticking by. She'd gotten the answers from Mason that she
had needed to hear, and she had to get back to the stone in case anyone
went looking for her.

Yet she couldn't seem to leave.

Sex with Genesis was still on the table as far as she was concerned,
but if she was going to go through with that, she needed something to
hold onto.

Something to remember, something to pretend she was living
instead of what she was doing.

She needed Mason.

Forcing herself not to hide the vulnerability she felt inside, Jessica
reached out and touched his length, it immediately stirred at her touch.
"Make love to me. Please."

"Jess," her name was said with such heavy emotion attached that a
tear very nearly slipped out. It had been so long since anyone cared
enough about her to worry like Mason was.

"It's not taking advantage," she assured him, knowing instinctively
what his concern was.

"Feels like it, baby."

"I want you, I need you, I ...." She wasn't even sure how to express
this burning need for his touch that she felt deep down inside her soul.
"Please."

After a hesitation, the hands that still framed her face swept down
her cheeks, over her shoulders, and settled on her breasts. When his
thumbs began to circle her nipples, making the little buds immediately
pebble as they responded to his touch. Even the thin material of her
white cotton bra wasn't enough to dull the sensations.

"Slow and sweet."

She never did slow and sweet sex.

Fast, hot, over and done with.

That's what she was used to.

But when she opened her mouth to protest, he cut her off with a
kiss. A lazy, sensual kiss.

"Slow and steady or not at all," he said against her lips, his big hands kneading her breasts making her moan and thrust her chest out, seeking more.

"That's blackmail."

The smile he gave her was pure sex. "Sure is. So ...?" He arched a brow and rolled one of her nipples between his thumb and forefinger.

"Mmm," the moan tumbled from her lips, giving her away. "Slow and sweet."

"That's my girl," Mason said, and as his mouth moved to claim one of her breasts, Jessica wasn't sure if it was the feel of his tongue flicking her budded nipple or his words that had something warm growing inside of her.

It was too hard to think about it because while one of his hands still played with the breast his mouth wasn't lavishing attention on, the other slipped between her legs and began to tease her. Long, lazy strokes across her soaked center, Mason appeared to be in no hurry to do anything to put out the fire he had set alight inside her.

He teased her entrance, perhaps slipped the tip of his finger inside, then withdrew it again and moved to her bundle of nerves that was crying out for attention. Attention he barely gave it as he'd tweak it, or roll the pad of a finger over it, but nothing that would bring her the release she wanted.

Each featherlight caress, each touch of his tongue to her nipple, each time he swirled around her entrance and she wondered if he was going to enter her this time, drove her wild. Sensations threw her equilibrium out the window, and she squirmed and panted, on the verge of begging for more.

Jessica didn't beg.

Ever.

She just got the job done herself if need be.

But this man ...

He did crazy things to her.

What the heck? She'd already bared more of her soul with Mason than she had any other person in her life.

"P-please," she whimpered as the tip of his finger teased her entrance.

Fire flared in Mason's brown eyes and a way too sexy smile curled his lips up. "You begging me, baby?"

Stubbornness had her wanting to say no, but she knew if she did, he could continue this slow, sweet torture for hours, keeping her body humming with need but not giving her any release.

Hadn't she already thrown her pride out the window?

The finger at her entrance slipped inside her. Just the tip, and already her body wanted to combust at the heat Mason managed to produce.

"Hmm? You 'didn't answer, baby." That finger edged a little further inside, and Mason scraped his teeth over her hard, wet nipple, and she about exploded on the spot.

"I-I'm begging," she agreed. Right now she'd say anything as long as that finger hurried up and got all the way inside her.

"Love it when you beg. I think you deserve a reward."

Finally, his finger filled her, stroking deep. Another joined it, stretching her as both curled and found that spot inside her that had her legs turning to Jell-O the second they brushed across it.

Her breathing hitched, and she threw out her hands to brace herself on his shoulders. "M-more, p-please, Mason."

"Baby, you're undoing me here," he groaned as he finally picked up the pace, stroking inside her, working her bud with his thumb, latching onto her breast, and suckling her nipple as his tongue swirled against the hard tip.

Sensations swirled inside her, more than just pleasure, although there was plenty of that. But there was so much more. A fullness that wasn't just because those big, thick fingers of his were buried inside her heat. It was like he had somehow found a way to patch the holes in her soul, and was slowly filling what years of being used and abused, and pushed beyond her limits, had drained out of her.

"M-Mason, I'm g-going to c-come," she panted. Not just come but scream her release aloud because it was too big for her to contain, alerting everyone in the guards' camp to her presence here.

"Come, baby," he coaxed as his lips claimed hers, catching her scream as his words pushed her over the edge and fiery hot ecstasy consumed her.

Throughout her orgasm, he continued to touch her, stroke her, drawing out her pleasure for as long as he could.

By the time she was floating back down to earth, his length was bulging in his boxers, straining to get out. Jessica expected him to plunge inside her, thrusting fast until he found his own release, but instead, he eased her panties down her legs, shoved his boxers aside, then lifted her, lowering her slowly, one delicious inch at a time, onto his erection.

It pulsed inside her, big and hard, filling her so perfectly it was like they had literally been made for one another.

His lips found hers, and he made love to her with his mouth as he thrust slowly in and out of her. As much as she wanted him to go faster and push her over the edge all over again, Jessica never wanted this moment to end.

It was too perfect.

Too special.

But each thrust of his hips brought her a little closer, each sweep of his tongue inside her mouth closer still.

When his hand moved to claim her still sensitive bud that was it. No way the combination of his hands, his mouth, and his penis couldn't have her hurtling toward an inevitable conclusion.

Just as her pleasure reached its peak and detonated inside her, Mason hit his own release. Together they clung to one another as they fell through a world that consisted of nothing but pleasure.

Turned out slow and sweet wasn't so bad after all.

Or maybe it was just that it was slow and sweet with this man.

Even as she knew she had to go, she clung to Mason. It was dangerous to allow him into her heart. She was messed up, she had trust issues, she had a job that required her to do things that made her ashamed, and she felt a compulsion to do what she believed was expected of her even if it hurt her. What good could she possibly bring to his life?

CHAPTER *Fifteen*

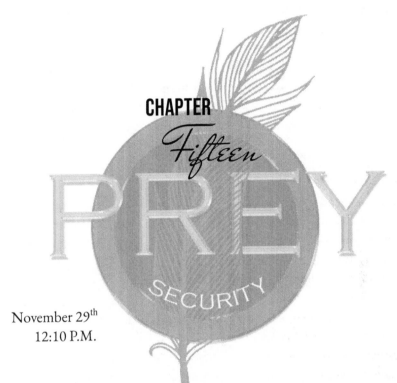

November 29th
12:10 P.M.

"Not ready to let you go yet," Scorpion told Jessica when she made a move to climb out of his lap.

She laughed and reached up to ruffle his hair. "I've already been gone for hours. I have to get back out there in case Genesis goes looking for me."

"It's still raining." Damn. He hated the idea of her out there all alone in the pouring rain not properly dressed for the cold night. The cult leader was going to kill his anointed one if he insisted on leaving her outside where, sooner rather than later, she would succumb to hypothermia.

"I'm not made of sugar."

"Smart mouth," he teased. Then since it seemed impossible to resist, he tucked his forefinger under her chin and nudged her face up so he could capture her lips. These were kisses he could drown in. "Sweet mouth," he murmured when he paused to take a breath.

"Was just thinking the same thing about you."

Her response warmed him, and he pulled her back against his chest and tucked the blanket over her shoulders. "Stay, at least a little longer. I don't like the idea of you out there in the pouring rain. And don't tell me again that you won't melt. You were freezing when you got here and its barely midnight, there are still hours to go until morning, and even then it won't warm up much."

"Who knew you were such a worrywart," she teased, eliciting a small smile.

"Can't seem to help it where you're concerned. Especially knowing the truth about the past."

Jessica sighed. "Mason, it's sweet that you worry, and I'm forever grateful that you called the cops and CPS and got me and my sisters out of that situation. But I think I've done okay with my life. I helped take care of my sisters even after we were put in foster care. I pay my bills, and my dad's medical bills, I have a job I'm good at even if it's not the one I would have chosen in a perfect world. I can handle the cold and the rain, same way you handled whatever you had to do to prove your loyalty." Her brows furrowed. "What *did* Exodus make you do?"

Something he'd rather not think about.

Something he wished he could forget.

Something that would haunt him for the rest of his life.

"Mason?" Worried blue eyes looked up at him, and she placed a hand on his chest, above his heart, her fingers gently caressing his skin. Skin that now felt chilled and clammy. "What did you have to do?"

"They took me to a quiet road, told me I had to pretend the car had broken down and shoot whoever stopped to help." Scorpion had to pause to drag in a ragged breath. "It was a young couple and their infant in the car."

Expecting horror, expecting shock, expecting judgment, expecting anything other than the sympathy but unwavering support in Jessica's expression, he couldn't have been more surprised with the question she asked.

"How did you convince Exodus and his men that you shot them?"

"How do you know I didn't?" he countered. At every turn this woman managed to do and be the opposite of what he expected.

Instead of answering, her fingers moved to brush around the gash on his forearm. "You let the bullet tear through your own flesh and then hid the wound and pretended the blood was theirs, didn't you?"

"I couldn't do it. Not even to protect my cover, not even to protect you. I'm sorry." If Exodus or any of his men had gone to the car to confirm the occupants were dead, it all would have been over. It was only by some miracle that his urgent plea to the couple to pretend they were dead and smearing his own blood on his hand as evidence of his kill had been enough to convince the men he'd done as ordered.

Crushing her lips to his, Jessica kissed him hard. "Don't be sorry for being a good man. You're not at all who I thought you were, Mason Markson."

"Ditto, Jessica Bowen."

"I like this Mason a whole lot better than the man I thought you were."

"Ditto again."

"But I still have to go," she said with a laugh when his hands curled around her backside and he attempted to shift her closer.

"I know, but I don't have to like it." When he gave an exaggerated pout, she laughed again, and Scorpion found he could listen to the sound forever. Not wanting to examine that thought too deeply, he watched as she climbed off him and picked up the still sodden material of her dress which lay on the floor of his tent.

Jessica made a face as she pulled it over her head. "Yuck. I hate wearing wet clothes," she muttered. "Oh, Mason. I keep wanting to ask you. Where did the nickname Scorpion come from?"

"I grew up in Nevada. When I was nine, I was out playing in the desert around Vegas one day with a couple of my friends. Got bitten by a scorpion. Started experiencing numbness in my limbs and was vomiting, I was in so much pain. Two of my friends went for help, two stayed with me, by the time help came, I was in pretty bad shape. Spent a week in the hospital recovering, and after surviving, my friends started calling me Scorpion. When I joined the military, it seemed only natural to have that as my nickname."

"Wow, you were lucky to survive. I'm glad that you did," she said shyly, and leaned over to give him a quick kiss.

It took a whole lot of effort not to grab her, hold her in his arms, and refuse to let her go back out into the rain. No way would he sleep tonight in his dry, warmish tent, with a cot, a pillow, and a blanket, knowing she was out there in the elements with no protection other than her dress.

When she went to kneel to crawl back out of the tent the same way she'd come in, she hesitated. "Mason, I don't know what's going to happen. I don't know if I'll get a chance to come and see you again, or when we'll get the intel we need to bring the cult down, or if I'll see you after we leave, but ... I want you to know, whatever happens, I'm glad I got to know the real you."

He was off his cot and beside her, dragging her into his arms, quicker than she could blink. "Won't ever regret coming here to get you, even if I didn't know why you were really here at first." As much as he wanted to offer her more, reassurances about the future, that he'd track her down after she closed her case, that there would be something more to their story than stolen moments while undercover in a dangerous cult, he couldn't. Because he didn't know what their future held.

But he did know that he liked this woman, respected her, was attracted to her, and cared about her. If there was a chance at more, he'd grab hold of it.

"Be careful, okay?" she said as she rested her cheek against his chest and held onto him.

"You, too. Don't feel like you have to do something you don't want to, okay? You're an amazing woman, Jess. So very selfless, always putting other people's needs above your own, but you deserve to be taken care of, too. You deserve to be shown your worth."

When she lifted her head and looked up at him there was guilt there. "I can't make any promises. This case ... it's too important to worry about my own needs."

That she believed that so completely only made him respect her more, even as it made him worry about her more. Assuming they both got out of this alive, he was going to do everything he could to help Jessica see that she had her own intrinsic worth that wasn't reliant on what she brought to the table for someone else to use.

Whatever wound up happening or not happening between them, he wanted that for her. Wanted her to know her worth so she could have the future she deserved and not the one she believed she had to have for the sake of the people around her.

Grasping her shoulders, he bent his knees so they were eye to eye. "Then promise me you'll be as careful as you can."

A small smile curled her lips up. "You'd miss me if I weren't around, huh?"

"Yes. I would," he replied honestly.

Surprise flitted through her eyes which seemed more green than blue now. "I promise to be as careful as I can be," she said solemnly.

It was all he could ask for, but it didn't seem like enough. Wrapping her in bubble wrap and putting her in a padded room without a single danger wasn't an option, so he was going to have to trust her.

Easier said than done as he gave her a final kiss, then held up the side of the tent so she could slip out. Scorpion watched as she quickly disappeared into the trees and the dark night, all too aware that was exactly how quickly and easily she could disappear from his life before he had a chance to figure out this thing developing between them.

~

November 29th
   6:50 A.M.

Shivering uncontrollably for hours had every muscle in her body aching.

Darn rain wouldn't go away either. It hadn't given her a break all night.

Jessica was cold, tired, wet, and hurting. All she wanted was a hot drink, a hot meal, a hot bath, and then a nice cozy bed to curl up in and sleep for a solid week.

Sounded like heaven.

Unfortunately, for the foreseeable future, she was trapped in hell.

If she clamped her jaw any tighter together in an attempt to stop her teeth from chattering, she was pretty sure she was going to break her teeth.

Felt like days had passed since she had been warm and dry inside

Mason's tent. His arms around her, his body solid, he'd felt so wonderful, and curled up on his lap she'd felt a sense of peace that had been lacking from her life for so many years.

It was a terrifying thing to be in charge of so much responsibility at such a young age. The pressure had worn away at her in ways she hadn't even realized until she had a brief reprieve from the weight of her world.

Mason was that reprieve.

What would life with him be like without the dangers of being undercover circling around them?

Not that he'd made her any promises. As much as it disappointed her, she respected that he didn't just tell her what he thought she wanted to hear. It made her feel respected, like if he took that step with her, it was because he truly wanted to and not because he felt bad about her past, or was letting the adrenalin of their current situation influence him.

The sound of approaching footsteps through the—thankfully—lightening rain had her straightening her back. Now wasn't the time to be trying to figure out things with Mason. There would be plenty of time for that later, when she didn't have so many people relying on her.

"Good morning, my angel," Genesis greeted her as he entered the clearing. Of course, he was wearing a raincoat. It was okay for her to sit out there for hours getting drenched, but he had to put on something to protect him to come and check on her.

Hypocrite.

"G-Genesis," she said, unable to keep her teeth from chattering completely as she said his name.

Like he hadn't even realized she might not be okay out here all night long in the cold and rain, his brow furrowed in confusion. "Are you cold, my angel?"

Lie or truth?

Problem was, she never knew which way was the right one, and she was all too aware that a single slip-up could be all it took to unravel everything she had set out to achieve.

"Y-yes," she replied. Surely it couldn't hurt for him to know that it wasn't okay to do this to her. Winter was fast approaching, and if he continued to leave her out there, she would eventually succumb to hypothermia.

Puzzled, he examined her as though the answer to why she was cold wasn't glaringly obvious. Then again, he truly believed she was an angel star gift from the moon. Eventually, his gaze settled on her stomach as his expression became thoughtful. "I am sorry, my angel, I wrongfully believed your light was enough to keep you warm, but I see I was mistaken. Perhaps it is because you have not yet received the seed."

At his words, her stomach clenched.

Wasn't like she hadn't known what she was getting herself in for. Although her original target had been Exodus, since she didn't believe she had what it took to reel in the cult leader himself, she had been aware that if she was pronounced the angel star, it would involve Genesis wanting her to get pregnant.

What was it about cult leaders and believing special babies were the key to bringing in a new world? Jessica knew all about Storm Gallagher and his cult that had been used as a front to cover up a plot to overthrow the government that included a Presidential candidate, the Russian Bratva, and a well-known and popular actress.

Maybe Genesis had been taking notes, only decided to tweak things to fit his own delusions.

Keeping her serene smile was difficult enough, cold as she was, but adding in her fear at being forced to offer her body as a sacrifice to get this job done made it that much worse. Still, she could tell by the smile Genesis gave her in return she'd managed to do it.

"Perhaps you are correct," she said sweetly.

"Come, let me warm you up." Genesis took her hand and helped her step down off the stone, then began to lead her back toward his camp.

The relief she felt when the trees began to block some of the rain was nothing compared to when they finally stepped inside his tent and water was no longer beating down upon her. Even her wet clothes sticking to her chilled skin weren't enough to completely dilute the feel of the warmer air now that she was inside.

"Why don't you take a bath, my sweet angel, while I go and take care of something."

Not needing to be told twice, the second Genesis left the room, Jessica yanked off the sodden material, and let it drop to the floor, then hurried over to the large tub. The water must have been prepared some time ago because it was lukewarm at best, yet as she stepped into the tub and sank down so the water covered her to her neck she swore nothing had ever felt this good.

Time faded as she sat there and slowly warmed up, but far too soon, Genesis joined her in his tent. Like he usually did, he picked up the soap that was made on the commune and a loofah, pulled up a chair beside the tub, and began to wash her.

Only unlike usual there was something different in his touch today.

Normally, he cleaned her like one might when giving a baby a bath. Done with wonder and joy, but there was nothing sexual about it.

Today she could feel the sexual undertones each time he swept the loofah across her skin.

It took all she had not to flinch or pull away. She couldn't, not when she was so close to getting the answers she needed. All it took was for her to learn the city where Seeds of Life planned to strike first, then she could get that intel to her boss, and it would all be over.

Mason was the only reason she was able to stay still and relaxed. Imagining him here beside her, encouraging her, and telling her believed in her. Who would have thought a man she'd hated for over a decade was now the one she mentally turned to when she needed strength?

Genesis' touch was clumsy, like he didn't have a lot of experience with women and wasn't quite sure how to approach this. Given his dedication to his delusions and desire to rebuild the world the way he thought it should be, it wasn't surprising that he hadn't spent much time around women.

"Time is drawing near," Genesis said as his hand settled between her legs. "The beginning of the end. As we prepare to march into battle to fight for our Goddess the Moon, we need to make sure we have everything working for us that we can. The people of the sun are strong and powerful, but they are wicked. They must fall. It is the only way. My soldiers are preparing for battle even as we speak. But I must do my part."

Jessica braced herself for him to pull her out of the tub and have sex with her. Reminded herself that she'd been through worse than this and survived. That sex could be nothing more than two bodies touching, it didn't have to involve any kind of feelings, positive or negative.

She could do this.

Keep her mind blank.

Don't think too much about it.

Let it join all the other times her body had been used by men in the past.

But Genesis didn't touch her. Instead, he straightened and shoved his pants down enough that he could free his length. It hung limply, obviously the sight of a naked woman didn't do much to harden him up.

With clumsy but determined strokes, he fisted his length and began to work it. Slowly the appendage began to harden. There wasn't a single look of enjoyment on his face even as his erection grew.

While she kept waiting for him to pounce on her, he never did. Instead, he pulled a metal cup from his pocket and held it at the end of his now fully erect penis, and with nothing more than a small grunt, came, semen spewing out in thick spurts, into the cup.

Triumphant now as though he had conquered a major task, he held up the cup. "This is the future. Soon it will be inside you, and a baby will be formed. Our baby. Angel star, gift from the moon, and the prophet, creating a child that will be unstoppable."

With every fiber of her being, Jessica prayed that the birth control implant she'd had before coming here would stop that from happening.

Because the last thing she wanted was to wind up pregnant to this man.

CHAPTER
Sixteen

December 3rd
4:23 P.M.

Days continued to tick by.

Scorpion hadn't gotten another glimpse of Jessica.

It seemed he was out of isolation now, while he still had his own tent for sleeping in—not that he was complaining about that—he was spending his days training with the other two dozen men that formed Seeds of Life small army. That also meant he ate with the others, sat around the fire with them before bed, and attended the daily stargazing sessions.

Of which Jessica had been notably absent.

Was it because someone discovered she'd left her stone the other night?

Obviously, they didn't know she was with him since he hadn't been punished, the opposite in fact. If someone had realized she had snuck off her stone and was out on her own somewhere around the camp, she could be being punished.

Could even have been killed.

Didn't matter to his imagination that if something had been done to Genesis' chosen one then it would be all over the camp. While talking in the main commune was mostly either outright against the rules or at the very least discouraged, it wasn't the same at the guards' camp. They were free to talk as much as they wanted as long as they were focused during training sessions.

If Jessica had been hurt, punished, or exiled he'd know.

He was sure of it.

Cold comfort though when he didn't actually know anything. When dealing with delusional men like Genesis and psychopaths like Exodus, nothing was off the table and the only predictable thing was that nothing was predictable.

Hard as it was, Scorpion had to keep reminding himself that Jessica was strong, smart, and capable. Plus, she had a knack of talking herself out of any situation she found herself stuck in.

There was no need to worry about her.

She was fine, doing her job, whatever it took to bring down Seeds of Life.

Which was exactly why he couldn't stop worrying about her. Jessica needed to learn the balance between taking care of the people that she loved, and doing what was best for them, but also what was best for her, too. Her needs and desires were every bit as important as those of the people in her life.

Scorpion was already thinking of ways to start rectifying that. Figuring out how to help ease Jessica's load so that maybe she could start doing things that were important to her. If she didn't, her whole life was going to pass her by and she wasn't going to have done anything that made her happy.

"Hey."

Looking up, he saw one of the younger soldiers come and sit beside him in front of the fire. They'd been training all day, running scenarios much the same way his team did when they were training on their property and the specially designed courses they'd set up.

While these men had some training, although likely most of it had been picked up while they were already here, they were nowhere close to the same level as him and his team. Since Exodus knew he had been in the military, he couldn't pretend he wasn't already proficient in using various weapons, including his own two hands, but he was also doing his best not to advertise just how skilled he was.

It was one thing to want to keep his cover, it was another to let a man like Exodus know just how big of a threat he really was.

"Hey there," he said, sliding over to make room on the wooden bench he was sitting on. Right now, he was doing the bare minimum to build relationships with these guys. He didn't need to be best friends with them in order to gather intel, Scorpion already had a team and he wasn't looking for another one. Especially men who had willingly joined a cult with the purpose of killing thousands of innocent people.

"Can I ... ask you a question?" the young man asked. Just because he didn't want to be best friends with these men, it didn't mean he wasn't learning everything he could about them. When it came time to turn the Seeds of Life cult members over to the authorities, he wanted to be able to share who the main perpetrators were. Some of the people here had no real idea of what Genesis actually planned to do, that couldn't be said of the men who were part of the army.

They knew everything.

They were the ones who would carry out the plans to poison water supplies.

"Sure thing, Tig," he said, patting the seat beside him. Bryce "Tig" Tigall was barely out of his teens. The best he could gather about the boy's past was he'd come here with his parents when the cult was still in its infancy. Back then, it had just been a couple of families, Genesis, and Exodus, and spending the last three years here listening to Genesis' ranting and delusions twenty-four-seven, it was no wonder the boy had aspired to join the ranks of the guards.

Sitting down on the bench, the man—more a boy really—fiddled with the tin cup he was holding. Whatever the kid wanted to ask about obviously had him nervous.

"What's up, kid?" Scorpion asked.

Glancing around, it looked like to make sure they weren't going to be overheard, Tig leaned in close. "Do you ... this stuff that Genesis says ... the moon, the stars, the angel ... what we're going to do to unbelievers ... you believe it all, right?"

There was a spark of something in the boy's eyes, almost as though he wanted to be convinced that there was nothing right about any of this.

Scorpion would never stand in judgment of the belief system someone wanted to follow. If this was just about living off the land, supporting yourself, worshiping the moon, and trying to find yourself a star twin, he would say these people should be left alone to do as they wished.

But it wasn't.

This was about so much more.

It was about punishing everyone who didn't agree with you. About power and control. Scorpion had grown up in the Baptist church, his dad had been a pastor, and while he believed in God, and in Jesus, he believed the best way to share his faith was to live it, not to kill all those who disagreed with him.

What should he say to the boy now?

Should he tell him all of this was insanity, and if he really wanted to prove he wasn't the kind of man who would kill innocent people just for not believing the stars talked to you, then he should get out of here now? Before he did something that couldn't be taken back.

But if he told the kid to get out of there and the boy told someone what he'd said, then he was putting not just his own life at risk but Jessica's and every single person who was at risk of drinking the contaminated water.

"Why you asking, kid?" Maybe if he knew for sure what the boy wanted to know, confirm he wasn't trying to trip Scorpion up, then he would know what answer to give. "Thought you been here longer than most all of us."

Tig nodded. "I've been here since I was seventeen. I turned twenty just a month ago. My parents really believe all of this. All my dad wanted was for me to be chosen to be one of Exodus' men. Little sisters are really into it all, too, but ..." The kid gave a nervous look around, then leaned in closer. "You ... there's ... I can't explain it. I've been having doubts, I don't think ... it's not right to kill people like they want to. You seem ... there's something about you. Are you here to stop Genesis?"

Whoa.

The kid was smart and observant.

But how did he answer that?

Scorpion had no idea if the boy was really trustworthy. If he was then he could be a worthy ally, someone to help gather intel, and someone he could use when this all went down. On the other hand, this could quite easily all be a set up. Just because he'd proven himself by "killing" the family in the car, it didn't mean Exodus wouldn't decide to test him all over again.

His gut said to trust the kid, that the boy had also taken a huge risk by opening up to him because if he wasn't here on Exodus' orders, and he was wrong about Scorpion, then nothing would stop him from turning the kid in. For now, he'd stick to being vague, say nothing that could be used against him, but also keep the boy on his side in case he needed him at some point.

Standing, he set his cup of coffee, long since gone cold, onto the wooden table, then he stood right in front of the kid. "You know how to follow orders, kid?"

The boy blinked, but then straightened and nodded enthusiastically. "Absolutely, sir."

Giving the kid a smile, he turned to walk away, pleased he might actually have someone on his side when the time came. "Good to know."

~

December 3rd
10:37 P.M.

The air seemed supercharged today.

Even stuck as she was indoors on her own, Jessica could feel it.

Apparently, potentially being the mother of Genesis' child meant she was no longer allowed contact with anyone but him, and the one maid who served him personally. She slept in his bed, stayed in his room. He bathed her daily, his touch lingering on her stomach, he fed her three times a day, and watched her at night.

It was beyond creepy and quite frankly annoying.

All she wanted was a few moments alone to herself without being watched, without being restricted on where she could go and what she could do. It was plain boring in here. Worry about Mason, listen for any intel, sit around and stare into space, that was all her days consisted of, and her nights weren't much better. Dreams of Mason, dreams of Genesis, blank and empty hours of nothing.

She was ready for a change.

Ready to find something to give to her bosses to end this.

So, she prayed she was right about this energy buzzing in the camp.

"You're wrong," Exodus' heated voice snapped like he was close to reaching the end of his rope.

Get in line, buddy.

Jessica had reached the end of her rope a long time ago.

"You dare to question me?!" Genesis roared like the idea was completely preposterous. Gotta love a cult leader thinking they actually were God and whatever they said was gospel law.

"You appointed me to this role for a reason. All I am asking you to do is remember that and trust me to know what I'm doing," Exodus said with the kind of over-the-top patience sometimes needed to deal with a small child.

"I trust you, but you're right, I did appoint you for a reason. My reasons. And one of them was that you were a loyal follower."

Even though she was inside the tent, she could all but see Exodus bristle at the comment.

The man might play at being a loyal follower, but the last thing Exodus saw himself as was anybody's yes-man. He liked his role as leader of Seeds of Life army because it meant he got to be in charge. Men like Exodus didn't like anyone trying to put them in their place.

Creeping across the room, she stood as close to the tent door as she could without leaning against it and alerting anyone to her presence. All she needed was for them to let something slip in their argument and she'd have what she needed to pass along to her bosses.

"I always have Seeds of Life best interest at heart," Exodus said, sounding like he was forcing the words out through clenched teeth.

"I know that, my child, which is why I need you to trust me."

"Normally I would, but in this instance, I don't think you are thinking clearly. It is a big risk to strike so close to home."

"You are wrong, my child, taking control of our home state is the first step to conquering the entire country, and then the world. We must start here, in Charleston, it is the right path."

Relief almost knocked her over. Jessica swayed, and since she had nothing to hold onto that wouldn't give away that she was listening in on a conversation not meant for her ears, she quickly hurried on shaking legs over to the table where she had been sitting and dropped into her chair.

Charleston.

Finally.

She had a location.

Something to pass along that could actually bring Seeds of Life crashing down. They already knew the plan was to hit up water treatment systems, so all the cops had to do was stake out the place and wait for the cult's people to show up.

Months of hard work, of toiling long days in the fields, caring for the animals, cooking for the few hundred people who lived here, pretending to believe what everyone else did, and of having to constantly be watching every move she made and every word she spoke, was now all about to pay off.

"If we hit Charleston first then they will know the approximate area we are in," Exodus continued to argue. "It is better to travel, to hit a target further away from us. We can come back for Charleston another time."

"Traveling puts our men at greater risk, and if we do not expand our territory slowly and carefully then we are doomed to failure."

"But—"

The sound of a fist hitting flesh cut off the argument before it could continue further, and Jessica winced along with Exodus who she knew was the one who had been struck. She knew the sound of a broken nose when she heard one, could identify it by the snap of the bone, the howl of pain muffled by the blood that was likely sliding down his throat as well as his face.

Not fun.

"Do not question me again, Exodus," Genesis warned in a voice she'd never heard him use before. He might pretend to be all light and godly but in the end, this was all his plan. He wanted to kill thousands of innocent people and took pleasure in it. A psychopath just like Exodus, only a delusional one. "You know what happens to those who turn their back on the moon, on me, on all we are trying to achieve."

"Yes, Prophet," Exodus muttered.

"Good. Now I don't want to hear any more about your thoughts on our plans. They have been made and they are not going to be changed. Go and prepare your men, I want them ready to move out in an hour."

One hour?

That didn't leave her much time to get a message to her boss. And Genesis would be in here soon to bid her goodnight then watch her while she slept. She'd have to stay awake, pray sooner rather than later he fell asleep and then make a run for it.

It was risky, but it was her only chance.

She hadn't spent all these months here to let this lead pass her by without doing everything in her power to get the word out. It was why she was here after all.

"Hello, my angel," Genesis said as he breezed into the room. His voice was back to normal, and he acted like he wasn't rubbing his knuckles and didn't have a smattering of blood on his shirt and face.

Taking her cue from him, Jessica also didn't acknowledge the blood. "Genesis, I'm so glad you're back."

He cast a quick glance at his shirt. "I'm afraid I must go and take a bath before I join you for the night. It's late though and you need your sleep, so why don't you go ahead and get into bed."

Thank you.

Sending that silent praise up into the universe, she stood and crossed to him, laying a hand on his shoulder, and touching a kiss to the clean side of his face. "Goodnight, Genesis. Thank you for always taking such good care of me."

Beaming at her, he swept his good hand across her cheek. "Always, my sweet angel star. Always. Now, into bed. You have a little one to be thinking of."

Of course, there was no way to know if she was pregnant, and since

Jessica knew she was on birth control she knew the chances were slim to none, but still she smiled, slipped off her shoes and climbed under the covers.

Closing her eyes when she wanted to track his every move was difficult.

Remaining in bed after he left the room was even harder.

After counting to one thousand she sat up, threw the covers back, and climbed out of bed. If she was caught it could mean her death, but it wasn't like she had a choice. Besides, if she was caught, she would pretend she had been in the bathroom and hope that nobody knew otherwise.

The woods were quiet. It was a cloudy night so there was no light from the moon to help guide her. Thankfully, she knew the way there well enough to walk it in the dark without crashing into anything. Last thing she needed was to be trying to explain away cuts and bruises.

It seemed to take an eternity to reach the place where she had hidden the satellite phone although she knew it hadn't been more than a few minutes.

Since every second could be the difference between getting the message out or failure, she didn't hesitate to pull the phone from its place inside an old tree trunk and dial the number she knew would be monitored twenty-four hours a day, seven days a week.

As soon as the call was answered she spoke. "Charleston. They're leaving in an hour."

Not bothering to wait for any kind of reply, she ended the call, hid the phone again, and took off for the tent. No sooner had she slipped under the covers and slowed her breathing than Genesis was walking in.

Success.

Now all she had to do was pray that the cops were able to take down the men who would be hitting the Charleston water treatment system tonight, and then raid the commune and arrest Genesis.

The end was in sight, but there was still so much that could go wrong.

CHAPTER

Seventeen

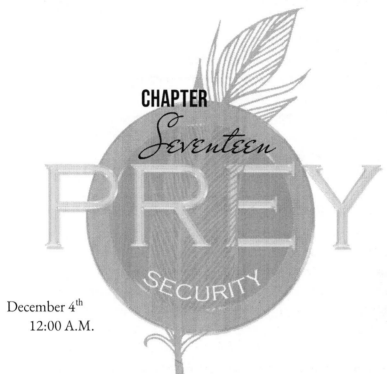

December 4th
12:00 A.M.

The sound of a siren yanked him from sleep.

Years of training had Scorpion snapping awake and alert instanta-
neously. On the battlefield, there was no time to wake slowly, leisurely, it
could get you killed.

Pulling on his clothes and shoving his feet into his boots, he grabbed
his weapon and headed out of his tent less than a minute after awaken-
ing. He was the first one out, so he stood at attention and noted Exodus'
nod of approval.

Within a couple more minutes, the rest of the soldiers had also come
out of their tents, most of them still looking half asleep.

"Men, it is time for the first phase to begin," Exodus announced.
"Six of you will be coming with me tonight, the rest of you will remain
here to protect the compound."

There were a few muted grumbles at the idea that not all of them
would be able to participate in poisoning the water supply.

You better choose me, Exodus.

He was the best the man had, and Scorpion knew Exodus was aware of it, even if the man didn't know just how skilled he truly was.

Even though nervous energy buzzed inside him, Scorpion stood still as Exodus walked up and down the line of men inspecting each one as though making his decision on the spot like he didn't already know exactly who he planned to take with him.

"Markson," Exodus said, and Scorpion sighed inwardly in relief.

Taking a step forward he acknowledged Exodus with a nod like a good little loyal soldier eager to serve and please.

"Peters, Abdulla, Simpson, Young," Exodus rattled off as he continued to walk up and down the line of two dozen men.

And Tigall.

Scorpion sent up another silent plea to the universe. Whatever was going down he was going in blind. He didn't know the location, or the exact plan. He didn't know if there would be workers at the water treatment system they would be striking who would be killed. He didn't know if Jessica was aware of the plans and had had a chance to warn her boss. He didn't know how he was going to get a message out if she hadn't.

He needed one thing in his favor.

That one thing was a disillusioned kid who seemed to not agree with Seeds of Life's view on the rest of the world.

"And, Tigall," Exodus said like the words had gone straight from Scorpion's thoughts and into the man's mouth. "Let's move out immediately."

Weapons in hand, they all piled into a truck. Exodus carried with him a bag that Scorpion assumed contained the poison, that once added to the water, would cause anyone who drank it or touched it in any way to die, or at the very least, become very ill. While chemistry was not his strong suit, from what he understood, the poison acted like a corrosive agent, destroying organs and tissues the moment it made contact.

Despite all the unknowns he was walking into, Scorpion relaxed as they drove away from the commune. This was what he did, this was what he was comfortable with. He was as adaptable as Jessica was when it came to combat, and whatever he found when he got to the water treatment system plant, he would be able to handle.

It soon became clear they were heading into Charleston, obviously deciding to hit the closest target first. Scorpion was a little surprised they hadn't aimed for something bigger to invoke the most fear possible, especially since New York City was so close, but he was glad. The sooner they got this over and done with the better.

The closer they got to the city, the more a plan began to formulate inside his head.

No matter what happened, he couldn't allow those chemicals to get into the water. The results would be catastrophic no matter how big or small the population of the city. Whatever he had to do to make that happen he would.

There was also no way he could allow Exodus and the others to go back to the commune. They needed to be apprehended now. Having gotten to know Exodus a little in the last few weeks, he knew the man would do whatever it took to achieve his goal. If he was stopped from poisoning the water now, when he did try again, it would for sure be on a bigger scale with more than six men accompanying him.

Since Exodus already knew that Scorpion had served in the military, there was no way he could blow this by pretending to be incompetent or freezing as some first-time soldiers did. After all, training and simulations could in no way fully prepare you for what it was like to truly put your life on the line, knowing you might very well lose it.

If he tried to do something stupid, freeze up, it would completely blow his cover, but there was somebody here with them who was both young and inexperienced.

Tig was the perfect man for the job.

All the kid had to do was mess things up and draw attention, and even if Jessica didn't know about tonight's planned hit someone else would call in the cops. If he could tell Tig to act like he was spooked and fire off a whole volley of shots because he "thought" he saw someone, then Scorpion was positive that someone would call 911. Even though the plant wasn't in a heavily populated area, there should be someone watching it, even if it was only via security cameras.

At one in the morning, everything was quiet as they drove into Charleston. With Thanksgiving over Christmas was well and truly on the way. Decorations had been put up, both houses and businesses getting in the Christmas spirit. It reminded him that while he'd missed out on the family vacation to go into Seeds of Life to help Jessica, he could always go home for the holidays.

No way did he regret his choice even if his reasons had been different before he knew who Jess really was and what she was really doing with the cult.

The van they were in had a logo for the water treatment plant on its side, so it would blend in with the others, and when they parked it out the front of the facility, he was sure nobody would think anything of it until it was too late.

"This should be a simple in and out. We get in, add the poison to the water, and get out," Exodus informed them. "You see anyone you shoot them. No witnesses."

Since he was sitting beside Tig he could feel the young man tense. The kid didn't want to kill anyone, he didn't want any part of this, but he didn't know a way out. Unless Scorpion could get the boy to help him, he would go down for Seeds of Life's crimes the same as Genesis, Exodus, and the rest of the men in the army.

They all piled out of the van, and Scorpion made it a point of placing himself next to Tig.

"Hey, kid," he whispered as they all pulled on their masks—with stars for faces since Seeds of Life wanted everyone to know they were responsible for this act of domestic terrorism—and headed toward the fence. He was hoping it set off an alarm when they went over it, or through it, or whatever Exodus had planned for them.

"Y-yeah?"

"Don't try to be quiet."

"But—"

"Trust me."

While he couldn't see the kid's face, he knew Tig would do as he said. After all, the boy had been the one to come to him with his concerns about the cult's plans. If he was wrong, Scorpion would just claim the boy misunderstood what he'd said and had been too young and green to go on such an important mission.

Turned out the fence was easier to get over than he'd anticipated, and they were in the facility, all except Exodus, who remained with the van. It was dark and quiet, and they hadn't seen even a hint of what might be another person.

Even though he'd been the one to tell the kid not to be quiet, there was a small part of him that startled when Tig started firing his weapon wildly.

"What are you doing?" Abdulla hissed as all the other men froze.

"Saw someone. Over there. No, over there," Tig said, pointing frantically in all directions.

The kid was on fire, his acting skills rivaling Jessica's.

Only then, Scorpion sensed the presence of other people outside the six of them and he knew the boy had been shooting at real people and not just to make a lot of noise and alert someone that something was going on.

All of a sudden, the world around them sprung to life. Bright lights lit up the night and at least three dozen men all dressed in black came running toward them, weapons aimed at them, shouting to them to get down on the ground.

There was no way anything he or Tig had done had brought in the cavalry.

Nope.

That had to be his Jessica.

Somehow, she'd gotten the word out before they'd shown up here.

As he lowered his weapon, put his hands on his head, and got down on his knees, he was both relieved and worried. They might have foiled the cult's plot, and might have Exodus and some of the guards in custody, but Jessica was far from safe. She was back at the commune, and when Genesis learned that things hadn't gone as planned, there was no telling how the delusional psychopath would react.

December 4th
    2:44 A.M.

Something touched her.

Jessica sprung from a deep sleep in that foggy, not quite aware of where you were or what you were doing, not even quite aware of who you were, kind of way.

She hadn't meant to fall asleep.

But she was so exhausted that when she finally did get back into the cot after calling in the intel to her boss, she must have just crashed. Her plan had been to stay awake and be ready to hear whenever Genesis did what had gone down.

Just because she expected that her colleagues had gotten to the water treatment plant first and were prepared and ready for Exodus and his men, it didn't mean everything had gone smoothly. She had no idea how many of the guards Exodus had planned on taking with him, and she had no idea how well trained those men were and if they were likely to shoot back at law enforcement or if they might panic. Sometimes, it was those who panicked who were the hardest to deal with since they were so unpredictable. An animal fighting for its life was a dangerous thing.

Now she blinked up to find Genesis standing beside her bed, his hand still on her shoulder.

As much as she hated his touch, she didn't shrug it off. Instead, she blinked away the sleep from her eyes and the fogginess from inside her head, and curved her lips up into a small smile.

"Genesis? Is something wrong?" she asked as she sat up.

The hand on her shoulder began to knead her muscles, yet he gave no answer. Just looked at her contemplatively for a long moment before releasing her and holding out his hand.

"Come with me?"

Since he had pronounced her the angel star gift from his Goddess the Moon, she found that he didn't order her around all that often. While she always complied with everything he asked, she found that he did actually ask most of the time rather than just telling her what he wanted her to do.

"Of course," she said, pushing the blankets back with one hand while placing her other in the one Genesis still had outstretched.

When his fingers curled around hers it was with an almost tentative touch. Like he was afraid if he was too rough with her then he might cause her harm. Jessica knew it wasn't just because he thought she was a gift from the goddess, but also that he was sure that his attempts to impregnant her had been successful.

Every day she prayed he was wrong.

"It's cold out," he said. Once she was standing, he released his hold on her and grabbed the woolen blanket from the bed and wrapped it around her almost tenderly.

Beneath his psychopathy and delusions there was a man who still had the ability to care about other people. It was an odd dichotomy, and since psychology had always held an interest to her, she wanted to be able to dig deeper and found out exactly what had shaped him. But that wasn't why she was here. She didn't need to know everything about him, just how to manipulate him and get the intel out of him she needed to destroy his plans.

"We need to protect the little one." A shaking hand reached out and briefly caressed her stomach.

Despite her best efforts, she trembled at his touch. It was bad enough thinking that she might have a living link inside her that would forever attach her to this man, but to have him touch her right where that baby could be was too much right now.

If she was ever going to have children, she wanted them to be with a man she loved. Who respected her, supported her, and loved her back. One who would be involved in every aspect of raising the child they had created together, and in running all the areas of their home as a team.

A partner.

That's what she really wanted.

She was so tired of having to always go it alone.

"The little one," she agreed, hoping he didn't call her on her tremble.

Instead of looking angry, Genesis smiled. "It's amazing to think about, isn't it? A very special child, unlike one the world has ever seen before is already beginning to form inside your womb. A child that will change everything for the better."

If her birth control had failed and allowed her to fall pregnant, then the best she could hope for was that it was Mason and not Genesis that had fathered the child. While she believed she wouldn't and hadn't gotten pregnant, she'd had unprotected sex with Mason on two separate occasions, and on the night spent in his tent, they'd made love three times. If she was pregnant, there was more chance the baby was his than this delusional psychopath's.

"Amazing," she mumbled in agreement. Whatever the reason Genesis had woken her it wasn't to discuss the fact that he believed a baby was currently growing inside of her. She wanted to know what that reason was, and not think about the horror of being pregnant when she wasn't anywhere near ready for another responsibility to be added to her already overbrimming plate.

"You'll need your shoes." Fussing like a first-time father worrying and caring about the mother of his child, he led her to the table, sat her down, and slipped her boots on for her, tying the laces firmly but not too tight. Then once again he claimed her hand as he guided her outside.

The night was cold. Cold enough that if he was still insisting on keeping her out there, she might not have made it through. Although winter was still a couple of weeks away, it was definitely making itself known. Any day now she expected to see snow, she wouldn't even be surprised to see a covering on the ground come morning.

Walking in silence, they weaved through the trees toward the clearing. As well as cold, the night was still every bit as dark as it had been when she'd crept through the woods a couple of hours ago to send out her message. Thick cloud cover blotted out everything else, and even though she knew the way to the clearing, it almost seemed too dark to find your way anywhere in the forest tonight.

There was something ominous in the air.

Something she didn't like.

Something that said whatever was happening next wasn't going to be good.

Jessica hoped this feeling of doom that was hovering over her wasn't because something bad was going to happen to Mason. She had no idea if he was with Exodus at the water treatment plant, but if he was, there were so many things that could go wrong and any one of them could claim his life.

Losing him would be ...

Not something she wanted to think about.

Crazy, since a month ago she didn't even think about him, and if someone had brought him up, she would have curled up her nose in disgust. But everything had changed since she learned who he really was, and she liked this guy. A lot.

"Sit," Genesis said when they entered the clearing with the stone he seemed to hold in high regard.

Once he'd lifted her on to it and made sure the blanket was tucked securely around her, protecting her from the worst of the cold, he stood, hands held high, and face tilted back as though drawing in the strength of nature all around them. This place was beautiful, and it did hold a sort of power, but not the kind he thought he had found.

Not the kind that was going to make the world the way he wanted it.

Not the kind that was going to save him when the cops came for him.

"Do you feel it?" he asked, eyes still closed, face still tipped up as though drinking in the moonlight, the clouds no barrier to where he believed his strength came from.

"I feel it," she echoed, injecting some enthusiasm she certainly didn't feel into her tone.

"Where?" Eyes opening, he eyed her curiously, and she knew exactly what he wanted to hear.

Pressing a hand to her stomach she met his gaze. "Right here."

Pleased with her answer he beamed. "I was right. I knew the time had come. Everything has aligned, and our battle has begun. Tonight, the first stage has taken place. Any moment now we will receive a call to tell us that our message has been taken out into the world. Now it is on them. Come to us, humbly and with a willingness to obey and be spared. Fight us and you will perish."

The last he screamed into the quiet night with a ferocity that made her flinch.

Standing before her might be a man who actually wholeheartedly believed he could speak to the stars, and that they spoke back, but he was a dangerous one. One who was not just prepared to, but was excited to kill all those who disagreed with him.

When the cell phone rang, she jerked in surprise. It had been so long since she'd heard one she'd almost forgotten the sound.

With a grin that could only be described as maniacal, Genesis answered. Jessica held her breath.

Good news for him or good news for her?

Relief filled her when the smile dropped from his lips, and he let out a howl of pain.

CHAPTER Eighteen

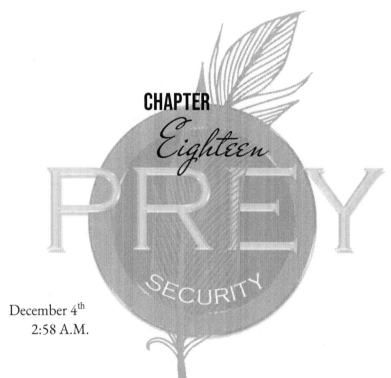

December 4th
2:58 A.M.

His howl echoed through the otherwise quiet forest.

Maybe he should be surprised by the volume and power behind his scream, but Genesis wasn't.

This was supposed to be one of the best days of his life, the culmination of so many years' work, and yet instead of celebrating what should be the first of many victories, everything he had worked so hard for was lying in shattered ruins at his feet.

"No!" he bellowed.

How could this be happening?

Everything had been planned so carefully. He had paid attention to every detail, no matter how small and insignificant it had seemed. The people around him were loyal, true believers just as he was. They all had the same goals, the same vision, so how was it possible that when he should be flying high, he had instead been plunged down into the depths of despair?

"Genesis?"

Lowering the phone from his ear, he saw his sweet angel star looking at him. Her large eyes seemed to sparkle like gray diamonds, although he knew that had to be his imagination as it was too dark to see anything more than the pale shadow of her face.

Still, the sight of her looking up at him as though he were her everything—her reason for breathing, her reason for living, her reason for existing at all—was enough to help him find it within himself to calm down. Something had gone wrong, there was no denying that, but the only way to fix it was to find out what that something was.

People were counting on him.

He was their leader.

Even this wonderful, amazing, magical gift from the Goddess Moon herself, his precious angel star was relying on him to bring in the new world for her.

There was no way he could fail.

No way.

"What's going on? You're scaring me," his angel star said anxiously.

Reaching out, he allowed himself a small moment of weakness and stroked his hand along the silky soft strands of her golden mane. She was so beautiful. Soft like silk, sweet like honey, and bright like the stars. And inside her was a tiny little baby that was going to change everything.

He had to hurry.

The woman and child had to be protected at all costs.

If their enemies had foiled them in the first battle, there was every chance they might be coming here next.

"I'll be right back, my angel star. Stay right here. Please. Don't move at all. Right now, we need all the power we can get. Just sit there and ask your mother the moon to please shine her light upon us."

Although her expression remained confused and concerned, she nodded and closed her eyes, and miraculously, before he even made it to the tree line, the clouds were clearing, and the moonlight beginning to stream down upon the woman on the stone.

His screams had roused the guards, and they were approaching him as he headed toward their camp.

"Prophet? What's going on?" Exodus' right-hand man, Delores, asked, looking around somewhat frantically as though he expected their enemies to jump right on out of the trees. "What's wrong?"

Everything, he wanted to wail.

Every single thing that meant anything to him was at risk, and he wasn't sure in this moment how to protect it all.

How to make things okay again.

"They failed," he said simply. Speaking aloud the words Exodus had uttered through the phone mere moments ago felt like giving them life. Power.

Staring at the phone, an object of evil he abhorred, but which he acknowledged was occasionally a necessity, he threw it away from him like it might rear up and strike him. Flung with force, when it connected with a tree, the plastic shattered, and the phone dropped to the ground with a muted thud.

"Failed?" Delores echoed.

Did the man need to hear it over and over again?

Every second they wasted was a second that the enemy could be using to draw closer.

"Gather everyone. Leave no one behind. Man, woman, and child. They are all to be in the clearing immediately. Go!" he shouted when Delores and the rest of the guards just stood there and stared at him, dumbfounded and utterly useless.

When Delores gave a nod and gestured to the other men and they all turned and disappeared, Genesis went back to the clearing. Back to where it had all begun. Back to the clearing where he had been conceived one beautiful, magical night.

A night of a Luna eclipse.

The moon hadn't shined that night because it had given a piece of itself to him. A piece he had treasured and nurtured. A piece he had watered like it was a tiny seed in need of his care until it had grown into something big, strong, and beautiful.

There was no way he would allow it to be cut down.

Running as fast as he could, as soon as he broke through the tree line, finding his angel star right where he had left her, only now bathed in a pool of moonlight, he snatched her up, clutching her tight.

"I won't let them hurt you," he vowed.

"Hurt me? Who? Who would hurt me?"

"The enemy." Sighing, he sat on the stone, holding his angel on his lap, rocking her, unable to let her go. "They failed tonight."

Admitting failure was never something anyone liked to do, but in this case, given who he was, what he was doing, and who he was talking to, it filled him with almost more shame than he could bear.

"I'm sorry," he muttered, burying his face against her neck as tears flowed freely down his cheeks.

After a beat of silence, his angel spoke. "It is not your fault. There is great evil in the light and those who call themselves her children. But success is still there, still within your reach, all you must do is hold onto your faith. For it is sometimes in the darkest moments that we realize our own strength."

Truer words had never been spoken.

Energy flowed from his angel into him.

Needing more, he pressed his palm against her stomach, seeking strength from their special child.

She was right. This wasn't his fault. But it was somebody's. There was someone here, someone who had been welcomed with open arms into their family who must have betrayed them.

"Genesis? Are you all right?"

Before he could assuage his angel's fears and tell her that he would always take care of her, the sound of approaching people stopped him. The others were here, it was time to figure out who had betrayed them all, and then make sure that person paid the ultimate price.

Leaning down, he touched a quick kiss to his angel's forehead. "All will be okay. I promise I won't ever let anyone hurt you. Won't ever let anyone take you away from me. Nothing can break our bond. We are forever one."

After another quick kiss—because he just couldn't seem to resist—Genesis stood on the stone so he could see everyone as they crammed into the clearing. There were so many of them now that the space was full, literally crammed to the brim with people. A few of the men even had to climb the trees ringing the clearing so they could hear him.

"My children," he began, projecting his voice so there wasn't a single one here who wouldn't be able to hear him. "Tonight was to have been the day we had all been waiting and praying for. The first battle. The beginning of the end. But our plans tonight were foiled."

A chorus of gasps went up from the crowd, and several of them turned to one another in shock and horror, offering words of comfort and encouragement to each other. Supporting one another as a family was supposed to.

"Our plans may have been foiled but this is not the end."

"Not the end!" a few voices yelled back to him.

"We will not give up. Are you with me?"

"We are with you!"

"Say it again. All of you together."

"We are with you!"

The roar of the voices all in unison was more fuel to the burning fire inside him. "We will prevail!"

"We will prevail!"

"We cannot be stopped!"

"We can't be stopped!"

The energy in the clearing was something special, something amazing, and he could feel the light of the moon growing as she beamed down her joy upon them.

"Before we can march back into battle there is one thing we must do," Genesis told his people.

"What is that, Prophet?" many called out.

"Amongst us is a traitor. One who used their powers against us tonight. One who worships the light and will fight against us again if we do not stop them."

Murmurs of fright echoed through the crowd as they all looked upon their neighbors with suspicion this time.

"I will find this traitor. Every one of you will stand before me, young and old, male and female. You will prove your allegiance to me, to my angel, and to our Goddess the Moon, and the one who does not will be proclaimed the traitor. Will be ripped apart by the hands of the righteous. Will die the death all unbelievers deserve. Then we will rule the world, a new world, a better world, and all who oppose us will die!"

CHAPTER

Nineteen

December 4th
   3:23 A.M.

Getting arrested wasn't fun.

Although Scorpion knew that the agents swarming around him and the Seeds of Life soldiers had to know exactly who he was, they had to make it look like he was just another domestic terrorist. No special treatment, because special treatment would tip off to the cult members that he wasn't who he had told them he was.

So, for now, he was shoved roughly onto the ground, his arms yanked none too gently behind his back, and wrists secured with handcuffs.

Beside him the other members of the cult—barring Tig who was lying every bit as quietly as Scorpion himself—were fighting against the men trying to arrest them. How they thought they were going to manage to outfight three dozen men when they were definitely outgunned as well as outmanned, he had no idea, but they had obviously been told not to go down without a fight.

Likely to take out as many as they could as well.

Although the chemical they had brought with them had been designed to be delivered in water, odorless, colorless, and tasteless, it was still a corrosive agent and could be dangerous enough on its own.

Just as he thought he was surprised that Young, who had been the one carrying the carefully packaged chemicals, hadn't tried to throw the vials at someone, he heard a muttered curse.

"You think that was funny?" one of the cops surrounding them muttered, and even from his position lying flat on his stomach on the ground he could see a man clutching the black case the vials had been transported in. Passing the case off to one of his colleagues the man grabbed Young, dragged him to his feet and literally lifted him off the ground. "No one is dying here today. Except you if you want to."

"Seeds of Life serves the Goddess Moon. All children of the light must submit to her or be destroyed," Young ranted like the indoctrinated soldier that he was.

"Yeah, yeah, heard it all before," the agent muttered, all but tossing Young onto the ground. "Get them all out of here."

The next hour or so passed in a time loop that felt like being trapped in quicksand, so close to where he wanted to be and yet not quite there yet. He didn't care about being shoved in the back of a police car like a criminal, didn't care about having his mug shot taken or his fingerprints, he knew both would be wiped from the system before they were ever even part of it.

Nor did he care about being left, cuffed in an interrogation room. He knew his team would be on their way and that this was only about keeping up appearances. The only thing he cared about was Jessica.

She was still there.

Still in danger.

And the need to get to her was clawing at him like a horde of angry ants.

It was a need. There was no other way to describe it. That woman did crazy things to him, and the thing was, he didn't even care.

Being obsessed with her was exciting and exhilarating. It was like hopping on a rollercoaster knowing the ride was going to be wild and crazy, but knowing the fun was going to far outweigh everything else.

It was more than just fun though. Jessica brought out every protective instinct he possessed, and a tender side he hadn't even realized was part of his makeup. Growing up with two sisters he'd been coddled, but he'd always been a mini alpha male, wanting to take care of them and his mom. He'd never been the kind of kid, or man, to sit and soothe someone when they were upset, he wanted to fix their problems for them not go on a journey of pain with them.

With Jessica it was different.

With Jess, he wanted to soothe every old hurt and kill anyone who tried to inflict new ones.

He was falling for her.

Hard and fast.

"Hey, criminal, want these?" Trick asked with a grin as he opened the door to the interrogation room and tossed the keys to the handcuffs around as though juggling them.

"What took you guys so long?" he grumbled, more than ready to get out of here and get back to the compound to get Jessica out.

"Ooh, grumpy and impatient are we?" Trick said, making the hand-cuff key disappear.

"Cut him a break," Panther said, nudging their team jokester out of the way. "He's spent the last three weeks in a cult."

"Surprised you gave up family time to go in after the sister of an old friend," Tank said as he followed the others into the room.

"Thought you were supposed to be bringing her out, not joining them in poisoning the water," Rock teased.

Since he knew Jessica sent regular updates to her bosses, he knew there was no way Prey didn't know that he had decided to stay and help bring them down. What he was surprised about was that nobody had told his team that Jessica was an undercover cop.

The weird looks Eagle and Olivia had given him that day when he'd been badmouthing Jessica now made sense. The couple had known who Jessica really was and what she was doing there, but they'd obviously been told not to tell him. And they obviously hadn't passed along to the rest of his team that Jessica was there for her job, and not because she'd joined the cult for real.

"You guys going to uncuff me or not?" he asked, holding up his bound hands.

"He's the one with the key," Tank said, pointing to Trick who just grinned and held up empty hands.

Not in the mood for the magician wannabe and his games, he jiggled the cuffs again. "Don't have all day here."

"Definitely grumpy and impatient," Trick said as he came over. "Let's see where those keys went. Ah, there they are." Pretending to pull them out from behind Scorpion's ear, Trick finally unlocked the handcuffs.

"If I was six, I would have thought that was real cool," he muttered. "Make sure whoever is doing the interrogations knows that the kid, Bryce Tigall, didn't want to go through with this. Family joined when he was young, they've been there since the beginning, but he has no loyalty. Smart kid, observant, knew I wasn't one of them. They might get something out of him."

As far as Scorpion knew, the cops had no idea who had been the one to actually create the poison. That person needed to be identified immediately. Anyone who would create such a deadly poison was a risk of selling it on to other terrorists.

"We'll let them know," Tank said. "You ready to get out of here."

"I'm not leaving," he said, shocked that his team were prepared to just walk away while Jessica was still there at the commune in danger.

"Thought you were anxious to get out of here," Rock said, brows furrowed in confusion.

"Out of these handcuffs, definitely. Out of the room, yes. But I'm not leaving. We need to talk to whoever is in charge of the raid on the commune."

"Don't think Prey was planning on being involved," Tank said. "I know you were trying to do a favor for a friend, but you can wipe your hands of the woman now. She'll be picked up with the rest of them."

"You don't know, do you?"

"Know what?" Panther asked.

"Jessica Bowen is an undercover cop who's the reason Seeds of Life didn't just succeed in poisoning a water supply and potentially killing thousands." It was his fault that his team had such a bad view of Jessica. After getting the call about her being in the cult, he'd let his team know he wouldn't be going on vacation, because instead, he had to go and rescue the spoiled brat sister of an old friend. Now Scorpion had to wonder whether it was her bosses who had wanted him to go in as back up for her. After all, she'd been there for six months alone, and David had known she was gone for months, yet the timing of him being called in, plus Eagle and Olivia knowing who Jess really was, led him to believe it was no accident that he went in when he did. They'd known things were about to blow up, and thought he was their best bet at providing back up to Jessica and helping to stop an attack from happening.

Surprise filled all his teammate's eyes. "Eagle didn't tell us that," Tank said.

"Didn't tell me either. I figured it out when I got there and the woman I thought I knew didn't exist. I was wrong about her, and I unwillingly played a part in hurting her in the past."

"I get it, man," Rock said. "But she knows what she's doing, and her team will be there when they raid the place. You went in to help her and you did. It's okay to walk away now."

"You guys don't get it. I *want* to go in after her. I *want* to make sure she's okay. I *want* to be the one who has her back as she breaks the biggest case of her career."

"Uh-oh," Trick muttered.

"Another one falls," Panther added.

Thing was, Scorpion had no problem with his team believing he had fallen for Jessica, no problem with the whole world hearing it. Because it was one hundred percent true, and as soon as he got her off that commune, he intended to do something about it.

December 5th
    3:05 A.M.

What was taking her colleagues so long to get here?

Jessica had been sure that as soon as they had Exodus and whoever else he'd taken with him to Charleston in custody, a team would be sent in to raid the commune. Only an entire day had already passed and ... nothing.

No raids.

No back up.

No anything at all.

While she was trying really hard not to let it hurt—although failing miserably—the fact that Mason had just up and walked away without a second glance was much worse than wondering why her team wasn't coming in for her. With Genesis on his witch hunt, completely strung out and manic about it, there had been no chance for her to slip away and get a moment to herself so she could place a call to her boss and find out what was going on.

So, all she could do was sit there, on the stone, with Genesis, and watch as he interrogated every single member of his cult in an attempt to find the one who had betrayed him.

Thing was, if she told him it was her who was the spy, she doubted he would believe her. Learning his plans hadn't been successful had pushed him off the deep end and he was no longer thinking clearly. Not that he ever really had been.

The clearing was still crammed with cult members. Genesis wouldn't let anyone leave, not even those who he had proclaimed to be innocent. He had no compassion for the elderly who hadn't eaten or had anything to drink all day after being dragged out of their beds in the middle of the light. Nor had the couple of pregnant women, or those with small children been given any consideration. If one of the little ones got fussy and cried, instead of excusing the child and its mother so it could run a bit, or play, or just have cuddles, both child and mother were reprimanded in front of the whole gathering.

No one wanted to say or do the wrong thing, her included, so they all just stood there and listened to Genesis rant.

It was only because everyone was here that she knew Mason had been with the group who went to Charleston. She'd suspected Exodus would have chosen him, Mason was too skilled not to. She had also suspected that Mason would want to be part of coming in here to arrest the rest of the cult and selfishly speaking to make sure she was okay.

Just as she was aching to know he was okay.

A million worries ran through her head. He could have been hurt, his cover could have been blown. Or he could have decided that sex with her while he was stuck here was one thing, but now that his responsibilities had been taken care of, he could just walk away.

What they had shared had been special, right?

To her it had, but had it to Mason?

Jessica had been doing fine taking care of herself for the last two decades, she didn't need Mason to come swooping in on his white horse to save her now, but there was a huge part of her that wanted him to.

If she just knew what her bosses' plans were, she would know what move she should make next. There was no point in her doing anything to blow her cover now if for whatever reason they had decided they weren't sending any one in to raid the commune just yet.

Really, her only option was to continue to sit by Genesis' side and let him do his thing. If anything changed and he started to become a real threat to the safety of the people here, she would have to rethink it, but for now, it was just playing a wait and see game.

Hopefully food and rest for all of them was on the agenda because they were all teetering on the brink of exhaustion.

Twenty-four hours they'd been in the clearing, and who knows how much longer before that it had been since Genesis had gotten any sleep. The man rarely slept, and she had to wonder if that played a part in his delusional behavior. Lack of sleep could hamper decision making, problem solving, controlling emotions and behaviors, and coping with change. All dangerous things when you were talking about a psychopath with delusions.

Especially one who was already angry that he hadn't gotten what he wanted.

Maybe she could at least prevent things from getting worse by suggesting he get some rest. So far, he hadn't settled on anyone as the betrayer, but he wanted to, that was plain to see. Jessica was worried that when he couldn't actually figure it out—and he wouldn't because he wasn't even looking at her—then when he got toward the end of the group he would just pick someone at random and proclaim it was them.

"Genesis," she said gently, reaching up to touch his knee as he stood behind her.

Immediately, he looked down at her, concern on his face. "Is something wrong?"

"I think maybe the baby needs rest."

The concern left. "They will rest when I tell them they can rest," he yelled into the crowd.

Tightening her hold on his knee to redirect his attention back to her, Jessica had to work hard to remain the sweet, submissive woman he believed her to be. Not an easy thing to do with his cold and callous attitude toward the vulnerable of the commune. "I meant *our* baby," she corrected, pressing a hand to her stomach.

Like a flip had been switched he went back to concerned. "I'm sorry, my sweet angel. I was so fixated on finding the one intent on destroying all of us with their betrayal that I forgot that you are growing our child. I will take you back to the tent to get some rest then continue the interrogations."

Torn between wanting to agree to that so she could get some time by herself to get to her phone, and not wanting to leave him unsupervised with so many innocent people when he was already so volatile, before she could decide on the best course of action, she felt it.

A change in the air.

Nothing you could actually ascribe to anything, it wasn't a sound, a sight, or a smell. It was just a feeling that they were no longer alone out there.

Back up.

Finally.

No sooner had the thought entered her mind than figures began to emerge from the trees, weapons in their hands.

"Everybody down!" a voice yelled. She recognized it as belonging to one of the men on the team, although it was hard to recognize anyone with them all dressed in black with their faces painted so they had blended into the night.

"No! We do not kneel at the feet of our enemies," Genesis screamed back. "We must fight for our beliefs."

Absolute chaos descended on the clearing as the Seeds of Life members heeded their prophet's words and began to attack the cops surrounding them. Between the elderly and the children, she knew her team would want to handle this as carefully as they could so an innocent didn't wind up caught in the crossfire.

The cult's soldiers were here along with the rest of them, and they immediately began to fire at the cops.

She wanted to call out some sort of warning, but what could she say that her team didn't already know?

When Genesis grabbed her and dragged her off the stone with him, she had no choice but to go with him. It was already bedlam, and the last thing she wanted to do was cause more of a distraction when her people were already trying to make sure they got everyone contained without any needless bloodshed.

"Jessica!"

Someone screamed her name as Genesis pulled her further away from the people and into the forest.

She could have sworn it was Mason's voice.

Had he come back for her?

"They can't have you," Genesis said, tightening his grip on her and yanking her feet off the ground. "I won't let them take you from me."

His voice told her everything she needed to know.

Rather than let her go, Genesis would rather kill her.

Trying to keep her cover now was pointless, he believed her to be his angel, nothing she could say or do would change that, not even telling him the truth.

"Mason!" she called back, scanning the sea of people for him, but they were already disappearing as Genesis ran with her through the woods.

Away from Mason, away from her colleagues, and away from the commune. Through the woods, past a large open pit that was filled with bodies, and into a small wooden house she'd never seen before.

The eyes that looked back at her were clouded with insanity. Genesis didn't release his hold on her as he grabbed a box of matches from on top of a fireplace mantle. "It's okay, my angel, it will be over quickly," he told her as she tried to yank her arm from his grip.

One strike of the match was all it took, and the cabin burst into flames.

CHAPTER *Twenty*

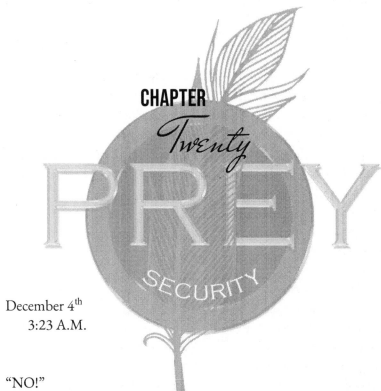

December 4th
3:23 A.M.

"NO!"

The scream felt torn from a place deep down in his soul as he watched fire spring to life less than fifty yards away from him through the forest.

Scorpion picked up his speed as he raced toward it. There was not a single doubt in his mind that Jessica was in that fire.

Damn everyone who had made him wait until the early hours of today before coming in to raid the cult rather than doing it right away yesterday morning. Those twenty-four hours had been an indescribable horror as time ticked by slower than he'd ever felt before. In that time, he'd thought over and over again about his future and what it looked like, who he wanted to see in it, and he was sure.

Jessica was it for him.

As soon as she wrapped up debriefing for her case, he wanted to ask her out and spend time getting to know her when they weren't under-cover. Wanted to make love to her sweet body properly, in a bed and a shower and any place else he could convince her to let him take her, then he wanted to go to sleep just holding her in his arms.

Nobody was taking her away from him.

Certainly not some delusional psychopath who believed she was an angel star.

"Whoa, man, hold up," Rock said, slamming into him when he would have made an attempt to run right through the burning front door of a small wooden cabin.

"She's in there," he growled, fighting against his friend's hold.

First it was just Rock's hands holding him back, but then others joined in. Tank, Panther, and Trick, all preventing him from getting where he needed to go.

From getting to Jessica.

Who needed him.

Who never had anyone there for her when she was in trouble.

Who fought every battle alone without a partner at her side.

Only this time she wasn't alone, he was right here and if his damn team would let go of him then he would come for her.

"Let go of me!" he howled, sounding more like an angry animal than a highly trained operator even to his own ears.

"You can't go in there, it's a death trap," Tank told him like he couldn't already see the flames and feel their heat.

"Jessica is in there." Were they stupid? Did they think he was going to just stand there and watch her burn?

"Would you go in if Ariel was in there?" he growled at Rock.

"If it was Ariel I'd walk through the very fires of Hell itself to get to her," Rock replied. The man hadn't just been willing to sacrifice his own life for a chance at saving the woman he loved or if he couldn't, at least be with her so she wouldn't be alone at the end, he had done it.

"And if it was Tillie?" he asked, raising a challenging brow at Tank as he managed to yank himself free from his teammates' restricting holds.

"Wouldn't care about the odds. If she was in there then I would be going in after her," Tank answered.

"Then stop wasting my time when the woman I'm falling for needs me." Scorpion loved these men unconditionally, but if Jessica died in there because they wouldn't let him at least try to save her life he wasn't sure he'd be able to forgive them.

With flames dancing around the walls of the building like the place had been rigged to catch fire, he scanned the area, searching for another way in. It had been less than a minute since Genesis set the cabin on fire, there was every chance that Jessica was alive in there. There had been no gunshots, and Jessica was trained, she knew he was here, she had to know he'd do whatever it took to get her out. She'd keep herself alive until then.

Not going to fail you, Jess.

With that vow sent out into the universe, his gaze fell on a large tree standing right beside the cabin. There was a dormer window in the roof, if he climbed the tree and jumped, he was pretty sure he could make it through that window. How he'd get Jessica out if she was hurt he wasn't sure yet, but one problem at a time.

Throwing himself at the tree, it didn't take him long to shimmy up the branches until he was on the one closest to the window. It was about a four-foot jump, not far by any means, but he'd have to aim just perfectly and hit with enough force to shatter the glass and make it inside.

There was no hesitation on his part.

The only thing running through his mind was that, injured or not, Jessica was running out of time.

Smoke inhalation could take you down quickly, and he wasn't going to lose his woman while he was this close to her.

Scorpion jumped.

Glass shards ripped at the exposed skin on his face as he broke through it, but he barely noticed the sting as he rolled and came up on his feet. He was in a small bedroom with a large wooden bedframe and little else.

Attention zeroing in on the stairs, Scorpion ran for them. Weapon raised, he made his way cautiously down to the main floor. The heat was awful, the smoke already thick, but the only thing he cared about was getting to Jessica.

Please don't let me lose her before she's even mine.

It was stupid to care so much about the woman when they didn't even know each other that well. Years of misperceptions would be hard for both of them to overcome, and he didn't even know if Jessica was looking for a relationship. Dedicating months of her life to this under-cover operation, she likely wasn't going to want to throw away whatever promotion they offered her for a chance at making something work with him.

Yet as he reached the bottom of the stairs and saw Jessica fighting for her life, he knew he wanted to try. He'd wait for her, take things slow, whatever she needed, but he wasn't walking away before he found out if they could have something special.

"Back away from her, Genesis," he ordered, leveling his weapon on the man.

Both Genesis and Jessica froze, turning to meet him.

For a second, he could have sworn he saw relief and something close to awe in Jessica's eyes, but in the glowing orange-red light of the flames it was hard to tell. Then she frowned. "Get out of here, Mason! I don't want you to die, too."

"No one's dying today, sweetheart," he promised her.

"I won't let her go!" Genesis shrieked. "She's mine. My angel star. Mine. I won't live without her!"

"You're right. Jess, drop."

She obeyed immediately, startling Genesis, who was clawing at her shoulders and leaving the man vulnerable to a shot without her body in the way.

A shot Scorpion took immediately.

Since the two had been locked in a fight, they both fell to the floor, and even though he knew he'd hit what he aimed at, his heart was in his throat as he ran toward the tangle of limbs.

"Jess?" he called her name as he went to his knees and reached for her.

"You shouldn't have come in here."

A grin broke out despite his fear. This woman never failed to amaze him. She was more worried about him coming in after her than that she'd been trapped in what would likely have become her tomb.

"No thank you?" he teased as he yanked her into his arms. There was no time to check her for injuries, so he steadfastly ignored the fact that there had been blood on her face.

Hands curled into his BDUs with surprising strength. "Thank you." Jessica touched a kiss to his cheek before she devolved into a coughing fit that sounded like she was going to cough up a lung.

Clutching his precious bundle in his arms, Scorpion ran back up the stairs. At the window he saw Panther and Rock waiting in the tree he'd used to jump into the burning cabin.

"She conscious?" Rock asked.

"She's—" Jessica started before another coughing fit stole her ability to speak.

"Throw her, we'll catch her. We won't let your girl fall," Panther vowed.

"I'm not his—"

"Would you just give me a chance to ask before you turn me down," he huffed, bemused as he touched a quick kiss to her forehead. This woman was going to keep him on his toes, no doubt about it. Fight him every step of the way, but life with Jessica would never be boring and he knew that she would love as big as she did everything else, with her whole entire heart, body, and soul.

Leaning as far out the window as he could, with Panther and Rock also leaning toward him, it was less of a throw and more a slight toss to get Jessica into their arms. One jump, and he joined them in the tree. His limbs were beginning to feel the weight of the smoke he had inhaled, but there was no way he wasn't going to hold his crazy woman.

With the guys' help, he got her safely down to the ground, and it was only then that he realized more people had shown up. There was an ambulance, and medics who immediately came running toward them, and several cops, the cavalry had come only if he'd waited it would have been too late for Jessica.

As much as he wanted to hold onto her, he relinquished her to the EMTs. There would be plenty of time to talk to her later, once he knew she was going to be okay.

"Sir, you can't come with us," a medic told him as they bundled Jessica into the back of an ambulance.

"Not leaving her side," he said, it was as simple as that.

"Policy is—"

"Don't care about policy. I'm not leaving her."

Jessica's shaky hand pulled the oxygen mask off her face, then reached out toward him. "Want him to stay," she croaked. "I think ... I think ... somewhere along the way ... don't quite know how ... he became my guy."

There was nothing she could have said that would have affected him more, and as he reached out to take her hand, following her into the back of the ambulance, he already knew it was a foregone conclusion.

She was his and he was hers.

~

December 6th
3:46 P.M.

"I can't wait to get home and into bed," Jessica said as Mason helped her into the front seat of his truck, and she relaxed back against the nice soft leather. Thirty-six hours had passed since he risked his life to save hers and he hadn't left her side yet.

Slowly she was beginning to believe that he wouldn't.

Well of course he *would*. They weren't going to spend every second of the rest of their lives side by side like they were running a three-legged race, but she also knew that Mason wasn't a liar. He was a good man, a brave one, strong too. He'd fought for her back when she was a kid and he hadn't even liked her, and he'd fought for her yesterday when he braved the inferno and literally walked through flames for her. Every time she looked at the small scratches on his face, she was reminded of the sacrifice he had been prepared to make for her.

As hard as it was for her to believe that she had someone volunteering—insisting really—to watch her back and be there for her, that's what Mason wanted to do.

Crazy man.

Crazy, wonderful man.

Why he thought she was worth the hassle Jessica had no idea, but it gave her a warm, kind of cozy feeling to know that he did. He didn't care that she could be high maintenance. Not in a prissy sort of way with shoes, makeup, and clothes, but she was used to working things alone. She didn't always play well with others because nobody ever really wanted to play with her, she had a job that would take up a lot of her time, and a whole lot of responsibilities.

But none of it seemed too daunting for Mason, he just took it all in stride.

"You spent the last day and a half in bed," he teased as he climbed into the driver's seat.

"You can't rest in a hospital. It's impossible." She huffed. When her hands trembled a little as she tried to do up her seatbelt, Mason merely reached over, took the buckle, and snapped it in place for her.

"You didn't even try," he reminded her.

"Uh-uh, I did so," she protested.

"Did you just stick your tongue out at me?" he asked on a laugh as he started the engine.

"Maybe." Okay so she had, but he was wrong, she had tried to sleep. It was just that between her sisters coming to visit, and her foster parents, and her bosses wanting statements, plus the nurses constantly checking on her, it was pretty much impossible.

"Crazy lady."

"Was just thinking *you* were the crazy one."

"For putting up with your sass?"

Even though she knew he was teasing, Jessica sobered. This deal really did seem to be pretty one-sided. What exactly was Mason getting out of being with her?

Not a whole lot as far as she could see.

Pretty much her entire paycheck went to her dad's medical bills and the cost of his care, most of what was left went to help her sisters. Other than paying her bills, she didn't spend a lot on herself, so she wouldn't have much to contribute financially. She'd been abandoned and betrayed by most of the people in her life when she was young, so she definitely had trust issues. She was used to doing everything alone so there were likely going to be times when Mason was only trying to help her, and she'd bristle and want to fight against that help because accepting it would be weird.

A large hand claimed her thigh, the fingers digging in just hard enough that it almost hurt. "Not going anywhere, Jess. I'll tell you that as many times as you need to hear it."

That was the problem.

She was going to need to hear it a lot.

Feeling insecure was new for her. At least lately. Her childhood had taught her to tackle anything life threw at her, but as an adult she only ever tackled obstacles she already knew how to handle.

This was all new to her.

But she wasn't going to wimp out.

"Sorry if I need to hear it a few times," she offered as she placed her hand on top of Mason's.

"Partners, Jess. That means we tackle this together. Okay?"

"Together." Still felt weird though, together wasn't a word she was used to, but it was nice to think she had a partner now.

At least it was until Mason had to go and open his mouth and ruin things.

"Hold that thought, okay?"

Suspicious now, she frowned at him. "Why? What are you going to do?"

"Nothing bad, just what partners do."

"You know this partnership is new, right? No need to go jumping in at the deep end when we're just learning how to doggy paddle."

All he did was give her an indulgent grin and keep his hand on her thigh as they drove the rest of the way to her apartment. The tiny one-bedroom apartment wasn't much, but it was clean and tidy and all hers. So, it wasn't in the best part of the city, at least it was cheap, and the furniture was all hers. Cheap pieces she'd picked up in secondhand stores and worked on herself. Medical care was expensive, and it was more important to take care of her dad than to have a big home to live in.

Still, when they pulled up outside her place and she saw the horror on Mason's face, her stomach soured.

Judgment.

Why was she not surprised to see that they were right back where they started?

Guess that togetherness lasted only long enough for him to see that she lived in a rundown apartment in a rundown street in a rundown neighborhood.

Jerk.

Fighting embarrassment, she quickly unbuckled her seatbelt and shoved her door open. "Thanks for the ride," she muttered already running for the stairs that would lead her up to her fifth-floor apartment.

"Whoa, no running on me already, Jess." Strong arms scooped her up, cradling her tenderly as Mason carried her up the five flights of stairs.

When they reached her door, there was a part of her that wanted to be stubborn and refuse to let him inside, but that would be childish. And she was tired, best to let him in, see in all its glory how she lived so he could just leave and get it over with.

So, when he set her down she unlocked the door, let him in, and closed and locked it again behind them.

"Well, this is it," she said, waving her hand around the cramped room, no longer proud of all the work she'd put into the place.

"Totally you," Mason said as he looked around.

"Yep, small, dirty, and cramped. Just what I deserve, right?" When she tried to turn her back on him and walk away, he grabbed her and spun her around to face him.

"Uh, uh, babe, we're not doing that. Don't run from me and don't put words in my mouth. I'm not looking down on you, nor am I putting you down, or judging you for living in a tiny apartment. I'm angry your brother hasn't stepped up to help in all these years, allowing you to shoulder the burden. I'm also angry your sisters haven't stepped up, but allowed you to keep taking care of them even though they're both adults now and should be contributing. I also think this place is cool. I love the bright colors, I love the flowers, I love stains you chose for the wood, and the only reason there's a layer or dust is because you've been undercover the last six months."

Unable to meet his eye, her voice shook when she spoke, and it had nothing to do with smoke inhalation or the minor injuries—mostly cuts and bruises—from fighting with Genesis to get out of the burning cabin. "So, you don't look down on me for living in a place like this?"

"Look at me."

His voice was pure command, and Jessica found she couldn't disobey. When she looked up at him there was no judgment in his gaze, and she wondered now if she had imagined the whole thing. Allowed the dirtiness that still seemed to cling to her skin all these years later to cloud her judgment. Had she seen what she expected to see from the Mason she'd thought he was all these years, instead of what the real Mason was showing her?

"Why would you think I would look down at you for spending all your money taking care of everyone else instead of yourself?"

She shrugged uncomfortably, wanting to run from this whole conversation. But Mason was here, he wasn't going to let it go without an answer, and she wasn't a coward who ran away from things that scared her.

Nothing had ever scared her as much as Mason and everything he was offering her did.

If he left, he could shatter her poor little heart, and then what use would she be to the people who counted on her?

Still, she jutted out her chin, forced her fears aside, and met his gaze with as much confidence as she could muster. "Because for years I thought you looked down on me, thought you believed you were better than me, thought I was nothing but a dirty whore, and I resented you for it because it was true."

CHAPTER

Twenty-One

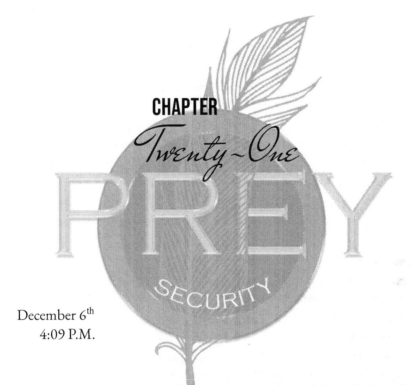

December 6th
4:09 P.M.

Counting to ten was the only way to ensure he didn't explode and say something he'd regret.

Something that Jessica would misinterpret and make her insecurities worse.

Scorpion hadn't really realized that she had insecurities, she seemed so confident, so sure of herself. She was comfortable going undercover alone with a dangerous cult, had fought for her life while surrounded by flames, and had been prepared to do whatever it took, including use her body to do things she didn't want to do but would do for her case. There was nothing about her that screamed she wasn't completely comfortable in her own skin.

Yet he had to remind himself—even though he hated thinking about it—that she had been forced to prostitute herself as a young teenager. She'd been raped, probably at least dozens of times, maybe more. Of course that was going to leave behind scars.

Scars he was going to have to help her see he didn't mind living alongside.

Of course, he hated she'd been through that. He hated she had scars at all, hated no one had been there when she needed them, hated even more it was her own family who had hurt her, but he certainly didn't look down on her, and he absolutely did not think she was a dirty whore.

"You are without a doubt the smartest, strongest, bravest, most self-less, and beautiful woman I have ever laid eyes on. I'm obsessed with you, with touching you, talking to you, hell, looking at you. I don't care what we're doing I just want to be around you." How did he make her see that? Was it even possible to overcome fifteen years of bad blood between them? Was he crazy thinking he could have a future with this amazing woman?

"You know what I did though, you knew then. I know you didn't know the why but you thought I was a prostitute and ... you weren't wrong." There was a vulnerability in her eyes that while he wasn't used to seeing, even through his anger and helplessness, he could see that it was actually a gift she was offering him. She trusted him enough to let him see that she wasn't always the competent and in control woman she presented to the world.

"No, baby," he said gently, giving her shoulders the smallest of shakes before he cupped her cheeks in his palms, his thumbs smoothing across her soft skin. "You weren't a prostitute, you were a victim. I can't go back and pretend I wasn't fooled by your brother. I didn't know you, all I had to go by was David. I wish I hadn't believed his lies, that I never for one second thought you were spoiled and selfish because you are the very antithesis of those things, but I did believe his lies. I can't take it back, baby. But please understand, that's my failing, and what happened to you was all your brother. You are not dirty. You're beautiful, and sassy, and sweet, and so amazing I can hardly stand it. I literally ache for you. Here." He grasped her hand and touched it to the bulge in his pants. "But also here." He moved her hand and pressed it to his chest. "I can't erase your past, but I can make sure you never feel dirty again. May I?"

When he nodded at the zippered hoodie she was wearing, and she gave him a shaky nod of her own, he very slowly eased the zipper down, wanting to both devour this amazing woman who was unaware of just how amazing she was, and wanting to take his time, make her feel special and not just give her pleasure which was all too fleeting.

"If you'll let me, every day I'll tell you how in awe I am of you," he said as he leaned in and feathered a kiss to her plump lips. Trailing a line of kisses down her neck, he stopped when he got to her chest. "Your heart is so big. You try to hide it behind a wall of sass, but you love so hard, so deep. You took care of your mom when she should have been the one to take care of you. You took care of your little sisters and made sure everything was taken care of, everything except yourself. I'm here now though, baby, and I'm going to take care of you. Make sure you never want for anything ever again. I want to take care of you, want to make sure you know that you were a victim, that there is nothing dirty about you. That I might have thought you were spoiled and selfish but that was my error, nothing to do with you."

"I feel dirty," Jessica whispered. "I don't know how not to."

"We're partners now, that means it's my job to help you learn how." Capturing one of her nipples, he sucked until it pebbled then pulled back and blew a breath of air on the wet little peak, making Jessica shiver. Heat sparked in her eyes, chasing away some of the insecurities and pain, and he vowed to do whatever it took to help her move past the trauma she had endured.

"What if you get tired of the job?"

Scorpion laughed. "Get tired of you, babe? Not possible. Never met a woman like you before, one who's guaranteed to keep me on my toes. You have too much sass, too much spirit. Life with you will never be boring."

Whatever she was about to say was cut off when he snatched her up, gripping her hips and grinding her center against his throbbing erection. What he'd said was completely true, whenever he was around her, he was aching to bury himself inside her tight, wet heat, but there was more to it than that. There was a pain in his chest he'd never experienced before. A knot that was a combination of worry—that she wasn't okay, that he was failing her somehow, that she needed something he hadn't given her—and something that he was pretty sure was the pre stages of love.

It was crazy, and exhilarating, and wonderful all rolled into one, and there was no one else he would want to walk this journey by his side.

"Mine," he growled as he carried her to the bed and tossed her down.

Heat grew in her eyes and more of the pain faded away.

"Say it," he ordered as he hooked his thumbs into the leggings she'd put on at the hospital and inched them down her legs.

"Pretty sure I said it to the paramedics, my colleagues, and the guys on your team already," she sassed.

A satisfied smirk hit his lips as he remembered. Yeah, she'd told everyone he was hers, but right now the caveman in him wanted to hear her say that every inch of her delectable body was his. His to pleasure, his to take care of, his to worship. In return, he would give her everything that he had, all of himself, holding nothing back.

"Yeah, you told them, now tell me." Throwing her leggings and panties onto the floor, he nudged her knees apart and settled between them, pressing his face to her center and inhaling.

"Already told you."

Touching his lips to her entrance, he allowed a chuckle to rumble through him, making Jessica's hips surge forward as the vibration hit her most sensitive flesh. "Stubborn girl. Tell me you're mine or this is going to go real slow."

"Fine, I'm yours." She huffed, making him laugh again and he rewarded her with a thrust of his tongue.

"Wasn't so hard now, was it?" Flicking at her bud with his tongue, he slid a finger inside her, teasing her with slow strokes. "This beautiful body is all mine. No one else touches it. You have a problem with that, babe?"

"You better not be letting any other woman touch what's mine," she shot back.

"No other woman I want touching me, babe. Only you."

"Only you," Jessica echoed, and he saw a soft look in the green-blue eyes that looked down at him.

Unable to hold back any longer, Scorpion went down on her. Suck-

ing, licking, and touching, needing to know he could bring his girl pleasure and undo a little of the pain in her past. While it wasn't like he
thought sex with him was going to solve the problem of her unresolved
past, he wanted her to know she was safe with him. Her body and her
heart.

All of her.

Whatever it took, whatever she needed, all she had to do was tell him
and it was hers, she'd have it.

"Come, baby. Come now. All over my face and my fingers," he
urged as he took a breath then circled his lips around her bundle of
nerves and sucked hard.

"Mason!" she screamed as she came hard.

Not wanting to stop until he got every last drop of pleasure he could
from her, Scorpion didn't let up. Continuing to suck on her overstimu-
lated bud, he added another finger, stroking so he could brush the pads
of his fingertips across the spot inside her he knew he could use to make
her come again.

She pushed at him and whimpered. "N-no more, c-can't take m-
more."

"Yes, you can, babe. You can take anything," he told her, absolutely
positive it was true. Switching so his mouth was on her entrance, his
tongue plunged inside her as his fingers rolled and tweaked her bud until
she was a writhing mess beneath him, begging and pleading, then
exploding for him all over again.

He was so hard he knew the only way he wasn't going to come the
second he was inside her was to let her take the lead. Scorpion grabbed
his girl's hips and spun them both so she was on top of him.

Greedy eyes took in his impressive length—if he did say so himself—
and he jerked when her fingers curled around him.

"This is huge. I can't believe it's already been inside me. I would
swear it's too big."

Scorpion grinned. "You're good for my ego."

Guiding his tip to her entrance, she took just his first inch inside her
and then began to rock her hips lazily.

It took all his restraint not to hurry her along, but he'd had his fun
and he wanted her to have hers. While she'd been getting tested and

treated in the ER, he'd been reading up on victims of rape, and one thing he had learned was that it was likely important to Jess to know she was in control, that anything that happened to her was because it was what she wanted.

Another inch entered her heat, and he groaned when she rocked her hips a little harder, a little faster.

Inch by inch she took him inside her, and once he was buried deep, she rolled her hip, hitting her bud against him as she did so and sucked in a breath. Even that first tremor of her building pleasure was almost more than he could take.

Heavy lidded eyes looked down at him and she smiled. That smile he felt deep down in his soul and Scorpion couldn't hold back any longer.

"Hold on, babe," he warned as he gripped her hips and began to thrust up frantically, desperate now to find his release. "Touch yourself, want you to come when I do."

One of her hands gripped his shoulder, the other went to where their bodies were joined together, and a moment later he felt her entire body go taut as pleasure rocketed through her. Only then did he join her, allowing himself to find his own release.

As their pleasure faded, Jessica slumped down against him, her fingers stroking his chest as she pressed her ear above his heart. "I could stay here forever," she said, giving a content sigh.

"You can, babe," he reminded her. They didn't have to rush, they had all the time in the world to get to know one another, but he knew they both felt that this thing between them was big. Was real. Was life changing for both of them.

"I think I like this better than what we just did, and I liked that a lot," Jessica said on a yawn as she snuggled closer.

He should get up, clean her up, tuck her in properly, but Scorpion found he couldn't make himself move. He was right where he wanted to be and the woman he craved was right where he wanted her to be.

~

December 7th

8:26 A.M.

"So ..."

Jessica stiffened as Mason dragged the word out, obviously having something he wanted to say that he already knew she wasn't going to like hearing. Propping her chin on his chest, she gave him her most scathing glare, mildly irritated when instead of looking properly chastised like he was supposed to, he merely grinned at her.

"No need to be frowning at me, I haven't even said anything yet," he teased.

"Yet I know from your tone, I'm not going to like wherever that so was going."

"Such a suspicious one." Tugging on a lock of hair, he leaned up to touch a kiss to the tip of her nose. "It's nothing bad, it's just ... remember earlier in the car when we were coming here, and we were talking about being partners and tackling things together from here on out, and how I told you to hold that thought?"

"Yes. I remember. I knew you were up to something then, and I can see whatever mischief it is you were cooking up then you aren't finished with."

"Nope, not finished with it. So, I, uh, know that medical bills can be overwhelming, especially when you're dealing with it all on your own."

"You don't think I'm going to let you help me with that, do you?" It was one thing for Mason to help pay her dad's bills if they were married, but they'd been together officially for like forty-eight hours, no way was she letting him take on that burden.

"Oh, babe, it's already done. I've paid all your dad's bills, and I've secured him a place at the best facility in the city. I'll pay for his care. I've also had my penthouse transferred into your name, I don't live in it anyway and it just sits empty, so I thought you could stay there until you're ready for us to move in together."

Jessica's head was spinning by the time Mason stopped talking.

He'd done what?

Invaded her privacy somehow to pay off all the debts that were her responsibility to take care of. Then he'd moved her dad from a place she could afford to something she would have to work around the clock to pay the bills. As if that wasn't enough, he had also given her a penthouse.

Just given it to her.

Like it was a box of chocolates or something.

Honestly, she would have felt like a box of chocolates was too much. All of this was new to her, and she'd thought they were going to take things slow. Exclusive, and she wasn't denying she liked Mason a whole lot and saw a future for them, but this was supposed to go slowly so she could get used to the idea of them as a couple.

That was blown out of the water now.

Shoving out of the bed, she didn't care in this moment that she was completely naked, she just needed to put some space between them.

How could he just take over like that?

Was he trying to rub it in her face that he had more to offer than she did and always would?

Dragging her hands through her long hair, Jessica was spinning around to give Mason a piece of her mind when she paused. There was worry in his deep brown eyes, and a heavy dose of uncertainty.

It was that moment when she got it.

Mason was nervous about this, too. It was new to both of them, and he was trying to show her that he cared, that she didn't have to take on everything on her own now. Mason wanted to be her partner, and he was trying to do it the best way he knew how. The small red scratches on his cheeks reminded her that he was a doer, a fixer, this was how he knew to help alleviate her burden.

Knowing that took the wind out of her sails.

"Are you doing all of this because you feel guilty about believing David's lies?"

"No."

The one word was all she needed to hear. With a weary nod, she walked back to the bed and slid under the covers, curling up against Mason's side.

"Well ... wasn't expecting that. I was all prepared for the fight of the century."

"I don't want this thing between us to be a fight. Do I like that you went and paid off my bills and made decisions about my dad without talking to me first? No. I don't. That's not being my partner. Partners work *together*, but I know I wasn't making working together very easy for you, and I appreciate what you were trying to do. You want me to know that you have my back."

"Always." There was such earnestness in his expression that it melted her heart.

"I think it's going to take us both a while to figure this thing out. Since I know your intentions were good ... thank you."

"Wasn't so hard to say, was it?" he teased before sobering. "Maybe I overstepped. Okay so no maybe," he added when she arched her brows at him. "But you've been on your own for so long, and I hate the idea of you working yourself to death to take care of everyone else. What about you? Taking care of you, that's my job now. I want you to be able to do whatever makes you happy, anything in the world, and not have to worry about it."

"Anything?"

"Anything. Whatever makes you happy, Jess. You just reach out and take it. I'm here to make sure you can make it happen."

A world of possibilities ... if she was brave enough to reach out and take them.

But ...

There was one thing she didn't understand.

"You own a penthouse? And you can just afford to wipe out tens of thousands of dollars of debt, and put my dad in a facility that probably charges more for a single day than I make in a month? What are you? Some sort of millionaire?"

"Yep," Mason agreed cheerfully.

"You're not kidding?"

"Nope. Grew up in Vegas. Dad was a minister, but he liked to gamble more than he should. He actually won big, not that it wound up making him happy. All he got were hundreds of people who wanted money from him. He died a year later from a heart attack and left it all to me. I bought the penthouse, but otherwise I just invested it all, I didn't need or want millions of dollars. Always thought that when I found something worthwhile to spend the money on I'd know. Guess I finally found something—some*one*—worthwhile."

Trust her to accidentally pick a millionaire, someone who could help in a practical sense and not just be a moral support kind of partner. "I don't ... I don't even know what to say. That's so generous of you to want to help me."

"Your future is yours, Jess. Take some time while you recover, think about what you want it to look like, then we can make it happen."

Her stomach chose that time to grumble loudly, making them both laugh. "Guess what I want right now is breakfast. There's this great little bakery just down the street. They make the most amazing bread, and they sell homemade jams that are to die for."

When she went to get out of the bed and look for her clothes, Mason stopped her. "You stay here. I'll go."

"How gentlemanly," she teased.

"Always." Mason winked as he climbed out of the bed and threw on his jeans and shirt. "Keep the bed warm."

After giving her a quick kiss, he disappeared out the door leaving her smiling, her body sore in all the very best of places, curled up under the covers warm and cozy on the outside and the inside. Mason did crazy things to her heart, making it accelerate and beat really hard in her chest like it was trying to scream something to her.

It wanted her to listen, and she was.

For once she was making a decision that wasn't logical, she was just following her heart.

Deciding she may as well make some coffee while Mason got them breakfast, Jessica got out of bed, not bothering to put any clothes on, and went to boil some water. What was the point? After they ate, she had no doubt that Mason would be ready to make love to her all over again. Even if he wasn't, she totally would be. Her body always seemed to be desperate for his touch even when she'd just had it.

Still as amazing as sex with Mason was, there was nothing better than falling asleep last night in his arms. She'd felt so safe, so secure, so protected. Mason kept proving over and over again that he would never leave her in the lurch, that he wanted to be there for her, and it was as amazing a feeling as it was surreal.

Part of her kept waiting for the bubble to pop.

When she heard her front door opening, she turned. She'd missed him and he'd only been gone a couple of minutes at the most. How crazy was that?

"Back already—"

Her words died when she saw that it wasn't Mason who'd just walked into her apartment.

It was Exodus.

And he held a gun pointed directly at her.

CHAPTER
Twenty~Two

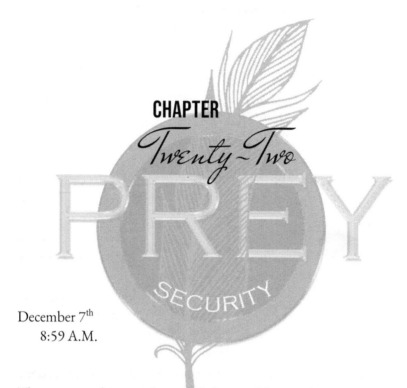

December 7th
8:59 A.M.

There was nothing in the world that could wipe the smile off his face this morning.

Absolutely nothing.

Scorpion was positive of it.

Not only was Jessica alive and mostly well—mild smoke inhalation, a couple of first-degree burns, and a few bruises and cuts, only one of which had been deep enough to require stitches—but she had been a whole lot more amenable to the idea of him helping her than he thought she would have been. He had been all geared up for a fight, aware that he had overstepped by making decisions for her life and the people in it without talking to her. But he also knew that it was the only way to make a stand and show her that partners had each other's backs.

If he'd offered to pay off her medical debt with money that was just sitting there doing nothing but earning interest, she would have refused. Would have made him wait at least until they were married before she allowed him to help contribute to her dad's medical care. That wasn't going to fly. She needed financial help now, and he was in a position to be able to offer it.

Still, he'd been shocked when she looked like she was gearing up for the fight he was expecting only to have her sag in defeat and thank him.

They both had a lot to learn about this partnership thing. Scorpion knew she wouldn't let him get away with taking over like he had again, which she shouldn't, partners discussed things, compromised, and worked out a plan together. But he thought they were off to a pretty good start.

Since he wasn't sure what Jessica's favorites were, he chose a few different loaves, white, multigrain, and whole meal, and one jar of each type of homemade jam they sold. Strawberry was a classic but his favorite, and he wondered what Jessica liked best. There were so many things he still had to learn about her, and he was as excited to learn the little things as he was the big ones.

Just as he finished paying, his cell phone began to ring. Balancing the bag filled with bread and jams in one arm, he answered.

"What's up?" he asked Tank.

"Are you still at Jessica's?"

There was a thread of concern in his friend's voice that immediately had him on edge, and he quickly dodged around a woman attempting to wrangle a stroller with a baby, a toddler, and a whining preschooler. Just seconds ago, he would have been imagining him and Jessica having kids one day, but now, he was too panicked to think of anything but why Tank was calling.

"I'm down the street at a local bakery," he replied. "Why?"

"Since Exodus managed to evade cops at the water treatment system, Panther was worried that he might go after either you or Jessica when he realized that the commune was raided, and she wasn't who she said she was. So, he hacked into security cameras and has been watching her place and your penthouse, since we weren't sure where you guys would go after you left the hospital. He just picked up a van with a water logo on the side pulling up across the street from Jessica's apartment."

"Exodus." He'd known the man was dangerous from the beginning, an absolute classic psychopath, but now if he knew that Jessica was actually a cop and had been at Seeds of Life undercover with the express purpose of bringing them down, there was no telling what the man would do.

Scorpion had no conscious memory of ending the call to Tank, or of taking off down the street.

He was consumed by only one thing.

Get to Jessica.

It ran on a loop inside his head as he sprinted down the sidewalk dodging around an elderly couple, a couple of chattering women, and a dad with a little girl on his shoulders. By the time he reached her apartment his weapon was already in his hand. He didn't care if he looked like a lunatic and the people he'd just run past called the cops. Scorpion *hoped* they called the cops, the more people to take down Exodus the better. Who knew what the man had planned.

The only reason he slowed as he ran up the five sets of stairs to Jessica's floor was because the last thing he wanted to do was make things worse by bursting in their like a crazy man.

Exodus was a dead man.

Simple as that.

Scorpion had no intention of letting him walk away alive this morning.

The door to Jess' apartment was partially open and as he approached, he could hear her voice. Relief almost took him to his knees. She was still alive. He hadn't lost her.

Yet.

"I don't know what you want me to say, Exodus," Jessica said. Her voice held a whole lot more calm than he was able to dredge up at the moment.

At least one of them was thinking clearly, because he was consumed with the need to destroy.

Destroy Exodus until he was no more.

That's all he cared about.

"I want you to admit everything," Exodus growled. It was obvious he was taking care to keep his voice quiet so as not to draw the attention of Jess' neighbors, but Scorpion could hear the fury, feel it even from out here.

"Admit what exactly?" Jessica asked. She seemed like she was going to try to keep him talking. She might not know that he already knew she was in trouble, but she knew he was only down the street and that he'd be back soon.

Hold on, baby. I'm right here.

"Admit you lied about everything," Exodus hissed.

"What did I lie about?"

"It was *you*, you ruined everything."

"What did I ruin? I wasn't even there when you failed to deliver the poison to our enemies."

"Lies! You told the police we were there!"

"How could I have done that?"

"I don't know, but I know it was you."

"I don't know what you're talking about. I was with Genesis the entire time. How could I possibly have told anyone anything?" Jessica's implacable calm was working Exodus up further, and he wondered if that was her plan.

Creeping closer to the door, Scorpion peeked inside and about had a heart attack when he saw Exodus brandishing a weapon.

Tone it down, babe, please, he begged. *Don't push him too hard.*

"Yet, you're not with Genesis now though, are you? You're here in this rundown apartment with that man. The man who keeps circling around. The man who was with us for less than a month before everything fell apart. The man who is the only one of my soldiers who isn't currently being held by the police. Do you think I am stupid?" The last was roared at full volume and Scorpion knew he was out of time.

Exodus had cracked and was about to explode.

Right as he shoved the door open, his own weapon drawn and aimed at Exodus, Jessica lunged at Exodus.

A howl of pain shrieked through the air.

Both weapons fired at the same time.

Scorpion threw himself sideways behind the sofa at the same time as he fired.

Normally, he would know for certain that he hit whatever he aimed at, but Exodus had moved just as he fired, and he wasn't sure that he had eliminated the threat.

Everything was silent.

No more screams of pain, no heavy breathing to indicate somebody was injured but alive.

Nothing.

Moving carefully, Scorpion edged out from behind the sofa. The first thing he saw were two people lying unmoving on the floor. Even from there, he could see that both Jessica and Exodus had blood on their heads.

Everything slowed down. He could feel each painfully slow thump of his heart and feel his pulse echoing much too loudly in his ears.

On shaky legs he stood, keeping his weapon aimed at Exodus as he crossed the floor. Empty eyes stared up at him, and from the hole in the man's forehead, he knew that this time had been no different and he'd hit his target with pinpoint accuracy.

There was no satisfaction in knowing the man was dead, only fear for Jessica.

He dropped to his knees beside her.

Reached out to touch her neck, searching for a pulse.

"Ow."

The moaned word, uttered a split second before he touched her still body, had his hand jerking back and a gasp falling from his lips.

"Jess?" he asked tentatively.

"Knocked my stitches when he fired at me." She groaned as she blinked open her eyes and reached up to brush at the bleeding wound on her cheekbone, pausing before she touched it. "Must have got some of the boiling water on my hand when I threw it at him."

Circling her wrist, he saw the skin on the back of her hand was red and already blistering. "You threw boiling water at him?"

She gave a one shouldered shrug. "Didn't know how busy the bakery was and when you'd be back. He had a gun, but I was boiling water to make coffee. Thought it would take him down long enough for me to get his weapon off him. Should have known my knight in shining armor was already there and ready to ride in to the rescue."

"Think you saved yourself this time, babe." If he hadn't of come in when he did and shot Exodus, he had no doubt that Jessica would have gotten her hands on the weapon and killed the man herself. Grabbing her, he dragged her into his lap, kissing her fiercely before giving her a gentle shake. "But don't you *ever* scare me like that again."

~

December 7th
9:11 A.M.

Because her heart was still racing, her face throbbing, hand burning, and how close both she and Mason had come to being killed by Exodus, she attempted a laugh that turned into something dangerously close to a sob. "I'll do my best."

"You'll do it, not just your best." Mason's hold on her tightened to the point it was almost painful, yet there was nothing in the world that would make her ask him to let her go.

Nothing.

This was absolutely right where she wanted to be.

"Kind of my job to be in danger," she reminded him. Just because she was with Mason now and he turned out to be a millionaire, it didn't mean she was going to give up work and let him take care of her. That wasn't who she was. Working was important to her, and just because Mason wanted to help it didn't mean she didn't still have responsibilities.

Mason froze. "It doesn't have to be."

"What do you mean?" Jessica pulled back just enough that she could see his face.

"You could quit. Being a cop isn't really what you ever wanted to do anyway."

"Yeah, and what else will I do? Wait tables? Work at MacDonalds? Being a cop is what I know how to do and I'm good at it. If you think I'm just going to quit and spend my life waiting on you hand and foot you have another thing coming, Mason Markson," she warned.

The smile he gave her managed to be both sexy enough she was willing to ignore the dead body on the floor of her apartment, and the pain in her face and hand, and have sex with him right here and now, and tender enough that tears stung her eyes. "I know you want to work, babe. But being a lawyer, that's your dream. A dream you gave up because you were so busy taking care of everybody else you let what you wanted slip away. I have more than enough money to pay for law school."

It was said hesitantly like he knew she was likely to argue with him.

Thing was, if he'd suggested it earlier this morning she would have. Being a couple didn't mean he had to pay for things for her and take care of her like she was helpless and couldn't do it on her own.

Now she understood.

Doing things for her wasn't just about him making up for what he perceived to be letting her down in the past, it was because he cared deeply for her, and he wanted to show her that in a practical way rather than just with words. He wanted to show her what it was like to have someone work alongside you, supporting you because there would be times when you would support them.

Unable to hold them back, tears that had been two decades in the making burst out of her. She flung her arms around Mason's neck and clung to him as she wept for everything that had been taken from her as a child, and everything Mason was offering her now.

Seeming to understand that she needed to purge this mess of emotions, Mason just held her, rocked her, and stroked her back, murmuring a string of soothing consolations in her ear.

It was everything that she needed.

"Uh … everything okay in here?"

The voice had her jerking back, embarrassed by her wet cheeks. And she realized far too slowly the fact that she was still naked. Four guys stood in her doorway. They all had weapons in their hands, and she recognized them from the fire and the hospital. They were Mason's teammates.

"We got it handled," Mason replied. "I haven't called it in, but I'm sure a neighbor has called the cops. What are you guys doing here? And don't any of you dare look at my naked woman."

"We stayed in the city and hung out with Alpha Team and their families. We wanted to be close by if you needed us," a guy with gray eyes said as he stepped forward, holding out a blanket he must have grabbed from the couch. "We need to call an ambulance?"

Since the man had nodded at her when he said it, Jessica shook her head. "I don't need to go to the hospital."

Apparently not believing her, gray eyes looked to Mason instead.

"I'd prefer you go to the hospital," Mason told her as he covered her with the blanket. "But if you're dead set against it, Rock is our team medic, he can probably restitch your wound."

"Rock," she said immediately. No way was she wasting another day at the hospital. Besides, she and Mason were both going to have to give statements about why there was a dead body in her apartment.

Lifting her into his arms, Mason stood, setting her down on the kitchen counter beside the sink and turning on the tap. Then his large hand circled her wrist, and he guided her burned hand under the cold water.

Pulling out a first aid kit from his pack, Rock stepped up beside her and gently probed at the reinjured gash on her cheek. "I'm no plastic surgeon," he warned.

"I'm not vain enough to care about a scar," she shot back. Jessica had no idea what—if anything—Mason had told these men about her, but she knew that for the last fifteen years Mason had believed her to be a spoiled, selfish princess, so there was every chance these men had a low opinion of her.

Instead of the reaction she expected, Rock grinned at her as he prepared a suture kit. "I like her, and Ariel is already itching to meet her."

"Who's Ariel?" she asked, trying to hide her wince as Rock injected a local anesthetic into her cheek so Mason didn't freak out. He was already watching her like a hawk.

"The woman I'm going to marry as soon as I'm sure she'll say yes," Rock replied.

"You're not sure?" she asked.

"Oh, I know she loves me, but Ariel went through something horrific this year and she's still recovering, I don't want to pressure her," Rock explained.

"Aww, that's sweet." What was also sweet was the way Mason

brushed his thumb across the inside of her wrist as he held her burned hand under the water. Jessica wasn't sure if he was even aware he was doing it because his attention appeared to be focused solely on the needle Rock was preparing to pierce through her skin. "Umm, maybe we should just go with a butterfly bandage," she suggested. The idea of Mason upset made her feel upset, it was the weirdest thing, she'd never experienced another person's emotions as keenly as she did with him.

"Stitches," Mason insisted.

"Fine, but don't squeeze my hand off, and don't rip your friend's hand off. Remember he's helping me," she told him.

Rock laughed. "Listen to her. I like my hands right where they are."

"So, do I get to meet Ariel?" she asked, kind of to Rock but also kind of to Mason. Just because they were together, it didn't mean he was ready to introduce her to all the people in his life. Although she hoped he wanted to.

"Dinner tonight at the compound if you guys are up to it," a huge man said, stepping forward. "Tillie is also anxious to meet the woman who Scorpion joined a cult for."

"Tank and Tillie are engaged," Mason supplied for her benefit.

"You guys live together on this compound, right?" she confirmed. Mason had told her a bit about his team and the targets on their back while they'd been in the hospital.

"Yes. We could do dinner somewhere else, but Beth and Axe aren't ready for Beth to leave the safety of the compound yet," Mason replied. "I'll tell you their story later, it's complicated."

Complicated she understood. These people weren't just Mason's friends, they were his family, and she wanted to get to know them. She was even a little nervous to meet the women in case they didn't like her. This was all new to her, she rarely dated because she was too busy, and when she did, she'd never felt anything close to what she felt for Mason with any of those men.

"Relax, darlin'," another huge man drawled. "They'll all love you. If you're important to our man Scorpion here, then you're important to us."

"Trick's right," Mason told her. "We're a family, we take care of one another. Which is why the guys will help me kill your brother if that's what you want."

"Mason!" she gasped. "You can't be saying things like that when cops are going to show up here any second. And I don't want any of you going to jail because of David."

"No one said anything about jail," the only guy she hadn't been introduced to yet said.

"Panther's right, none of us would go to jail. We know how to make someone disappear and leave nothing behind." Mason looked and sounded so deadly serious that she shivered. Never in her life had she had a group of men—four of whom didn't even know her—offer to commit murder for her.

It was a weird, but oddly comforting feeling.

Still ...

"I don't want David dead. Honestly, he's not worth it. What I want is for one night just to be a normal woman. No responsibility, no worries, nothing but spending time with my man and his family, like a regular person."

Leaning in, Mason brushed a kiss to her lips. "You are a regular woman, Jess. You and me are partners now, we handle everything together. That means you'll never have to worry about too many responsibilities slowly crushing the life out of you again."

It was way too early to say it, and yet ...

Jessica knew she was falling in love with this man.

He'd offered her everything she needed and everything she'd ever wanted, and she knew she was one lucky woman to have Mason Markson by her side.

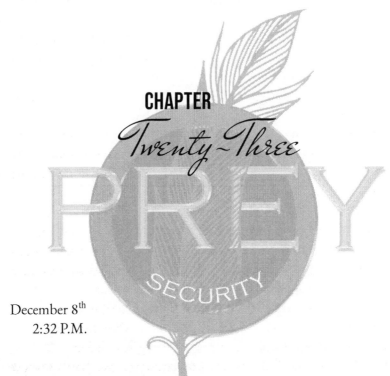

CHAPTER

Twenty-Three

December 8th
2:32 P.M.

"Are you sure you want to do this?"

"Oh, yeah," Scorpion answered.

"Mason, don't ... don't do anything stupid, okay?" Jessica said, sounding worried. She didn't just sound it she looked it, too. She was chewing on her bottom lip and eyeing the house they stood outside nervously, like the last thing she wanted to do was go inside.

"Honey, if you want to wait in the car, I don't mind," he offered. Confronting David wasn't an option. There was no way he was letting the man get away with what he'd done, pimping a minor—his own sister no less—wasn't just wrong it was a crime, and one Scorpion intended to see his old friend charged with.

"I'm not leaving you two alone," Jessica said quickly. Still, despite how adamant she was, he could see her nervousness. It was likely that she hadn't even had any contact with her brother since she and their younger sisters were put in foster care, there would be no reason for her to see him, and he couldn't imagine she would want to after what he had done to her.

If he was honest, there was a part of him that knew he ought to be punished right alongside David. Just because he hadn't known exactly what was going on, and he had tried to do something to stop it, it hadn't been enough. He should have known, should have seen that David wasn't who he pretended to be.

Knowing Jessica had been hurt so badly left him with this ache in his chest he couldn't seem to dislodge. Wasn't sure he ever could, even if he did whatever it took to make sure David was punished for the pain he had inflicted on her.

"If you can't face him, Jess, it's okay. I promise I won't do anything stupid." A harder promise to make than she could ever know, because he was pretty sure his fists were going to fly the second he saw his old friend. But for her, he would find a way to control himself so she didn't have to put herself into a situation she wasn't ready for.

"I can do it." Her chin had that stubborn tilt to it, but it trembled ever so slightly, and he knew she was in fact afraid to face her brother.

"Together," he reminded her, lacing their fingers together.

"Together," she echoed, voice a little stronger now. "Let's just get this over with."

"If he won't agree to turn himself in, then I'm calling the cops," he reminded her as they walked up the short path to the front porch.

"Isn't the statute of limitations up? It's been thirteen years since my sisters and I were taken in by CPS and David could no longer get to me."

"Eagle has a lawyer already lined up, and a team digging into David. Whatever he's been up to these last few years you can bet he's done something illegal. Men like him don't just stop because one of their victims is taken out of their reach. He's going to pay for what he did to you, Jess. That's a promise."

She nodded distractedly. "CPS thought it was my mom, and I let them," she said in a small voice. "There was part of me that blamed her for what David was doing. She was my mom, and she just checked out after Dad's injury, left everything on my shoulders. She didn't even notice what her son was doing to her daughter. I was so angry at her."

Her whispered declaration broke his heart. She'd been so young, so vulnerable, so helpless. There had been no one to watch over her and make sure she was okay. No one who noticed that someone was hurting her, and he knew that abandonment had left deep scars. Scars he was determined to help her heal one day at a time.

"It's okay to blame your mom, too, Jess," he assured her. "She did let you down, she did fail you. But I promise you I won't ever do the same."

Although a couple of tears slipped free, rolling down her bruised cheeks, she managed a smile for him. Those smiles of hers did weird things to his heart, and there wasn't anything he wasn't prepared to do to make her smile.

His Jessica.

His to love and protect and care for.

"You ready to do this?" he asked as he lifted his hand to knock on the door.

"Ready. Hopefully knowing David is being punished for what he did can bring me some closure so I can stop letting the past dictate my future."

"Coming," David's voice called out from inside the house when Scorpion gave a single hard rap on the wooden door.

A moment later, the door was flung open, and his old friend stood there. Time hadn't been kind to David Bowen. Although the man was only thirty-three, same age as Scorpion was, he was mostly bald, and what hair he had left was stringy and dirty looking. David had put on a lot of weight, his stomach bulging out over the top of a dirty pair of jeans. With a half-unbuttoned shirt on and bare feet, he looked unkempt, like he didn't care much about his appearance.

"Scorpion." David looked shocked for a moment, but then his gaze landed on his sister. The slow perusal he gave as he looked her over from head to toe, and the way his gaze lingered a little too long on the bandage on her hand and the stitches on her cheek, had Scorpion's blood pressure rising.

There was so much judgment in David's gaze. Especially for a man who knew he had been lying about his sister. That Jessica wasn't a spoiled princess who refused to step up and help out her family when they needed her. David knew she had been the one to cook and clean, do the laundry, care for her little sisters, and shoulder the responsibility of paying for it.

It was David who was the selfish one. David who had inflicted pain and trauma on a young, innocent girl.

That he could stand there now, looking down his nose at his victim, had Scorpion's blood boiling.

"You found her," David sneered. "Looks like it was just in time. What ridiculous trouble did you get yourself in this time, Jessica? Did you at least thank Scorpion for going out of his way to rescue you?"

The strong, confident woman he knew Jessica to be seemed to shrivel under her brother's condescending sneer, and it was the final straw.

Shifting Jessica so she was tucked safely behind him, Scorpion threw a punch.

It felt so good when his knuckles connected with David's face. His old friend's howl of shocked pain was music to his ears. It was one thing to pick on his little sister to make himself feel like a big man, but Scorpion would show him how a real man behaved. A real man protected and cared for those smaller than himself he didn't take advantage of them.

The second punch felt even better because this time David made a pathetic attempt to defend himself.

The third punch had David stumbling further back into the house, slipping as he wildly swung his fists about as though he hadn't gone through basic training and learned how to defend himself, and landing flat on his backside.

When he pulled back for a fourth punch, Jessica's small hands caught his elbow. "Enough," she said softly. "He's not worth anymore."

Standing over the now cowering man, Scorpion drew himself up to his full six-foot-three height. "He's not worth anything."

"Wh-what was that for, man?" David whined.

"For everything you did to your sister, and it wasn't enough. Nothing I could do to you would be enough."

David's worried gaze bounced between him and Jessica. "Whatever she said, man, she lied. You know her. You know what she's like. It's what she does. She plays the sweet and innocent card but she'd not.

She'd vindictive and evil. She's spoiled and selfish, only cares about herself. Whatever she told you, you can't believe."

If Jessica wasn't tucked against his side, he would have beaten on David until he was nothing but a bloody pulp.

Instead, he settled for taking a threatening step forward. "Insult your sister again and see what happens."

"Oh, I see how it is," David sneered. "She got her hooks into you now. Never thought you were stupid enough to fall for her lies."

"The only lie I ever told was one of omission, David. And that was not telling the cops what you did to me," Jessica said softly, and he was so proud of her for standing up to her tormentor, it took more guts than she realized. "Mason knows everything. Every horrible thing you did to me. It's over. The truth is finally going to come out. You can go to the police station and turn yourself in, or we're going to call 911 and have you arrested."

For a moment, David just stared at his little sister in shock, obviously not used to her standing up to him.

"Turn myself in?" He sneered. "Why would I do that? You don't have any proof I did anything to you. You're the same stupid girl you've always been, and if you think you can destroy me you're even stupider than I thought."

"Call your sister stupid again and you won't like what happens," Scorpion warned. "Your smart little sister kept a record of what happened to her. Every man you sold her to, photos of the bruises they inflicted, names and addresses, the clothes you put on her when you pimped her out that I'm sure are a treasure trove of DNA. How long do you think those men are going to keep quiet when the cops go to speak with them? You think they're going to protect you over saving their own skins?"

"They'll never believe her over me," David mocked. "Who would believe a stupid woman who contributes nothing to society, over a former soldier who risked his life to serve his country?"

From what he knew of David's military career, he'd been dishonorably discharged and never put his life on the line. It was further evidence that this narcissist was living in his own delusional land that was as far from reality as the Seeds of Life cult.

"Your sister is a highly decorated cop," he informed David.

Shock had the man's mouth dropping open, and fear slowly began to creep into his face as reality sank in. As David deflated, Jessica's spine grew straighter, and he could feel an infusion of confidence slowly enter her.

His beautiful, brave warrior never gave up. She faced each challenge that came her way with a strength and grace he admired. Wishing he had never believed a single lie David had told wouldn't change the past, but in the future, nothing would come before this amazing woman.

His woman.

~

December 8th
3:09 P.M.

Jessica was sure she had never seen a more satisfying sight in her life than that of her brother in handcuffs.

She'd never thought this day would actually come.

Her own fault of course. There had been nothing but fear and shame stopping her from going to the cops the first time her brother forced her to have sex with a man so he could get himself some money. Back then she'd been a traumatized thirteen-year-old girl, she hadn't had anyone to have her back, to tell her the right thing to do, to help her do it, or to make sure she got the support and assistance that she needed.

Not the case now.

Now she had a man at her back, literally standing behind her, his arms wrapped loosely around her waist as she rested against his solid chest.

Mason was so much more than she had spent the last fifteen years believing him to be. He'd been her rock today and her support those last couple of weeks undercover. He'd saved her life more than once, and in helping her finally get closure for her past, he'd saved her all over again.

"You doing okay?" Mason asked, his breath warm against the top of her head as he touched a kiss to her crown.

"Better than okay. I never thought this could happen. So long had passed, and I thought everyone would look down on me if they knew what I'd been through, but I don't care what other people think anymore." Wriggling in his hold she turned so she was facing him. "I only care what *you* think of me. If anyone else wants to think I was stupid for not going to the cops right away, or that I was weak and pathetic, or nothing but a victim, or anything else, I don't care."

"If anyone thinks that way about you, I'll gladly school them, but, sweetheart." He gently grasped her chin between his thumb and fore-finger and made sure she was looking at him. "No one thinks any of those things. People understand you were a traumatized child with no one looking out for her. Victims keep their secrets for whatever reasons they choose, it doesn't make them weak or stupid. No one else has walked in your shoes so no one has the right to judge you, and if they try it only says something about them, not you. And for the record, I think you're amazing."

Warmth unfurled inside her. It could have been one hundred degrees out in the middle of summer rather than the late fall day with a hint of coming snow in the air. "I think you're amazing, too. What you've helped me do, it means a lot. I feel like the past isn't holding onto me quite so tightly anymore. You've given me so much. You've shown me what it's like to have a partner at my side, you've taken care of me financially, given me a beautiful place to live—although I'm yet to see this penthouse—you've taken care of my dad and my sisters, you've saved my life, you've given me a chance to work toward my dream job, and you gave me this."

She looked over her shoulder just as David was shoved into the back of a police car. It might not be easy to have David convicted of crimes that were a decade and a half old, but she was up for the challenge. Even if he wasn't ever found guilty, she'd finally had an opportunity to stand up to her abuser and that meant more than she could put into words.

It was freeing.

Those chains that had bound her so tightly to the past had loosened enough that she could slip out of them now.

"This is right where I want to be," Mason told her. "But, you're right, we do have to rectify the penthouse problem since it's yours now. Are you ready to get out of here?"

"More than." She didn't need to follow David to the station, watch him get booked, or listen in on the interview. This wasn't about humiliating him, or getting revenge, or making him suffer like he'd made her suffer, it was about moving on and laying the past to rest so her future could be whatever she wanted it to be.

"Then let's get out of here." With a hand on the small of her back, Mason guided her off the sidewalk and over to his truck. He opened her door for her, helped her inside, and then buckled her seatbelt for her, not because he thought she couldn't do any of those things for herself, but because he enjoyed showing her in big and small ways how much he cared.

In the car they were both quiet as Mason drove them into the city. It had been a long day, so much had happened, and there was a lot to process. But the silence was a comfortable one, and Mason's hand rested on her thigh the entire drive, its heat seeping into her, filling her more and more with love for this man.

Was she in a hurry to marry him?

No, they still had too much to learn about one another and about how they would work as a couple.

But she knew it was happening, that she was falling in love with him.

Knew it was happening for him, too.

She caught all the little glances he threw her way when he thought she wasn't looking. In those unguarded moments, she could see reflected in his eyes the same feelings she was having.

It had been a while since she'd been right in the heart of New York City. She lived and worked in the outer boroughs, and it had been six months since she went to the West Virginian mountains to be part of Seeds of Life. The hustle and bustle of the city seemed so different from those quiet days in the forest. Those days had been full of hard manual labor on top of the undercover game she was playing, but she'd become accustomed to the quiet. It was going to take some getting used to being in the city again.

They pulled up outside a building opposite Central Park, and a doorman immediately came to greet them. Mason handed over the keys and helped her out. His hand settled on the small of her back again as he guided her into the building and over to an elevator. If he kept touching her like that, all alpha and possessive, she wasn't going to make it to a tour of the penthouse because she was going to rip his clothes off the second they got to his place.

From the heat in his eyes when he looked down at her, she knew he was thinking the same thing she was. Her need for this man was insatiable. Just after she had him, she wanted him all over again.

Still, the view caught her attention the second the private lift opened onto the penthouse. "Wow," she murmured as she hurried over to the huge wall of glass with the most stunning view of the park and the Manhattan skyline. "I can't believe you own this place."

"Technically, I already signed the papers so *you* own it now."

This was an amazing gift, totally topping the extravagant list, and the last thing she wanted Mason to feel was like she was ungrateful. Jessica knew he'd given her this place so she had a nice, stable home base. A place that was just hers, that nobody could take from her, a place she could put down roots if she wanted to.

"How come you've never lived here?" she asked.

Mason shrugged, looked over her shoulder out the window, and then around the tastefully and expensively furnished living room. "It's not me. Not how I grew up and not who I am now. I like the peace and quiet of the compound. I love the little log cabin I built with my own two hands. It's not much, but it's ... home."

"How is it going to work when we decide we're ready to move in together? Are you going to be comfortable living here in the city, away from your team?"

"Home is wherever you are now. So, yes, when we move in together, I'll be okay being here because you'll be here."

"But you'll miss them."

"My team will make it work. Tank has when he and Tillie got together, and Rock has with Ariel."

"They both live out on the compound though." She'd met both women last night when Mason took her out to the compound. Both women were lovely, and she already knew they would become great friends. It was obvious as he showed her around how proud Mason and his teammates were of the place they had built. It was their home, and she couldn't see Mason being happy here in the city in this ostentatious penthouse.

"I don't care where I live, babe, as long as I'm with you."

"The compound is so peaceful, so beautiful, so much nature out there."

"What are you saying, Jess?"

She dragged in a slow breath and hoped he understood where she was coming from. "I'm saying this is the most amazing gift anyone has ever given me. The penthouse is gorgeous, and I'm going to love living here while we get to know each other. You can come and pick me up for dates like a normal couple, and sometimes I'll let you stay the night. It'll be close to school when I go back to study for my law degree, and it's a great place for my sisters to stay while they're in school, too. But when we move in together, I'd love for it to be in the cabin you built."

"You'd give up all of this to live in a small one living room, two-bedroom cabin in the middle of nowhere?" Mason asked like he couldn't quite believe it.

"Yes. Because it's where *you* really want to be, and home is wherever you are now," she said, using his own words.

Dragging her up flush against his body, he grinned down at her. "You're something else, you know that?"

"I'm falling in love with you, Mason," she admitted.

Relief filled his face, and he dipped his head and kissed her hungrily. "Happy to hear that, babe, because I'm falling, too."

"Together. We're falling together."

"Together," he agreed.

For someone who had been alone for so long, it was the best feeling in the world to now have someone who would walk by her side no matter what. Through the highs and lows of life, through whatever was thrown their way.

Together had become her favorite word in the English language.

CHAPTER
Twenty~Four

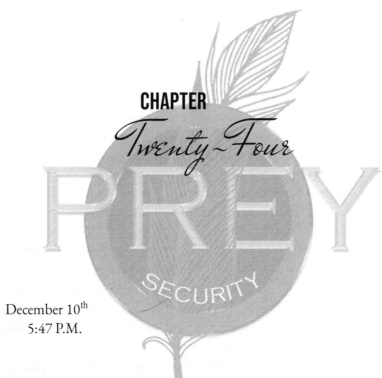

December 10th
5:47 P.M.

"Yep, it's love."

Scorpion looked over his shoulder at Trick who was watching him with amusement. "Nobody was talking to you," he said with an eye roll.

"I know, I just like to state the obvious," Trick said with one of his trademark grins.

"I never said I was in love," he said, even as he returned his gaze to the only thing in the room worth looking at. They were at the compound, at his cabin, decorating it for Christmas. It had been a while since he bothered putting up decorations. In fact, none of them usually did except for Panther since he had a little boy. Axe and Beth used to decorate, but this year had been so rough on them that neither had felt in the mood.

Apparently, the rest of them were going to make up for that.

The girls had gotten together and decided to decorate all the cabins this year, so the last two days had been spent moving from place to place setting up Christmas trees, putting garlands around the doors, wreaths and fairy lights outside, and of course mistletoe which nobody seemed to mind.

Not that any of them really minded decorating the cabins for Christmas. Seeing the smile on Tillie's face when they'd put the finishing touches on her and Tank's cabin had been worth it. Then seeing that same smile on Ariel's face when her and Rock's cabin was transformed into a Christmas wonderland, was even better.

Now they were here at his cabin and Jessica was having a ball decorating the tree, taking care to make sure the decorations were spaced evenly, and they didn't have two shiny baubles right next to one another. He and the guys were putting garlands around the banister, and then they would be moving on to the porch. As he worked, his gaze kept returning to Jessica. Her smile was brighter than the Christmas lights glowing on the tree in the corner beside the fireplace, and every time he heard her laugh, he couldn't help but smile.

"I know the look," Trick continued. "Seen it on Axe's face for years, every time he looks at Bethie. Then saw it on Tank, then on Rock when he finally got his girl back. Now it's written all over your face every time you look at Jess. It's love. For sure."

The rest of the guys were nodding at him, and he just shrugged, no point in denying it, he was falling further for his woman every day. Hell, every minute he liked her more, respected her more, and admired her more. She was stubborn for sure, and she was going to keep him on his toes, but she was so strong, and she tackled every problem that came her way with a confidence he knew had been born out of being thrown into the deep end too soon but learning you could swim.

"You know, man, you could be next," Rock teased Trick who looked so aghast at the very prospect of falling in love that they all laughed.

"Not me," Trick said confidently. "I much prefer my women on a casual basis. Hot sex, lots of fun, then time to move on to the next one. Too many women out there to limit yourself to just one. And for the entire rest of your life? No thank you. Not for me."

"It'll happen when you least expect it," Tank said, his gaze soft as he watched Tillie string tinsel around the branches of the Christmas tree.

"At the most inconvenient time," Scorpion added. When he'd agreed to give up family vacation time to go in and help out the sister of an old friend, the last thing he had expected was to fall for a woman he hadn't even liked back then. But things had changed, the real Jessica was someone he couldn't not fall for, and he didn't regret a thing. He'd already spoken to his family, and they were all going to fly in for Christmas. His family and Jessica's sisters would all be staying at the penthouse while his girl spent Christmas here with him.

"But once you fall, they become your whole world," Rock said. It had been a long and bumpy journey for Rock and Ariel, but the two were finally in a good place, healing from old wounds as well as newer ones from Ariel's abduction earlier in the year.

Happy.

This Christmas Axe had his wife back where she belonged, even if things continued to remain strained between them as Beth still had no memory of her husband or the love they had shared. Rock finally had the woman he had pined over since he was a teenager in his life and his home, and both Scorpion and Tank had fallen in love this past year. Panther had his little boy, and Trick seemed happy with his life the way it was.

All of them were right where they wanted to be, with the people they loved not just in their lives but in their homes. If he was a sappier guy, Scorpion would definitely say this was going to be the best Christmas ever.

Didn't mean things were perfect.

A glance at Beth, who sat a little away from the others as she unwrapped decorations for Jessica, Tillie, and Ariel to put on the tree, was all he needed to see to know that.

But even with Beth's amnesia, she was loved and supported. She had a whole family that kept growing and growing, surrounding her, and none of them were going to let her sink. Sooner or later, she would get her memories back, and when she did, Scorpion hoped that she and Axe could finally be happy together again.

Panther's phone dinged, and he pulled it from his pocket. As soon as he read whatever had caused the alert, he looked up at them, eyes wide.

"What is it?" Axe asked, immediately straightening. Even though there was no indication this had anything to do with Beth, any time their tech guru got an alert they all knew that Axe was hoping it was something that would give them answers as to who had kidnapped Beth, hurt her, and caused her to lose her memory in her brain's attempt to protect itself.

"It's a program I've been running," Panther replied, shoving his phone back into his pocket as he went to the kitchen table to retrieve his laptop. The man brought the thing with him pretty much everywhere he went. Now he sat at Scorpion's table, opened it up, and began hammering away on the keys.

"And?" Axe prompted as he followed Panther to the table.

"Is this about me?" Beth asked as the room went silent and everyone came to stand around the table.

Jessica came right to him, slipping a supportive arm around his waist. He'd filled her in on all the details surrounding Beth, and she had offered to do anything she could to help. Likewise, Tillie didn't hesitate to go to Tank, snuggling her cheek against his chest as her small arms circled his huge frame. Ariel slipped under one of Rock's arms that went easily around her shoulders, anchoring her against his side.

While Beth joined them at the table, she didn't go to stand beside her husband, in fact, she kept herself as far away from Axe as she could. From the way he watched her with such naked pain and longing in his eyes, they all knew that Axe wished that for once Beth would go to him, allow him to comfort her.

But she wasn't ready for that yet, and Axe had to find a way to respect her needs even as he hated them.

"As we all know, there are only four known survivors of Leonid Baranov's house of horrors. One who committed suicide not long after being rescued, one who was given a new identity, one who was killed a few months back, and Beth." Panther's gaze met Beth's, softening when she wrapped her arms around her waist in a gesture of self-comfort. "Since Bethie doesn't remember what happened to her when she was taken last year, and we suspect it's connected to Baranov, that only leaves us one other person who might be able to help us. I've been trying to find her. It isn't easy, whoever gave her a new identity did a good job. I haven't been able to figure out where she went after she gave her statement and was debriefed."

While there was no guarantee that this other survivor knew anything more than she had when they'd rescued her and Beth all those years ago, she was the only link left to Baranov. With the other two survivors dead, she was the only other person left who knew more about Baranov than he wanted them to.

The woman was also in danger.

If Baranov was cleaning house, going after Beth, and then killing his only male survivor, a man who had dedicated himself to bringing down the Russian oligarch, then it made sense Baranov would go for this other woman as well if he could figure out her new identity.

Panther tapped away on his keyboard for a minute, then looked up. "I think I might have finally gotten her new name."

Can love bloom from the darkness for Trick and a woman he finds himself held captive with in the fourth book in the action packed and emotionally charged Prey Security: Bravo Team series!

Cruel Scars (Prey Security: Bravo Team #4)

Also by Jane Blythe

CRUSHED RUBY

FRACTURED DIAMOND

SHATTERED AMETHYST

SPLINTERED EMERALD

SALVAGING MARIGOLD

River's End Rescues Series

COCKY SAVIOR

SOME REGRETS ARE FOREVER

SOME FEARS CAN CONTROL YOU

SOME LIES WILL HAUNT YOU

SOME QUESTIONS HAVE NO ANSWERS

SOME TRUTH CAN BE DISTORTED

SOME TRUST CAN BE REBUILT

SOME MISTAKES ARE UNFORGIVABLE

Candella Sisters' Heroes Series

LITTLE DOLLS

LITTLE HEARTS

LITTLE BALLERINA

Storybook Murders Series

NURSERY RHYME KILLER

FAIRYTALE KILLER

FABLE KILLER

Saving SEALs Series

SAVING RYDER

SAVING ERIC

SAVING OWEN

SAVING LOGAN

SAVING GRAYSON

SAVING CHARLIE

Prey Security Series

PROTECTING EAGLE

PROTECTING RAVEN

PROTECTING FALCON

PROTECTING SPARROW

PROTECTING HAWK

PROTECTING DOVE

Prey Security: Alpha Team Series

DEADLY RISK

LETHAL RISK

EXTREME RISK

FATAL RISK

COVERT RISK

SAVAGE RISK

Prey Security: Artemis Team Series

IVORY'S FIGHT

PEARL'S FIGHT

LACEY'S FIGHT

OPAL'S FIGHT

Prey Security: Bravo Team Series

VICIOUS SCARS

RUTHLESS SCARS

Christmas Romantic Suspense Series

CHRISTMAS HOSTAGE

CHRISTMAS CAPTIVE

CHRISTMAS VICTIM

YULETIDE PROTECTOR

YULETIDE GUARD

YULETIDE HERO

HOLIDAY GRIEF

Conquering Fear Series (Co-written with Amanda Siegrist)

DROWNING IN YOU

OUT OF THE DARKNESS

CLOSING IN

About the Author

USA Today bestselling author Jane Blythe writes action-packed romantic suspense and military romance featuring protective heroes and heroines who are survivors. One of Jane's most popular series includes Prey Security, part of Susan Stoker's OPERATION ALPHA world! Writing in that world alongside authors such as Janie Crouch and Riley Edwards has been a blast, and she looks forward to bringing more books to this genre, both within and outside of Stoker's world. When Jane isn't binge-reading she's counting down to Christmas and adding to her 200+ teddy bear collection!

To connect and keep up to date please visit any of the following

Made in the USA
Monee, IL
31 March 2024

56147660R10134